MALFON

WALT POLZIN

Walt Polzin

MALFON

WALT POLZIN

Malfon

Mockingbird Lane Press—Maynard, Arkansas
ISBN: 978-1-6341599-9-9
Library of Congress Control Number in publication data

0 9 8 7 6 5 4 3 2 1
www.mockingbirdlanepress.com
Cover: Jamie Johnson

TO KAREN:
SOMEONE TO WRITE FOR,
AND AN INSPIRATION TO WRITE.

CHAPTER 1

"Private Koch, Private Rafan here to relieve you of guard duty," Este Rafan said formally.

"Where is the Corporal of the Guard?" Koch asked. It was customary for the corporal to literally change the guard.

"He had an unexpected and undeniable call to the latrine. So I came on without him," Rafan answered. "I feel uncomfortable breaking tradition and protocol, but Corporal M'hut told me to come ahead. Besides, I didn't want you to have to stay on duty any longer than your shift."

"It's not a problem, Rafan. Don't be so tight. You don't need to do everything strictly by the rules," the more relaxed guard said.

"Well, as usual, there is nothing up here on the palace roof but dry, dusty desert air. You're welcome to it for the next duty period." With that, Private Koch swung his rifle over his shoulder and walked past Rafan unceremoniously on his way down through the palace below them, on his way home.

Something about the moment, perhaps the dry dusty air and the vision of Koch's carefree demeanor, reminded Rafan of his school days among the other children. One day in particular stood out in his mind.

It was the usual hot day for Malfon, perhaps 105 degrees, and the only smell was that of the tan dust. The other children were playing in the sun, careless about the harm such activity could cause. Running about, playing tag was not a suitable pastime, but that is what the children were playing. Rafan knew the kids were being stupid. They were working up a sweat that he could smell from the shady corner of the school building where he stood. He could have joined them, but he had no desire to do so.

The dust they kicked up added an additional hue to their already tan skin tone as it clung to them.

Rafan would exercise, by himself, when the day cooled a little in the late afternoon or early evening. That day was shortly after his parents had died and he was being cared for by various others, mostly one aunt. Since their death, he had trained himself to be precise in everything he did. He avoided anything that would sentence him to the same premature death they had suffered. He had a strict regimen for exercising. Just so many of each activity, no more or less. He demanded healthy food and anything else that he felt would serve his purpose of longevity. That had been true up through the time he'd become a young man in the Malfon army.

He remembered that day because of the pain he'd felt from losing his parents. There was something that brought the memory of that day back to him just then. But, he wasn't sure what it was.

Maybe it was the fact that his parents had warned him about heat stroke and he'd watched the playful attitude of the other kids in the same way he'd watched Private Koch meander away from the guard post, seemingly carefree, unconcerned about any consequences. Whatever triggered the memory, Rafan had no room for informalities in his life. He would shrug at the memory, just as he did the carefreeness of Private Koch. Serious attention to every detail was the only way to succeed. He knew that for sure. His parents had taught him that.

CHAPTER 2

I can see why Malfon has been such a poor country, Este Rafan said to himself, looking out over the parapet of his castle rooftop guard post. His eyes took in a desert bowl surrounded by mountains. He had seen those mountains everyday of his life but had never been to them. They were in other countries, like Talon, Malfon's Eastern neighbor. His family was too poor to travel.

Besides, Malfonies were not exactly welcome, even for visits, in Talon. That realization came to Este's thoughts out loud. "Fine. They can have their mountains. Malfonies don't need mountains. This desert is our home." He shook his head in disbelief that grew daily concerning the amalgamation of unrelated building styles that made up the capital city, Creche.

The government building he was guarding belonged to the middle ages of Central Europe, but Malfon was in the Middle East of the twenty-first century. The rest of the city was traditional desert dwellings, including tents, and spartan commercial buildings, spattered with occasional other European influences.

There were some steel and glass towers, though of moderate size, built in the 1900s. There were occasional Christian churches, and a Jewish synagogue to go along with the Muslim mosques.

The mountains in the distance were low and barren. They provided mineral deposits for other countries around Malfon.

But, there had been no minerals or oil found in the flat desert sand of Malfon. That unending sand indicated that Malfon also didn't have irrigation. So, there were no agricultural green spots of money crops to bolster Malfon's economy.

"Malfonies have been nomads over the centuries, but now our neighboring countries have put restraints on our wanderings," Rafan said out loud wistfully. "Now, Malfonies are forced to find other ways to subsist within this arid bowl.

"We used to wander with the winds to find new sources of food, or at least temporary ones to replace those that gave out with overuse or with the season. When a well ran dry, my ancestors moved to where they knew another watering hole existed, perhaps with date palms, or fig trees. But, now we stay put and try to bring food and water out of the same places day after day, week after week. Some people have to kill the cow that gives milk in order to have meat. I am too young to have known those nomadic days, but my parents knew it. Sometimes I long for those days to return. But, they cannot." Rafan had a habit of speaking aloud when he was alone.

In the mid-twentieth century, the natives had been joined by immigrants from Europe. That accounted for the unlikely names found in Malfon, as well as the architectural oddities. There were as many Helmuts and Lisls in Malfon as there were Alis and Abduls.

The Europeans had built buildings in the styles they knew back home. These immigrants had money brought from questionable resources. That allowed extravagances. But soon these immigrants, many of noble status, learned that all their currency would not help them to survive in the desert. Importing food became more important than showy architecture and the other extravagances.

These princes and their families soon had to adjust to the life of the nomads in many respects. However, some of the Teutonic fore-bearers of Rafan's blood managed to squirrel some money away into present times.

The nomadic Malfonies accepted the newcomers hesitatingly, perhaps assuming they would eventually leave once their reason for leaving their homelands was no longer prevalent.

But, that time had never come, and while the natives found their religion, their buildings, their dress and way of life, strange, their adoption of the Malfony language did much to ease the melding of the two societies into a whole new reality for Malfon.

The nomads were slow to realize their world had, in actuality, been invaded and their control of the area would be forever shared. After World War II, when the arbitrary boundaries of the Middle East had created new countries, the line between native and European Malfonies was already only a vague shadow. All parties involved realized the future had to belong to all of them working together in a new life of restricted nomadic style within the new lines on the map.

"It's not right," Rafan continued speaking aloud. "What is happening to our country...to our people?"

Some people did secure rights to work in adjoining countries. They worked in the industries there, or labored in the irrigated fields. The population of Norova, Malfon's neighbor to the West, and the other neighboring countries, like Talon to the East, was not sufficient to run the oil drilling and pumping rigs on the pipelines and keep them in repair. Nor were there enough people to grow the olives, artichokes, melons, and other produce their more mountainous and moist soils could support. So, a few Malfonies crossed borders each day to earn wages to buy, in many cases, that same food to feed their families.

The host countries benefited from the Malfony labors, and then sold them the fruit, and fuel for their cooking appliances and vehicles. Some Malfonies would probably have emigrated, a choice Talon, Norova, and the other countries didn't allow. But, most Malfonies loved their desert home even with its rugged harshness and short lifespans, and never dreamed of leaving permanently. Most were resigned to their lives of poverty.

Of course, Talon, the leading oil producer to the East of Malfon, faired immensely better than most of the host countries in having this work force to aid their production of the very profitable petroleum and ease the lives of its citizens. All of the countries adjoining Malfon enjoyed many advantages made possible by revenues from their oil wells, mines, and farms, thanks to the day laborers from Malfon. None of these countries cared to show their appreciation to Malfon.

Rafan paced back and forth. "Why stay at home and struggle for scraps? Why fight over the few things we can grow to feed ourselves or use to trade for other needs, when you can go to Norova and do so much better? It's not right!" Rafan clinched his fist and shook it in the direction of Malfon's border with seaported Norova. Our people shouldn't have to leave our homeland in order to live a decent life!" Rafan knew too well that the short periods of time migrant workers spent out of the country easily became cherished, especially since the money they brought home went a long way in Malfon.

Rafan dreamed of the period of time when Malfon had been moderately prosperous. When the Europeans had come, Malfon boasted a merchant fleet at the ports it then had. In truth, back then there were no nationalistic boundaries. The Europeans had brought money and some of it was used to pay for the stone and masonry to build the types of buildings with which they were familiar. Expensive Carera marble was brought in from Italy, and the cement for mixing with the plentiful but painstakingly washed Malfony sand, was shipped from England. But, after World War II, among the many changes brought to the world, was the annexation of those ports by the newly formed nation of Norova. The Malfonies had remained neutral in memory of the obscenities of the Great War that the immigrants had fled. But, Malfon was nominally aligned with the Axis powers by heritage, a forgotten partner of the fascists. Malfon had assisted a Balkan country that figured only minutely in the war on the losing side.

The Balkans had asked for a landing zone for their aircraft. None of that country's sparse outdated planes had ever used the strip.

So, the Allies had never bothered with it. The only use the field had ever seen was from Malfony citizens maintaining a fuel supply there in case it needed to be used in the war. The payment Malfon was to receive never arrived, as the war in Europe ended shortly after the tiny player in the conflict made the arrangements with Malfon.

After the war, the Allies and the fledgling United Nations, in their ignorance of the realities of the area, had drawn the lines forming post-war Norova and Malfon with the coast exclusively in Norovan territory as the price for that alignment.

"What did we do to deserve losing our ocean ports? We were not really fascists. Why did we have to pay a penalty? Why did we lose? Why do we have to suffer?" Private Este Rafan surveyed his dry homeland from his rooftop perch. The words of his parents still echoed in the ears of the dark haired slender young man.

"We deserve a simple life such as the nomadic Malfonies knew, or at least the prosperous life we had when the Europeans first came and we had a seaport." That was what both his parents had lamentingly said, in different ways, many times during his childhood.

"Take pride in yourself, your achievements, and your country, for whatever reasons you can find," his father had said. His parents had raised a few crops on a dry patch of land that only enabled them to feed themselves, and not well. Consequently, the family's diet consisted mostly of dates and figs. Sometimes the family would hoard their crops, restricting their intake, so they could have enough saved up to trade for other food. But, even with the paltry results their efforts brought forth, Rafan had always been healthy and strong. That may have been made possible at the sacrifice of his parents' own health.

The memory of his parent's poverty, he hoped, would drive him to make a difference in his own life and the future of his country. In his heart, he was sure of it.

"You are a very good student, Rafan. You make me proud," both his parents and his teachers often told him. But, as a young boy he had no idea what that would mean to him. Schooling was an honor in itself and Rafan made the most of it.

"Thank you," he would say. "But, what good will it do me to be a good student?" His parents and teachers would just smile at this common question from young people.

Rafan had begun to understand what his education could do for him. Little advantages from his academic achievements and the discipline he taught himself to accomplish them had started to accumulate. For instance, on this night he would surprise his friend, the corporal of the guard, Mahumud M'hut. His merits had gotten him a new appointment.

Rafan's mind slipped back to the day he'd been called from the playground at school to be told of his parents' deaths.

"Este, I am sorry. I have to tell you something very difficult," his teacher began.

"What is it?" Rafan asked, already guessing, for both of his parents had been ill for some time. A neighbor had summoned a doctor for them just that morning, while they were encouraging Este to go on to school.

"Este, your parents have died," the teacher finished simply.

In a simple act to encourage Rafan to do well at school, his parents had once rewarded him with a gift. They had spent much more than they could afford and bought him a bird. It was a finch in a cage. Rafan had been thrilled and understood that this gift was given to him because he was doing well in school. Even at that early age he understood that if he wanted more surprises he needed to continue to do well. He had no idea of his parents' sacrifices.

As he grew older he recognized that this was a false benefit of education. But, for a while, Este applied himself like never before. Then the bird died, probably from starvation. The family could barely afford to feed itself, let alone perhaps a poorly chosen symbol of achievement for the boy.

Rafan took the death in stride. He'd not had a bird before. Now he had no bird again. That was a simple adjustment for him. He took his parents' deaths in much the same stoic manner, silent and alone.

Rafan's head had bowed and he had shuffled back to the playground while the school awaited a responsible party to pick up the boy. But he didn't rejoin the other children. Arrangements would be made for relatives to raise Este. Rafan had only two friends, Mahumud and a girl named Anna. They, like everyone else, seemed to know Rafan wanted to be left alone to handle his loss. His parents had left a young child to carry on in life basically by himself, and Este seemed intent upon doing that.

Even at the moment he'd been told of his mother and father passing away, he knew what he would do with his education.

He did not even require the later return of his friendships with the other orphan boy, Mahumud, or the girl he would eventually tutor and encourage to marry Mahumud. Este made himself totally self-sufficient. Now, looking over the parapet, running his hand along the rough surface there, he remembered the feel of the bird's feathers on his hand as he held it.

"I'll be all right," he told himself. "I will live to make this a better place, where no one will have to live in poverty and die as young as my parents did."

Rafan's uniformed presence on the roof of the capitol, or palace, was hardly a necessity. The uneven top of the roof wall did nothing so much as remind Rafan of the grittiness of the desert below and of the life Malfonies led. There was no threat, military or otherwise, which required an army. But, the army remained as a limited paying job available to the few ambitious Malfonies who sought employment.

Rafan took a deep breath of the arid atmosphere and fingered the medal that adorned the front of his uniform. The medal meant nothing. Everyone in the army had one. It was part of the appeal, colorful decorations in a drab land. The fabric of the ribbon holding the medal had none of the silky feel that the clothes Premier Sabu would be wearing on his body at that moment, he knew. For there were some in this country who didn't have it so gritty and rough. This angered Rafan.

The army positions were highly sought because they offered better clothing and nutrition than the general public could expect, and there were fewer positions than men who wanted them. Rafan considered himself fortunate, but not lucky, to be in his place at his age. He had overstepped other candidates in his undeniable drive to his future. His attention to his studies had served him well. He felt that was as it should be.

"I know the Palace Guards are prestigious appointments," Rafan had told the leader of his unit at the barracks. "I know there are others who have been waiting a long time for a position to open up, but they are willing to wait. I am not. No one deserves this position more than I do. No one wants it more than I do."

But, as Rafan fingered the flashy Royal Guard Braid on his shoulder and looked out from his post, over the sand stretching fifty miles into the distance, he was not smug, nor satisfied.

There had never been an attack on Malfon. There was nothing here that anyone would fight over, Rafan knew. The non-violent annexation of the seacoast had robbed Malfon of the last enviable thing it had possessed. The Guard was honorary. It was a reward for excellence in the army service. In most cases that meant no sick days, no resistance to following orders, and taking good care of the uniform. But, in Rafan's case, it meant much more.

Rafan had gained his position in the honor unit by offering to improve dedication of the troops, to cut costs for maintaining and encouraging other guards to be at their best at all times.

Such an offer was unheard of from an army private, and well beyond what any one considered possible, even from an officer.

The leader of Malfon, Malat Sabu, had his headquarters in the building Rafan was guarding. A more incapable leader would be hard to imagine. His achievements amounted to zero.

No attention was paid to the problems facing the country and its people. He paid little attention to anything of consequence.

Sabu simply let time pass. But, he knew of Rafan. Word of this ambitious soldier had reached the highest levels.

A dust devil lifted itself to the rooftop level, bringing a little discomfort to Rafan's breathing. Sabu's ennui was well documented in the foreign press, which sometimes filtered into Malfon. But, any Malfony could tell the tale of the do nothing Premier.

Again, Rafan spoke aloud. "Why should I pace this roof, guarding a man who does nothing but listen to his ministers babble out 'nothings' that have no bearing on the needs of the country, since that is all he will allow them to discuss? Why protect a man who is not in danger and that I do not respect? When occasionally someone does try bringing up something that really needs to be handled, someone like Minister Arat, Sabu says, 'Well, I don't know about this concern. Perhaps we'd be better off not doing anything without knowing more about it.' The subject is rarely brought up again. Too many attempts have been thwarted by Sabu's ennui to allow anyone the ambition to try any more. Sabu is in power only because no one has any ambition left, after Sabu drains it with his lack of activity, to try to take his place. The other leaders tell themselves, 'who wants to be the ruler of a fourth rate nation?'

"Sabu gained his position because he is distantly related to the royal family that put together the infant nation from European immigrants. He was born in Malfon, but he is a traitor to our heritage, both European and Arab."

Rafan had taken to lengthy discussion with himself shortly after losing his parents. In a world where he had virtually no one, he became his own best friend. Here was someone for him to tell his plans for his life, someone who shared those plans completely. No other human being had ever been nearly as close to him as he was to himself.

Rafan continued to pace the palace roof, occasionally running his hand along the rough texture of the parapet. He reviewed the rest of his knowledge of Malfon's history, and the lives of its rulers.

Prince Sabu, Malat's ancestor, after being overthrown in his home country, had come to an unclaimed desert patch. His former countrymen had opted for a more democratic rule, but had fallen to a dictatorship without a royal line within a short time. Their misfortune must have seemed slightly humorous to the deposed Prince Sabu. But, he had felt it prudent to drop the royal title in his adopted land and perhaps forestall persecution from the Old Country. The riches that had left the old homeland with him were converted into the stone and other materials brought in to build the sort of edifices he was used to seeing from his European castle.

The local nomads had been impressed with this visible progress in their desert. The newcomer and his associates left the Arabs alone and they in turn brought no hostilities upon the Europeans. Little by little, the nomadic way of life altered to include new aspects that gave rise to a sense of pride they hadn't known existed. There was some prosperity for all.

Rafan's mind shifted to more present circumstances.

"Those piers at sea should be ours," Rafan again was audible. "Prince Sabu built them. My ancestors had no need of them, but in today's world they are important. But, Premier Malat Sabu does nothing about getting them back, or at least getting some use from them. Their loss was the main reason Malfon has fallen into such dire straits. When we had a port we brought things in that we needed more cheaply and traveled more freely. Now we pay duties to Norova and are restricted from leaving the area from their seaports. The airstrip from World War II is abandoned and unusable. So, no one leaves the country except to work in Norova or Talon for the day. The port belongs to Malfon!"

But Rafan's anger was muted, for he knew Malfon had remained invisible to the limited community of the Middle Eastern world. No one cared who built the piers. Unto the present day, Malfon was ignored. Not the U.N. or anyone else was about to give Malfon back its former port. There would be no easy way to do that. So, Rafan let that slight smolder while he dealt with his immediate situation.

His anger at Malat Sabu and the outside world did not always reach back to his nomadic ancestors' view of Malfon. For decades, Prince Sabu had made great strides in bringing his new country into the modern world. Shipping and ship refitting, naval enlistment, and regional trade brought his nomadic subjects a level of luxury they had never before known. Albeit, few others would have called it luxury. The varied religious factions all realized that they were unthreatened and better off than before Prince Sabu's arrival. The Prince kept the lion's share of the benefits for himself. But, even those who chose to continue the old way of life were undeniably better off than ever. There was some employment for those who wanted it and more goods available for everyone to share at some level.

But, the world was totally unaware of the changes in the desert. When the time had come for the United Nations to draw the post-World War II national boundaries, they had no guide as to where to put the lines on the map. Still preferring a low profile, the Prince allowed Malfon's yet to be formed neighbor, Norova, to make the most noise, and it was allocated the port.

In the generations that followed Prince Sabu's death, the leaders of Malfon, of mixed European and Arab blood, allowed the country to deteriorate into a weak sister to the global community. While no credit can be given this procession of untalented leaders for furthering prosperity in their country, it must be said that they were successful in avoiding any religious confrontation. With European Christians and the Muslim native population side-by-side, a holy war could have taken place.

However, whether by chance or design, both factions were content to lumber on in their own direction, even while the economical and political aspects of their lives crumbled.

"If only Malat Sabu had some of the Prince's capabilities," Rafan muttered. His gaze over the desert saw more than was there.

Then there was Defense Minister Aturk, one of the country's senior officials. Since he was minister of defense, his professional life was well known to Private Rafan. The talk of his own brand of obstructionism was voluminous. Rafan knew he was not perfect.

He had a memory of a painful lashing out at someone close. But, he felt he was nowhere close to Aturk in ineffectiveness. Rafan knew any flaws he had would interfere with the future he saw.

So, he worked hard to be secure in knowing that he'd outgrown the violent tendency that had made him lash out in the past.

There had only been one event and he had reconciled that with himself, changing what needed to be changed in order to reach out for what he wanted to achieve. He wanted to avoid anything that would occlude him from moving forward toward his ideals and goals.

Private Este Rafan had set his sights. He would change all the deterioration Malat Sabu allowed to continue. He was quite sure he could do it. He knew he would be the salvation of his country.

His life would be dedicated to that purpose. No other interests could be allowed to divert him from his path to that goal. He knew he had the ability and the drive. He just wasn't exactly sure how he could use it yet.

"One day, Sabu, I will undo all the wrongs this country has suffered," Rafan muttered aloud. "I am not yet sure exactly how, but I will do it."

Rafan had enrolled in an almost non-existent and forgotten officer's candidate school. Classes began irregularly because Rafan's countrymen rarely made the effort to do more than just take a military position at the bottom of the ranks when one opened. Promotions, when they occurred, were simply to fill voids caused by death or other absences. There were virtually no students to fill a class with those wanting to become officers, let alone a review board for promotions. Only Rafan had the incentive among his peers to achieve. The few others who made up the numbers necessary to form a class were only willing due to Rafan encouraging them to make a minimal effort in hopes of more income. Rafan needed the class for his own purposes, but he also felt that urging the others to enroll could possibly equip some other soldiers to benefit Malfon more adequately.

Rafan was self-educated well beyond the level the academic system of Malfon provided. The old brick school house Prince Sabu had built decades before was only a frame for Rafan's innate intelligence. He liked to think he had inherited genes that made the acquisition of knowledge simple for him. He was proud of his parents. They'd done much better than most by applying themselves appropriately to get ahead. Rafan's parents had seen his potential and encouraged it. They had given him personal instruction and opportunities to curry knowledge even at an early age. But, the ambition was all his own.

"Soon I will be an officer and many steps closer to my goals," he said.

Este Rafan was a distant relative of Malat Sabu. That had helped in obtaining his military appointment, his ascension to the Royal Guard, and now his admittance to the officer's school.

He had excelled in his army role, as he had done in nearly all his efforts during his short life. He was a fair athlete and a quick study at mental tests. He had been in the military only a month before he had earned the privileged post of Palace Guard. He felt his ancestry gave him the right to scratch his way toward the top. But, most importantly he felt he was worthy because he put out the effort to do what felt was needed by Malfon. He knew his previous successes in all he took on showed him capable of that goal. However, the obstructions that Malfon politics presented made that goal difficult to attain. That was the part of the future that infuriated him. He knew he had to struggle for all he hoped to achieve. He hoped that as an army officer he would have a little more help in overcoming the dissatisfaction those blockades presented.

He was startled by the sound of someone approaching.

"Good evening, Rafan," the corporal of the guard announced.

"Do you always pay such good attention while on guard duty?"

"I'm sorry, Corporal M'hut."

"You are supposed to challenge anyone who approaches," M'hut said in a semi-serious tone, knowing full well the joke of such protocol under the circumstances.

"No one comes up here. Who would want to? There's no threat."

"Uhummm."

"Forgive me. I know. It won't happen again," Rafan told his friend. He was much more offended by his lapse of military bearing than the corporal.

M'hut's tone relaxed even further. "I'm sure it won't," the corporal said. "You aren't being promoted tomorrow because you have bad habits. You've shown nothing but praiseworthy attributes since you've joined the army."

M'hut smiled. Of course he knew of Rafan's past, as they had grown up together. M'hut too had lost his parents at a young age and had lived in poverty all of his life until he had dredged up enough ambition from within to find a position in the army.

Rafan felt it was a shame that M'hut didn't apply himself more thoroughly, for he was surely capable of being more than a corporal in the army. Rafan cared about his friend, though his stiff manner and lack of sharing any intimacy made that hard to believe. Only sightly older than Rafan, the slim, lanky, mustachioed, M'hut was the person who was closest to being a friend to the private. There was some distance between them, perhaps caused by the fact that Rafan was a Christian and

M'hut was a Muslim, but their early years had shared some intense events.

"Did you say promotion, sir?"

"Don't call me sir. I'm just a corporal, the same as you'll be tomorrow. It was supposed to be a surprise, but since there is no ceremony, I wanted to be the first to tell you. Well, I guess it still is a surprise," M'hut stated.

"Thank you, sir," Rafan responded uncomfortably in his formal manner.

Noting Rafan's discomfort on the announcement of the promotion, M'hut continued. "You know it took me two years to make corporal."

"Yes." Rafan smiled slightly. "But, there were more people in the army then. It was harder to make rank." Rafan made an excuse for his friend.

"Not so," M'hut corrected. "Is that why you are acting so strange about your promotion? I thought you would be excited. You're so ambitious, I thought you'd be thrilled with the news. The leadership singled you out for this honor. Do you feel guilty that it was so much easier for you than it was for me to make corporal? Don't feel that way. When we had more soldiers, we needed more leaders, so rank wasn't any harder to get than it is now. We both know you're an exception, Rafan. That's why you're being promoted so soon. You've always been special. I am happy for you." M'hut paused a moment and then smiled at his young private. "But, thank you for trying to help soothe my ego."

"It's a shame Premier Sabu couldn't keep the military at its former level so there would be fewer people without jobs," Rafan sighed.

"Yes. Well, you know the country is too poor to do that. We've talked about this before. What we need is real jobs. In war time we could keep men in the army and they'd be happy to have food and a place to live. But, in peace time it is hard to justify that kind of thing. There are many who would call that slavery," M'hut finished softly. The sadness in his voice belied the laugh at his light attempt to be humorous.

Both men knew that Malfon's defense minister, Mustafah Aturk, loved to point out just that argument when military employment was discussed. "We cannot condone slavery under the guise of military duty just so that we can give people food and shelter," he would say. "We cannot afford to do that anyway. The people must find their own way to support themselves. The government is not their nanny! Let them go work in Norova, if they must."

That was something, perhaps the only thing, that Rafan and M'hut more or less agreed with Aturk on, but the minister always overlooked the fact that there was nothing citizens of Malfon could do to support themselves. Additionally, Rafan did not like the idea of Malfonies having to work in Norova, or Talon, or any other neighboring country. Rafan's dislike of Norova was obvious as he often called the Norovan's greedy opportunists.

Aturk wasn't dumb, he just couldn't offer a solution to the employment problem. So he omitted any part of the equation that addressed solving the need for jobs. Perhaps, left on his own, he might have come up with a solution. But, he had to answer to Sabu. After years of being batted down by the premier, Aturk's lethargy matched Sabu's. There was nothing to be gained by being persistent, so no more effort was made.

"Well, it is time to change The Guard," M'hut said. A soldier appeared and assumed Rafan's post.

"I'll see you tomorrow, Rafan."

"But, you see," Rafan began hesitantly, "I won't be here tomorrow."

"No? You're not going to desert are you?" M'hut asked with a laugh.

"No. I've been accepted into Officers' School. I start tomorrow. Sorry I kept it so secret."

"Only in this army could a secret like that be kept. I'm not surprised, Rafan. I am only surprised that there is still an Officers' School," M'hut replied with a laugh of mild sarcasm. "I knew something good was bound to happen to you. But, I thought the promotion to corporal was it. Well, I'll see you sometime in the future then, if not tomorrow. Perhaps we'll have a meal together, if an officer candidate can still eat with an enlisted man." M'hut turned to go, then turned back to Rafan. He was smiling. He put his hands on the private's shoulders. "It was a good idea to keep this a secret. Some of the other soldiers would be sore that the new boy was exceeding them again. It's their own fault for being inambitious, of course."

"That's what I felt," Rafan agreed. He also felt that M'hut suffered from the same malady as most of the other soldiers. He thought for a moment, then voiced his thoughts. "Perhaps you should apply."

M'hut laughed. "I don't think so." Then in afterthought he said, "But, you never know."

"Well, good night, 'sir'," M'hut said. "Now I guess I'll have to redo the duty roster for tomorrow. Oh, by the way, is it the army Officers' School, or the navy's?"

Rafan laughed lightly. There was only one Officers' School.

"No, I haven't forgotten your crazy dream of a navy for a landlocked Malfon," M'hut said.

Rafan sobered quickly. "I am aware that we have no navy." Regardless of any tension caused by the exchange, M'hut left Rafan smiling. Este Rafan was on his way to destiny. The corporal was proud of him, and a thought had been put in M'hut's mind as well.

CHAPTER 3

The Officers' School was almost a lark for Rafan. The regimens were easy for him. The regulations and challenges were easily coped with, and the self-disciplined confidence necessary for being an officer was already in Rafan's character.

Rafan was offended by the decaying slate boards on the walls of the classrooms and the missing tiles on the floor. After his suggestion, his class chose to fill the floor voids with cement they found discarded in a back room. There was no reason no one else had leveled the floor. It was just that no one else had bothered.

But, Rafan did.

Rafan's first class was map reading. What fool couldn't read a map, he had wondered. Then he realized that most Malfonies had no need for maps, maybe had never seen one. General education was poor and any travel was solely to reach work and return home. The schools barely touched geography, and apparently apathy for knowing of the world flowed down from Sabu himself.

The premier oversaw curriculum, or at least pretended to direct it. The Officers' School instructor was formal and uninteresting, until he recognized Rafan's devout interest. The student soon had the teacher caring about the course.

The special attention his parents had given his education and the physical preparation he had forced upon himself, his whole life, paid off handsomely. Together with his other innate abilities, they helped to make Officers' School solely a passage of eight weeks' time. Many times the scenario played out in the map reading course was repeated in his other classes.

One instructor objected to Rafan's constant suggestions.

"Why can't you be content to just take the course as it is Rafan?" The instructor asked.

"Are you afraid I'll learn too much?" Rafan had countered. "Some of the other cadets are starting to care a little more about the course. Isn't that a good thing?"

The instructor hadn't replied. His demeanor said he felt it an unfair burden to have to take on any more effort than he normally put out just to satisfy this young man. But, whether from internal sources or from guidance higher in the chain of command, the instructor indeed ceased stifling Rafan in class.

CHAPTER 4

"There is little to learn here," Rafan told one of the other young men who cared enough to become a cadet, enabling a class to be formed. "I hunger for the eight weeks to be over, so that I can start gaining accessibility to the military leaders and have the opportunity to study the paths to power and change."

"Whatever for?" The cadet responded. "Isn't it enough to just be officers and draw a bigger salary and get to avoid the work enlisted men have to do?"

"No," Rafan answered. "No, it is not. Once in the halls of power, I intend to achieve great things. This is but one step in that direction." The response left the other cadet shaking his head, not understanding Rafan's drive. He knew that long before graduation Rafan had already been able to mark himself as an exceptional candidate for anything he wished to undertake.

Rafan's fellow cadet had no doubt that Este Rafan could do whatever it was that he was aiming to do, he just couldn't see why he wanted to do anything at all.

"This part of your training is probably unnecessary," the instructor told Rafan on the firing range. "You'll probably never have to use your weapon. But, this is the military. So, you need to qualify with a pistol. That is what officers wear."

Rafan was lined up on an indoor range with a target fifty yards away. "This is about the maximum range for our little weapon," the instructor told Rafan and the other cadets.

Rafan removed his weapon from the holster he had on his hip and drew an eye-hand sight on the target as he'd been taught earlier in the class, before live ammunition had been issued. He awaited the command to fire.

"Fire," the instructor finally said. "Remember what you've been taught. Don't aim. Just point and shoot..."

The rest of his words were lost among the ringing echoes of the gun shots. That din, in addition to the hearing protection that everyone was wearing made the red and green flags displayed down range, which signaled 'fire' and 'cease fire' definitely a necessity.

The bullets from Rafan's pistol flew true to the target and perforated the paper bullseye over and over.

The cease fire command was given and the red flag came up. The cadets set their guns down, dutifully pointed down range, and pressed the button to retrieve their targets. Then removed their hearing protection gear.

The instructor came to Rafan's side as Este examined the results of his shooting.

"Multiple hits dead center," the instructor said. "Your usual result."

"Yes. But, a few hits were outside the cluster," Rafan complained. He demanded excellence of himself, whether the instructor did or not.

"Well, you will have no problem qualifying next week when we test...Unlike some of the other cadets." The officer looked down the line at the other men. "I can't tell if some of them are just bad shots or trying to miss on purpose." The instructor shook his head and moved on to the next cadet.

In a few days qualifying took place and Rafan applied himself fully.

"You've already hit the qualifying score, Rafan. You can quit now after the second round of firing," the testing officer told him, knowing Rafan wouldn't consider quitting.

"No, thank you, sir. I'll continue." Rafan turned his attention to the target, only ten yards distant for the third round. Precision was the deciding point at that distance, Rafan knew. So, he concentrated hard on the bullseye for each of his shots.

Women were not allowed in Malfon's army. But, there were a few civilian women who did certain chores for the military. They did things like cook, and clerical work, the chores chauvinistic Malfon had always deemed 'womans work'. Of course, only the men of Malfon held this view. But, the women generally acquiesced.

In the corner of the firing range one of those women sat recording scores in a ledger. She was struck by Rafan's good looks and impressed by his weapon skill. She tried to catch the eye of the physically robust young man on the far end of the line.

It was to no avail. Rafan was only interested in his shooting and wasn't allowing any distraction. It wouldn't do, of course, for her to approach him. So, she reconciled herself to the role of women in Malfon, and just admired the young man from a distance.

A few days later the weapons instructor told Rafan, "Another feather in your cap. You exceeded the best score ever achieved in marksmanship. That's three new records you've set here in Officers' School." The fact that there hadn't been many previous classes did not dull the instructor's awe. It was a repetition of other days of accolades. Rafan could not resist a swelling of pride, despite the fact he knew these achievements required no particular effort from him. These were the kind of rewards that had awed M'hut while he and Rafan were at school. Sometimes people accused Rafan of having an enlarged ego. But, they couldn't deny he had a right to having one. By the end of his time in the army school, he had earned a coveted position as Personal Aide to General Umbarik, the senior member of the military establishment of Malfon, second only to Minister Aturk. It was exactly what Rafan wanted.

"Lieutenant Rafan, I have some good news for you," the school leader told him at graduation. "General Umbarik has asked for you to be appointed as his aide de camp. He has heard of your ambition and has been impressed with your abilities. Since his former aide was recently removed in an attempt to shrink the military, you should feel especially honored that the general fought to have the deleted position reinstated and offered to you.

"It took the general some lobbying with Minister Aturk. But, the general usually gets what he wants if he cares enough to fight for it."

Rafan spent the time between the graduation ceremony and the Monday morning he was to report to General Umbarik preparing for his initial contact with the man he considered the greatest man in his country, with the exception of himself. Most of the few small improvements that had been made in Malfon in the previous twenty years could be traced directly to the general.

Rafan made sure his uniform was neatly pressed and all of his medals were polished. He had his hair trimmed, and on Monday morning, he shaved carefully. He and the general were both Christians and did not share the Muslim fondness for facial hair.

Thus, the special care with a functional activity that could have resulted in unsightly nicks he could have avoided by growing a beard and mustache. He knew the general would appreciate his clean shaven look, and Rafan wanted to make a good first impression with this contact.

Rafan walked, in nearly a marching fashion, down the concrete hall of the palace, taking in the beige wall color that offended him with its blandness. The floor was ceramic tile. At least that had some class, Rafan thought.

He found himself at the door of General Umbarik's office. No one was there. The aide's position inside the door, which was to be his, was bare. The young lieutenant approached an inner door, the general's private office. The door was open, so Rafan entered.

Rafan's mind flashed back to the conversation with the leader of the Officers' School, when he'd been told of his appointment.

"That is wonderful news, sir," Rafan had said.

"Yes, it is. The general had to work hard to get Aturk to rescind the order to abolish the position of aide de camp. Now Aturk is aware of you too. Watch yourself. Aturk is known to cherish a chance to claim he was forced to do something that didn't work out. Just a friendly warning, Lieutenant."

"Thank you, sir."

Now, Rafan faced the general's desk. "Lieutenant Rafan reporting for duty assignment, sir," He said with a snappy salute, encountering the general for the first time.

"Yes. Yes, Lieutenant Rafan. I've been looking forward to this day," the general said, returning the salute. "I have heard some very good things about you. I was also personally impressed with you at the graduation ceremonies." The general stayed at his big mahogany desk and eyed the man in front of him. He looked good in his green uniform with gold braid, the general thought to himself. He fits well with these drab walls. He decorates the office quite nicely. Of course, the general expected more from him than decoration.

Rafan had delivered the class address. That was an honor that Rafan did not consider diluted by the fact that there was no one else that could have been chosen to deliver the address. None of the few in Rafan's class had graduated, except Rafan.

He had spoken in a proud vocal projection of words that spelled out a future for Malfon that was quite different from its present.

"I love my country. That is why I have entered the army. That is why I have become an officer in that army." His delivery was unaffected by the lack of other graduates. He was addressing the assembled dignitaries, consisting mainly of the few senior officers and Minister of Defense Aturk. "I have accepted a position as aide to General Umbarik, a man that I consider capable of bringing to this country many of the things it is missing, among them national pride. I intend to help the general overcome the malaise that affects our countrymen. I have no doubt that my vision will come about. The same ambition and abilities that allowed me to set various school records will make it possible to give the general the support he will need to bring the brighter future of our country about, with pride, employment, and health, for all who stir their own patriotism and belief in Malfon."

The new lieutenant's ego was obvious and the fact that he had only been informed of his appointment earlier that day only highlighted the thought he'd already put into his future. Notably, the only member of the audience that didn't seem impressed was Minister Aturk. Whether the lack of enthusiasm he showed stemmed from not believing in Rafan's capabilities to use what he suspected would be limited opportunities, or from memories of long past frustrations he'd witnessed in his youth, even Aturk wasn't sure.

***

"Perhaps you think a general shouldn't show such admiration for a new lieutenant,' the general was saying in his office. "You'll find there are a lot of things about me that might not fit the stereotype of a general. But, I've done my homework, Rafan. I'm a good judge of men. What's more, your record shows nothing but dedication, ambition, and creative innovation." Umbarik had become an officer during World War II without the need or advantage of a training school. In the ensuing years he had seen little of the spark Rafan showed.

"I'll level with you, Rafan. I've lost my ambition, dedication, and innovativeness. I want us to have the kind of relationship that allows those things to prosper in you. I am old and I've grown stagnant. My ambitions for our country and our people have not come about under my leadership. I'm tired of being ashamed of my homeland.

"I don't think that it is all my fault, by any means. But, I think I may lack that special something that could have made it happen. I was ready to just give up and finish out my life inconsequentially.

"But, now, I see you showing all the same signs as I did at your age, and I'm charged up again. I'm hoping that with my power and your ambition, dedication, and 'special something', we may yet be able to see some great achievements in my lifetime. Maybe what I lacked was the combination of power and youthful energy.

"Together, you and I have that. You by yourself wouldn't have the access to the conduits necessary to make the changes you obviously want. I'd lost my belief that change could be brought about at all. I told myself that I was tired, old, done. But, it was just frustration bogging down a man with vision but no youthful persistence left to carry on the battle. I can give you what I never had at your age...power."

General Umbarik was heavy-set, but spry for his advancing age. He was also well known for speaking his mind. The spryness and the boldness now seemed to be at a peak unseen for a decade.

"I'm flattered, sir," Rafan said, uncharacteristically abashed. "I'll certainly try to help however I can..."

"Don't give me any false modesty or denial, Rafan. One thing your record shows clearly is that you want the same things I want. You want more Malfonies to have a job, in this country, so they can support their families while staying home. You want Malfonies to have a better diet and thus better health and a longer life span. I know about your parents, Rafan. I also know about others in the same situation. The things you brought up in Officers'

School tell me that you have ideas. You want Malfon not to be ignored by our neighbors anymore. You want Malfonies to have pride in their country, to have something to be proud of...

"So do I. You want Malfon in a place of honor in the community of the world. Your achievements so far leave no room for denial. Your statements, public and private, leave no fog on your vision."

"But, all I've done so far, sir, is attend school."

"Yes, and when you were at school, and saw a need for change, you spoke up and got attention. You pointed out that the school was using outdated manuals. We were teaching soldiers how to use rifles we hadn't used in the field for forty years! We taught them how to disassemble and care for those weapons.

"But, they had no use for that manual and knowledge when it came to assembling the weapons we actually have. No one else seemed to care. When I heard about your concern, I managed to budget some zlots for newer material. That's just one example. The worthwhile instructors at that school acted on your ideas.

"They say, thanks to you, there actually is another class of officer candidates behind yours. Some of the washouts from your group have been allowed to re-enter, and the word of mouth that's been spread around has caused a few others to sign up. The things your former classmates tell them about you and how things are improving in the school because of you give others hope there might be something better in their lives if they make an effort to move forward and upward.

"The new class is small, still, but there is a rippling of interest in self-improvement. Even the instructors are showing more motivation. So, don't give me any modesty."

"There were some, however, sir, that were not appreciative. I was often told to sit down and shut up, to stop rocking the boat."

"But, you didn't. Perseverance is important. My, boy, there will be people like that in your way all through life. Just ask me. I know. Those people will be left behind eventually.

"You have to weigh your convictions against the obstructions. If you're sure you're right, then you have to go forward. Handle each situation individually. Find the unique route to success for each, whether it's straight ahead bullheadedness or around-the corner finesse. Sometimes the person standing in your way just wants recognition of his own importance. Some people enjoy being difficult...I don't understand why. But, whatever the case, if you believe in it, your instincts will not fail to give you the prevailing hand. I have that much faith in your abilities...Because they mirror mine, from what I've already seen. I believe in you because I believe in myself. I also believe that as time goes by that faith will be vindicated when I get to know you personally. As I said, I am a good judge of people, and that judgment says I am not wrong about you, even with just your record to go on at this point. Take my advice. Do not let the nay-sayers bother you."

"Yes, sir." Rafan could think of nothing more to say. His mind was envisioning horizons he'd been sure he could reach, but hadn't known how to reach. Now, he knew the path he would take, if the general's words panned out. His temporary self-restraint was overcome and his heart soared.

"Dismissed, lieutenant," Umbarik barked from behind his desk. "Oh, by the way, get to work right away on some of the things I've posted memos on. You'll find them in your communications basket. That's your desk right outside the door. Make yourself comfortable and get to work...Any questions, ask."

Umbarik smiled. He was envisioning a new world around him. That world was the one he and his new protégé would create. Remembering his parents digging in the dust back in the 1930s, trying to grow something, dulled the enthusiasm he felt.

But, he knew that at last there was a chance to keep others from having the same disturbing memories.

Umbarik was well respected inside and outside the government. He never tarnished his image as a fair and likable soldier. He hoped he would be able to build on that image with Rafan's help. That would aid in making dreams into achievements.

He leaned back in his chair as Rafan exited. The buttons on the general's tunic strained, and the big man chuckled under his breath.

Umbarik didn't socialize much. But, he always looked forward to his occasional visits to his favorite bar for a beer. This was a reward his Muslim companions were deprived of, in his opinion. The practice didn't harm his standing with that group.

Now, Umbarik felt, there was much more to which he could look forward. Perhaps Rafan, also a Christian, Umbarik knew, would join him for that occasional drink.

A beer was nice. But, a better future for Malfon would be much more wonderful!

***

Rafan's first day went by, with the new aide settling in at his desk and getting accustomed to the flow of the office. There were no other soldiers in the area. It was just the general and Rafan.

By the end of the day there were more memos leaving the office than arriving, thanks to Rafan's efficiency.

"Lieutenant, I have a folder with a memo from the Premier for General Umbarik," a soldier told Rafan early on his first day in his new job. Rafan thanked the soldier and the enlisted man turned back as he was about to leave.

"Lieutenant," the man said. "I just wanted you to know I'm signing up for Officers' School. It's because of you, sir."

Rafan didn't color, he was getting used to flattery and compliments. "Well, good luck, soldier," Rafan said evenly.

When the man was gone, Rafan opened the folder. The Premier wanted to know how the general was doing on solving some of the paperwork flow problems that required excessive man power to handle. From things the general had said already and that Rafan had picked up on his own, he was surprised the Premier actually cared about anything. Perhaps these problems were causing costs that cut into his personal extravagance, Rafan thought.

Rafan found the general's memos dealt with the same sort of ideas Rafan himself had, in addition to routine correspondence. He had already seen a preliminary memo on the paperwork problem. The general had sent a memo telling the premier that he was working on it. The effort was concentrated on a blockade at the start of the paper trail. That was about all the general could tell the premier so far. But, Rafan saw a simple solution he couldn't believe the general missed.

The office routine became Rafan's routine. One day the general called Rafan into his office. "Rafan, I want you to turn your attention to streamlining our procedures," the general said.

As this was one of the projects some of the out-going memos had been about, and there had been no additional incoming memos about it in the time Rafan had been there, he knew he was being asked to come up with an answer to the paper flow problem.

"As you know, I report directly to Minister Aturk, and he has not come up with any suggestions for improvement, nor approved any of my ideas to this point. He is not helping in giving Sabu what he wants. But, we need to speed up the everyday business so we can tackle some of those things that you and I want to spend our time on...Right? It's up to us, you and I. So, I want you to come up with a better plan that Aturk will accept. I haven't bothered to keep him completely in the loop recently because I've had nothing to tell him. It's been hard enough to come up with memos to keep Sabu at bay." The general paused. Then with a smile, he said, "As a side project, perhaps you can find the time to do some work on the problem of feeding our people...Not just the military, all our people."

Though offered as a joke, Rafan knew it was not. He left the inner office smiling with a smirk that verged on laughter.

Weeks went by and the general and Rafan grew closer.

"Rafan, you don't have to say anything for me to know what's on your mind anymore," the general told his aide one hot day, a day much like all the days in Creche. There were few drizzly days and no cool ones.

"I know you always make sure your uniform is spotless and properly pressed, not because you think I might disapprove otherwise, but because of pride. I know you care about your appearance and want to be as close to perfect as you can every day, in every way. I know your mind is working on the maladies we're trying to cure, all day long, and at night too, I'm sure."

"Those cures need to be achieved, sir."

"Yes. But, beware of the cost to yourself. Don't put too much pressure on yourself. I certainly don't want to dim your ambition. But, don't burn yourself out," the general cautioned.

"I'll try not to, sir," Rafan replied. The general smiled and snuffled quietly.

"I know it's military courtesy, but I almost wish you'd stop calling me 'sir'," Umbarik said, smiling even more.

"I couldn't do that, sir."

"I know you couldn't, Rafan. It wouldn't be proper, would it?" The general chuckled again at an inner thought. "But, don't be surprised if someday I start calling you Este, Lieutenant."

The two men got along so famously it was almost a father and son relationship. The general replaced Rafan's parents in his heart. But, no father ever expected so much of his son.

***

"I know you hate these piddly routine details, Este, but they're part of the job." The general was indeed calling Rafan by his first name in just a short time. "It may not even be necessary to do these things, but that's the way things are done under this regime," the general told Rafan.

He felt sorry for the general, knowing that this paper bog and outdated way of doing unnecessary things solely for the sake of doing something, sifted down from Sabu and Aturk. Important things were left undone and 'make work' projects proceeded, albeit slowly, to serve Sabu's preference for not making changes in anything. The poor general had been putting up with this for years, Rafan knew.

Money would not be allocated for modern equipment and no attention was paid to anyone who made any noise about this road block to progress...Except by Rafan and Umbarik.

Sabu resisted change, and for whatever reason, Aturk went along with it. In reality, there wasn't much choice, short of tackling the whole system along with Sabu. Everything had to pass through the premier. Umbarik and Rafan chose to press everything possible that didn't actually directly threaten Sabu.

Their worthless work load kept the two from achieving the great things they wished to accomplish, and it bothered both men. But, it was indeed part of the job, as it stood. Both men knew that when your brain is occupied ad tedium with nonsense, you never have the chance to explore the scenery along the route of life. Perhaps somewhere along the line someone had instigated this paper maze for just that purpose. If underlings were not allowed to be creative, change would not occur and people in power would not be threatened. It took an extraordinary amount of time for a simple requisition to reach Minister Aturk because it first had to clear the general's desk. Even a requisition for materials like toilet paper or soap followed this path. That was the situation that Rafan and General Umbarik faced. They had no chance for innovation or creativity and couldn't find a solution for that when they couldn't clearly see the problem through the obstructions.

"I understand, sir," Rafan replied. "You won't find my attention to duties lacking."

Umbarik had never married. He felt he owed total dedication to the army and his country. But, his pride in Rafan took the place of the family life he'd missed.

"General, I hate to ask you this, but I need your help." Rafan approached the general with his head in an unaccustomed downward droop.

"What is the problem, Rafan?"

"Sir, there is a private that is being totally insubordinate to me. He refuses to salute. He's surly in his comments and declines making any effort to being a good soldier. I've tried being stern with him, threatened a court martial, tried to cajole him into a better repertoire that could possibly improve his willingness to have a different demeanor and be a better soldier. I've tried reasoning with him and explaining why discipline and protocol are important. I've tried to show him the value of pride. But, nothing works. I don't know what to do. I can't just let him get away with this disrespect."

"I know the man you mean. I've been wondering what to do with him myself. I guess there is only one thing left to do, Rafan. I'll take care of it."

The offending private was never seen by Rafan again.

Unknown to the lieutenant, the enlisted man was removed from the army and its benefits and was paying the price for his surliness by having to scratch for survival as a civilian. Umbarik had felt the need to handle the situation that was causing Rafan discomfort personally. There was little Umbarik wouldn't do for Rafan as time went by.

There was minor jealousy on the part of others over the relationship Rafan had with the general. There were those who resented his rapid promotion and the advance appointment in the first place. But, Rafan possessed the ability to get along with nearly anyone with whom he wished to get along. Umbarik was well respected and most by-standers were happy to see the general enjoying his circumstances at last. Eventually, Rafan made admirers of his detractors and was gaining respect for himself, as well. The one major exception to this was Minister Aturk.

"Rafan," an officer told him, "when you were first given your plush assignment, I was upset that you got the position I might have attained if you hadn't shown up. But, I've come to accept that it's my own fault I didn't get the appointment. If I'd have shown the initiative and qualities you exhibit, I'd have gotten that position before you even got here. If you hadn't come along, I might have gotten that appointment, but it wouldn't have been deserved. I can't say I'm glad I didn't get the appointment, but I'm hoping that your example has inspired me to do better so that the next time a position opens up, I will deserve it. Everyone I've talked to feels a little that way. We're all interested in performing better. I can't think of anyone who doesn't feel we're better off than we were before the general picked you as his aide. I'm sure there are some who are claiming sour grapes, but I don't know anyone who is."

"Well, there's Minister Aturk," Rafan supplied. "The general was already a thorn in Aturk's side. Now, I'm a sword in his gut!"

The other soldier laughed. Rafan slapped his shoulder. Rafan used that comradic contact to encourage, not because he felt emotionally close.

"Yes. I'd forgotten about Minister Aturk. He certainly doesn't share our opinion of you. I'm not sure why..." The soldier laughed again.

Rafan only smiled. He had occasional outbursts of levity, but his lighter moments were generally more a tool to manipulate a situation...Unless he was dealing with General Umbarik.

***

Another officer Rafan encountered said, "it's come to mean a lot more to me to work here since you came. I feel like we're accomplishing something here at the palace now. There's an excitement in the air I've never experienced."

A door nearby slammed and Rafan saw another face that had been hidden behind it.

"Hi, Hans," Rafan said, surprised to see him there, since neither of the two men was known to haunt the area. Rafan recovered from his surprise and responded to the light-hearted revelry that was pervading the athletic facility where they were.

"I can't say that we've accomplished much yet," he went on, "but, I promise you we will." All three of the other officers nodded and went about their business. They didn't know Rafan wasn't including them in what he felt the general and he were solely responsible for undertaking. His statement had been delivered like a rallying speech. He only needed these men to carry out their assigned roles, and spurring them on was his intention.

"Oh, Hans. I hear you're being considered for a post with the premier. Good luck," Rafan called after the men as he exited.

"Thank you, Rafan," Hans replied.

Rafan knew that he, Rafan, was also being considered for that job, but he had no desire to be Sabu's puppy. He knew General Umbarik was his key to the future. The general kept Rafan's work load as light as he could so that he would have the chance for creative ideas to develop. Rafan put that opportunity to good use. It was just the opportunity he wanted. He would refuse the position that Sabu was sure to offer him as the most distinctive candidate. The position would be good for Hans, or whoever else got the job, but not for him.

CHAPTER 5

Soon after his appointment as General Umbarik's aide, Rafan had started offering suggestions to his co-workers on how to improve their efficiency, on how to ease their labor. This was part of how he encouraged their personal support. It was what engendered the type of intercourse that had transpired in the locker room. When he found two soldiers doing a job together, he explained to them how each of them could be doing a separate task and thus achieving twice as much. Or, if one person was found doing a job that could be done much faster and easier by two, he counseled them to share the work load. Much of the camaraderie of working in pairs or teams was basically socializing, so Rafan reinforced having each individual apply himself to his own task as much as was feasible. One of the breaks with tradition that Rafan pressed the General to approve was to grant an extra day off with pay for meritorious achievement. It cost the establishment nothing and those left taking up the slack for the missing coworker strived to achieve even harder so they might be the one rewarded the next time.

The men obviously appreciated this, although there had been initial resistance. When he did run into objections occasionally, Rafan managed to finish with the thanks of the parties involved. When he ran into situations dealing with tradition or legalities, he referred the problem to General Umbarik.

The old man would light up with a smile, sensing that Rafan was settling into doing what he wanted him to do; trouble shooting, fixing his little chunk of the country's woes, as it were.

More often than not, the general would see the thing through and get the changes Rafan wanted approved and implemented.

One day, the general called Lieutenant Rafan into his office, where another man Rafan hadn't seen enter was seated.

"Lieutenant Rafan," the general began, rising from his chair. "I'd like you to meet Premier Sabu."

Rafan, of course, recognized the man. He was not overwhelmed. It was not Rafan's nature to be overwhelmed by anything. Working in the government, in the same building as the premier, he had assumed he would meet him some day. Indeed, he had intended to meet him, sooner or later.

"Premier Sabu, I'd like to introduce the most shining star in our army, Lieutenant Este Rafan. I expect nothing but great things from this young man, as I have explained to you."

"How do you do, young man," the premier said from his chair across the room. "It has indeed been brought to my attention that you are our shining star, as the general put it. You are our link to the future, I am told. Some of your proposals have reached my desk...The tandem paper processing idea, for example. Now, we can sort our red tape with half the manpower. Commendable."

"But, that was not the intention, sir. The proposal was made so that twice as much work could be done by the same amount of staff. We are so bogged down that we needed that new process just to bring our paperwork flow up to a reasonable speed. There are other things we need to use that time for. As it was, we needed weeks to process simple re-supply requests. Now, the procedure will only take half that amount of time." Rafan was cut off by a hand motion from the general.

"Yes, I realize that, young man. But, I took the proposal one step further." Sabu appeared unwilling to show this soldier any compassion. "You can see that our budget is way out of line. Malfon is a poor country. We cannot support people by giving them jobs that aren't necessary any longer..." Premier Sabu let his voice drift into silence. "Incidentally, Minister Aturk concurs, and as you know, he directly oversees the military."

"But, sir," Rafan sputtered. "We can't take jobs away from more people. This is not just an army issue. This is a problem for the whole country!"

"Lieutenant, where would we get more productive work for these people to do? With a reduction in the work load made possible by ideas like the Tandem Paper Processing, there is no more. We can get all necessary work done with less people.

Your new method is a wonderful solution to a problem we've been facing in the military for some time. As for the rest of the country...we just can't afford to employ any more people in the government in any segment. Reducing the payroll is the best thing that could happen."

Rafan started to protest, but the general again agitatedly stopped him, this time with a word.

"Rafan!" The general roared. Rafan subsided immediately, out of respect for Umbarik. The tandem paper processing project was simply one of several ideas of Rafan's that allowed work to be implemented at two entry points instead of one. The more urgent work entered one level above the more mundane items.

Thus, cutting the approval process to one less step and speeding it up. The TPP was only a small part of the improvements Rafan had come up with, but apparently the one that had really struck the premier.

Rafan was secretly glad that no one knew of the naval diagrams he had in his notebook. That plan would not have made a favorable impression on the premier; more likely an uncontrollable laugh.

Rafan held no great esteem for Sabu. Rafan wanted to say that he was tired of hearing about Malfon's plight. When Prince Sabu had arrived from Europe, money was spread around freely.

Malfonies enjoyed being paid to do menial tasks required to keep the country running comfortably. That money was spent to import good food and drinking water. There was a salt water port that Malfonies were paid to keep shining. Both native Malfonies and, increasingly, immigrants from Europe had access to these jobs. But, it was Prince Sabu's money and it soon began to dwindle. His country had no way to replenish it. There were no resources. Then came World War II and Malfon began to decay.

Rafan wanted to tell Premier Sabu that now was the time to do something about this downfall. But, Rafan knew that alienation would not serve his purpose, and as yet he didn't have a plan himself. He knew nothing would goad Sabu into action and if he and the general were to make any difference down the road, it was best to hold his tongue in the present circumstance.

The premier slouched in his chair. "The reason I am here today, Lieutenant, is to act on a suggestion by General Umbarik," the premier continued. Rafan heard a tone in the voice of his country's leader that he didn't like. Rafan sensed fear on the part of Sabu. Perhaps Sabu knew he was face to face with his destiny. Perhaps he felt he had good reason to fear Rafan.

"Este Rafan, by special recommendation of General Umbarik, you are being promoted on waivers of regulation, to captain."

"Thank you, sir," replied the surprised Rafan. His voice showed no excitement and his face showed puzzlement. Rafan glanced at the general.

"Who knows, perhaps one day you will be the head of this country," the premier suggested without much graciousness.

"You do share my bloodlines. Of course, this would be after my death," he hastily added with a smirk. Prince Sabu had married a native Malfony after his first, a European, wife had died, thus starting a blended royal family. Premier Sabu was part Arab, part European.

The idea Sabu mentioned, certainly facetiously, hadn't been precisely formed in Rafan's mind. He hadn't been sure where his path would lead. But, Sabu had presented Rafan with the distinct possibility of direction, Rafan thought. Sabu apparently had no doubt about Rafan's intention, regardless of how seriously he took it. Rafan wondered if there were others who felt this way about him. Of course, Sabu was just jostling this newly promoted mere captain in his army. But, obviously the thought was in Sabu's mind.

Rafan had been seen frequently in the streets talking to people, giving a sort of impromptu pep rally. He was known to the people on a personal level. His efforts on this front would now increase. He wanted people to know what was possible for their country.

"The word on you is spreading quickly through the country. You have started to become famous in our small little community," Sabu stated with obvious displeasure at the idea. "I welcome this spark of life to my administration." It was unlikely that Sabu didn't know why there were no other sparks, and surely he was not truly happy about this one. Sabu subdued ambition. Once, Rafan had heard someone had suggested bringing in foreign advisors to help find solutions for Malfon's problems, like unemployment.

Sabu had vetoed the plan. However, manuals had been brought in on how to keep stock alive in arid conditions. Improvement had been difficult, but the results had been moderately successful.

There were a few more sheep and even a few cows now living in Malfon. Sabu hadn't been appreciative of this improvement. He felt his veto had been circumvented.

Sabu was always uncharitable about the accomplishments of his cabinet. But, he had to know that he was the reason his ministers didn't perform better. The problem lay in what Sabu determined as better. He railed at any effort they put out to improve things, then complained when they accomplished no change. The complaining was mild because he definitely found change threatening.

Word of his fame was news to Rafan. He had no idea that his street talks, or anything else, had made him known beyond the ranks of the army. But, he supposed the other officers and men talked to their wives and relatives, and word of mouth from those who talked to him on the street apparently complimented him and sang his praise.

Rafan wondered how Sabu had overlooked his own displeasure with this spreading fame to allow himself to be persuaded to bestow the unprecedented promotion on him. The promotion was a contrary direction for Sabu's usual action on this sort of situation, or more closely, contrary to Sabu's usual ennui on the part of his government.

Rafan knew the promotion had to be the result of the general doing a lot of lobbying. He wasn't sure how the higher rank would help him, but apparently the general felt it would. If nothing else, it was a reward. Rafan wondered what the general had used as leverage to achieve the promotion for him. He knew it would do no harm, and it surely would mean more than the increase in pay he would receive. Perhaps the higher rank would make it easier for Sabu to keep Rafan under his eyes. With his new rank he would be more visible to everyone and that might make it harder to challenge the regime. Perhaps as well, Sabu thought that a little salve would give Rafan less reason to mount that challenge.

Maybe Sabu thought that a little reward would make Rafan feel a sense of debt and cause him to ease up on his motivation, thus becoming in a way, Sabu's slave.

Malfon was not a heavily populated country. Families knew that each mouth to feed could be the difference between the ability to survive and perishing. So the birth rate was low, achieved by every economical means possible. Some Malfonies emigrated to other places and easier lives, if they were accepted elsewhere.

But, they had no special skills that were sought after and weren't welcome most places. But, that minor emigration dampened the population figures further. There were other problems that kept the census low. Poor nutrition causing infertility was one. That also accounted for a high rate of infant deaths.

A few weeks after his promotion, still side by side with the general, but with more pull on his own, Rafan drew up a plan to build a better economy and improve the lives of his countrymen.

"Malnutrition causes far too many deaths in Malfon," Rafan told the general. That's just part of the generally poor living conditions. As you know, aside from here in Creche, there is little in the way of life sustaining land in the entire country. With water at a premium, sanitation is nearly unknown. That leads to disease. Coupled with lack of a decent diet, we have a double threat to life in Malfon."

Rafan had some ideas on how to change things and solve some of the problems. He had not aired them with the general before because they hadn't been completed.

The old man's eyebrows arched. "Rafan, I am well aware of the situation we live in, what's on your mind?" the general asked.

"General," Rafan continued, "we need to improve our ability to grow things, to feed our people. We need sewage facilities. Those things take water. At present we don't have any way to get the water we need. I'll work on that. The few wells we have are not enough. I'm sure something can be done. But, for now we just need a start at improving our standard of living. The people need to be shown a sign of hope. We need pride in ourselves. We need to find jobs for more Malfonies. The only way to increase jobs is to expand our business base. Right now, the government is just about the only business. Back during the war, the army supplied people with a means to survive. That was a long time ago. We don't have that any more. We don't have the money Prince Sabu used to spend. We need water, we need jobs, and those things will improve our lives and give us a positive outlook for the first time in decades..."

"Captain, have you forgotten that Malfon is heavily in debt from those times? Paying on those debts is part of the reason we cannot afford the military payroll we had then. There were countries that were willing to underwrite those expenses then, so they could count on our loyalty. That is not so now. We cannot afford to enlarge the army again, if that is what you are thinking.

Surely, you learned in school that Prince Sabu used his treasury to enable the spending that went on then, and as you said, that money is gone, along with the Prince." General Umbarik attempted to head off Rafan. General Ari Umbarik was, if one thing, practical.

"General, I am funneling my ideas on how to create jobs through you. You can sort out the flaws as you find them. But, I am going ahead on my own volition out of firm belief that they will work."

"Rafan, I know that many of our people leave here and take any sympathy for our condition with them. They have no fond memories of Malfon. But, perhaps the best thing to do is to encourage more emigration. The smaller population remaining would be able to live much more comfortably," the general suggested. That would only be a temporary solution. We still wouldn't be able to grow our own food. We would have to enforce birth control. How would we choose who got to stay and who got to leave, or had to leave? Where would the money for improvements to serve even the smaller number remaining come from?"

"Then what do you have in mind?"

"We can still get an international loan. I've checked," Rafan answered. "The military is the only nationwide entity we have, but the army is not part of my plan. We need a large, widespread base to benefit all our people. It has to be a nation-wide project. The World Bank will lend us the money, and I want to create a navy!"

General Umbarik almost laughed, but he knew Rafan was serious. "My dear boy, I don't have to remind you, we don't have so much as a harbor! We're landlocked."

Rafan lost none of his enthusiasm. "What I am getting at is that a navy can help us economically without military action.

My plan is to rent moorage in Norova for our navy. Putting men on the sea will give them pride in having a job to help support their families and their country. Many of our people, who have left, went because they were ashamed to be unproductive here. If these men could be providers and stay at home here in Malfon and feed their families, they would prefer to do that. Norova will like the idea because Norova is greedy as hell and it means more income for Norova!"

"But, where does our income come from? I don't see it. We'd have to borrow to pay the sailors and the moorage fees. We'd be worse off than we are now. We'd have more expenses. Besides, having a home port in someone else's country..."

"Lots of navies have bases in other countries! This will just happen to be our only base. We can raise money with our navy. I don't want to just give more men an unnecessary job. I can't really spell it out right now, but we could ferry soldiers from other armies from base to base all over the region, for instance. There are other navy-less countries around here. We can do specialized detail work like dredging, diving, salvage, and that sort of thing. We can offer to do the jobs that the more powerful countries can't afford to bother with. Our standard of living is so low, our costs will be well below that of our neighbors. Yet, the wages we'll pay will seem like a king's ransom to our poor, formerly unemployed sailors."

"You mean we'd be able to pay our sailors next to nothing and they'd still be happy," the general dryly interpreted.

"We'll have men back to work."

"I still don't know. That sounds more like a merchant marine than a navy..." the general started to say.

"That's why I don't want to detail it right now. I will work out a way to make joining the navy attractive.

"Our navy has to be military-like or it won't have great appeal. Our people know our army. It has prestige. We need to transfer that to the navy as well. If our men focus on the humdrum work our navy will be doing, it will be worse than the make-work the army does and they might not sign on, even though they need jobs. Joining a military force will give them a source of pride if we do it right. They'll be proud of themselves, and of Malfon. We have to do merchant marine type things in order to make an income, and that's the whole idea. But, there is limited appeal in a merchant marine. There has to be some appearance of glory. The palace guards get those flashy uniforms and the honor of guarding the leader of our country, such as he is. Even the smallest cog in our army has some prestige. I just have to find some source of pride to call on to make the naval service enviable. Certainly, the uniforms will part of it..."

Umbarik had never married, and Rafan was certainly the child he would have wanted if he'd had children, but, sometimes Rafan just frustrated the general. His pride in Rafan was often tempered.

"You probably have a good idea, Rafan. It seems you're rarely wrong. Your ideas are usually fresh and on the mark. The general sighed with resolve. "I don't see it. Still, I'll take it to the cabinet meeting with Premier Sabu tomorrow. I'll back you on this, even though I'm not sure about it. But, I have to warn you. I don't think the premier will go for it."

"I think he will," Rafan insisted. "He wants to look good. He'd love to have a better image for Malfon, if he didn't have to make any effort to get it, or take responsibility for any failures. I know he'd love to take credit for something like this. He has no ideas and no ambition of his own. But, putting more Malfonies to work in a flashy navy will appeal to him. I know it. If anything goes wrong, he can blame you...And me. I think he'd love that too. It seems he fears me. He'll go along, maybe half hoping we'll fail so it would hurt my standing with our citizens, and yours too. But, he will do it. I'm sure he will! All we need is the money and some time and the idea will work! Malfon will have a navy and more Malfonies will have jobs."

"I don't know that you are so important that the premier fears you, Rafan. Should he be afraid that you'll shoot him? Your reputation is certainly growing, that much is true. If this idea of yours for a navy happens, your name is going to be on everyone's lips. That won't please Sabu." General Umbarik let out a laugh.

"Yes, I'm sure that stirring up the feelings our people have subdued since the end of World War II doesn't make the premier happy," Rafan spat out counter-pointing the general's laughter.

"Now, now. Diplomacy. We don't need another war. Let's not be saying things like that." The general paused a moment. He had to remind himself that Rafan was just twenty-five years old. There naturally would be some youthful brashness at that age.

"We don't need another war? Maybe another war would be just what we need." Rafan fumed, then settled down. "Sorry, sir," Rafan apologized. "I'm not looking for a war. Although, I get very upset when I think about the way Malfon has been treated in the past. A war could be a positive influence on our economy. I'm not sure how..." he looked at the shocked face of the general and stopped again. "I'm really sorry, sir. I know no benefits could offset the loss of life and other costs from a war. I'm just so frustrated by the premier's attitude toward our problems."

CHAPTER 6

"Rafan, it is not your business to worry about why your memo on some scheme to offer an hour's time each week to some citizen to use speaking to the cabinet about his concerns and wishes was rejected," Aturk told Rafan one day when Este requested an answer to why he'd had no response to his suggestion. He had been walking down the masonry hallway past Aturk's office and decided to find out.

He burst into the inner office, past the minister's aide and immediately recognized the memo in question in Aturk's 'in' basket. The captain was able to recognize it because he used a different shade of paper for each day of the month on a rotating basis. He was the only one in the palace who didn't use standard white paper for everything. This memo of his was on orange paper. That had been the color for the first day of the month. It was now the last day of May. Rafan felt this eccentricity allowed him to keep track of his memos and correspondences with not only members of the government, but everyone he contacted in print. He felt it gave him a feel for the flow of the paperwork at the palace and it just overflowed into use for his other writing.

"It's been over three weeks, Minister! This is something we should already be doing."

"Rafan, I do not appreciate being told how to do my job, you should know that by now. I do not share your sense of urgency on your ideas. Nor do I appreciate you barging into my office. Now get out!"

Rafan had no choice but to exit. Aturk's aide was standing by the doorway waiting to see if any action would be required of him and was relieved when he saw that it wouldn't. He shared Rafan's enthusiasm for change, but Aturk was his boss! His actions would have been carried out with mixed allegiances.

Rafan spent months working out his navy plan, and even when General Umbarik forced a final decision by the cabinet, it took another year before any actual physical work could be done.

Sabu was reluctant in his support. Obviously, it was not Rafan's only embedded project, but it was the one he cared the most about.

"It will be impossible to get a loan for a landlocked navy," one minister complained.

"We will worry about that, Minister Arat," the general told the Commerce Minister. "We only need the approval of the Commerce Ministry to complete the go-ahead for the project.

"Captain Rafan and I will see to all the necessary details. The premier has given his consent, if you will go along with the idea. It falls under Commerce in some aspects, of course. So we need your approval."

However, it was true only Sabu had the authority to let things proceed. The premier wanted to be able to point a finger if something went wrong. That was Arat's concern. Sabu didn't want to look bad in the eyes of the world and this project would draw more than local attention. He'd gladly take the praise for success, but not the blame for failure.

Sabu had cleverly side-stepped responsibility for the project by pointing out that various ministers had control over the functions the general and Rafan required.

Finding allies with the power to help push the navy plan through was not easy.

Everyone in the government was afraid to be Sabu's scapegoat. Sabu was only concerned with not having to put out any effort. It was a characteristic even his wife complained of in their bedroom chamber.

"I have been reluctant to put my approval on this endeavor, but your Captain Rafan has a way of charging those around him with enthusiasm. I now realize that he may indeed succeed in this. So, I give my okay."

"Minister Arat, I need your help securing an international loan for the start-up money. You have the connections with the world community and the World Bank. I have talked to several individuals and they refuse to deal with me. They are familiar with you due to the arrangements on the debt payments we make. I am told only you can speak for Malfon in this instance. It has been pointed out that I am only an army captain."

"So, you've run into a roadblock, Rafan. You wish to count me among your allies. Well what is it that the money would be used for?" Arat asked.

"I want to buy an old ship and pay Norova for port space. I have talked to the Norovan authorities and we've agreed on a fee. They were very receptive to the idea, as I assumed they would be. But, you need to make the formal arrangements for the money. I have located an old pre-World War II Italian battleship which I feel would fit our needs."

"Since Defense Minister Aturk and the Foreign Affairs Minister have already told me they have begrudgingly given their signatures to the proposal they said you would be bringing to me, I know only my okay is left to obtain. I can now make those necessary contacts to raise the money," Arat said. "I was not told what the proposal was about and I must say I'm quite surprised. A battleship for a desert nation? I hope you realize General Umbarik has burned a lot of favors bringing the cabinet in line for this, I'm sure. General Umbarik, do you think we should let this army captain go around making arrangements with other nations?" Arat asked.

"As I reminded Minister Aturk, Captain Rafan is the second highest ranking officer in our army now, after some retirements recently. We only have one general, me, and one captain, Rafan. We have nine first and second lieutenants. So Rafan packs a lot of military power and responsibility on his two silver bars," the general told Arat. "But, talking to the World Bank, and the Norovan government? These are things even you wouldn't deign to do. It was his idea to start a navy, so who better to work out the pathways to getting one started? Who better to sort out the problems?"

"But, a navy?"

"The other ministers are supporting the effort."

I know. I know, and I'm not contesting the project. But, I've heard some of the tales about buttering the bread among the ministers that has been going on, like assigning an army private as a personal guard. Since when does a cabinet member need personal protection? Can you explain that little gift to me, general? I pride myself on a certain amount of integrity and it bothers me to see this going forward by that sort of means."

"I understand, Minister. But, Rafan has gotten me to really believe in this project and sometimes less than purely ethical means are necessary to bring about an ethical end," the general explained.

"Yes, unfortunately you're right," Arat agreed. "I understand Minister Aturk was particularly resistant to allowing this proposal to go forward. I believe only the indication that Premier Sabu wished him to co-operate brought Aturk around. You see, this is a military undertaking as I see it now, as well as a commercial one, and an international undertaking. So, Aturk naturally feels he has to be heavily involved. He wants to put his stamp on the purchase of this vessel, I'm sure. That would also go for the port facilities. He will want to share the credit for any success you have. It would be a wise move on your part to include him in your transactions in as great a degree as you can. You do not want to give him a reason to disrupt your project.

"You know, Rafan," Arat continued. "Aturk seems to take a great deal of interest in you. I might add, it's not a favorable interest. There was a time when Aturk was young and had some of your energy. But, as the years went by, he seemed to lose interest in everything. Now, he just more or less goes through the motions. He plays the part of 'yes man' to Sabu. Even his marriage fell apart from apathy. He remains a lonely man. I guess it's just the malady that this country gives everyone. It's easy to feel there is no use in caring about anything when the future holds only more of the same...poverty, unemployment for most people, starvation for many, shame..." Arat stopped talking. He rose from his chair. "Just more of the same things we have now. There, you see, even I have been infected," he said with disgust.

“Rafan will never succumb,” General Umbarik said. He looked over at his aide.

“I have noticed Minister Aturk’s interest in this project and in me. He has been quite obstructive already,” Rafan said. “I have found my memos still in his ‘IN’ basket after three weeks. Sometimes I never get an answer to my requests. Aturk balked at the purchase of the ship and renting the port in Norova until Sabu made him realize he liked the idea, as you guessed. He has blocked my ideas time and time again. He even stopped me from directly approaching the premier with any of my plans. I don’t know why. But, be assured, whatever his reasons for the way he confronts me, I will not let it dampen my spirit. I will not succumb to the lethargic malaise that holds the country down. I do appreciate your approval on this proposal, be aware of that. Thank you.”

CHAPTER 7

Enlistments began for duty aboard the sea-going workplace. Sailors-to-be signed for a tour of foreign ports, which unknown to them, were the two harbors Norova had agreed to let Malfon use. The enlistment office featured waiting lines most days. But, sadly only a few of the applicants could be signed on for duty.

There were only so many positions. Not everyone was suitable, either.

The uniforms Rafan designed were a big hit. Chances to travel, and a job, were all the incentives needed to fill the ranks of Rafan's navy. What the travel incentives lacked by way of exotic ports of call, Rafan hoped the green and gold braided uniforms would make up for in flash.

"Rafan, my boy," General Umbarik said the day the refitted ship hit the water, "you've got your ship. You've gotten your port. You even got full enlistment in your navy. But, there's still something that bothers me."

"What's that, sir?" Rafan asked with concern.

"It's just that there's no one to run this navy."

"Sir, luckily I found a few men who had served on board ship during the war. They're pretty old, but they have the knowledge that's needed. They have been placed as officers and are training the other men on how to run a ship. It's sort of like basic training afloat. In the future, hopefully, we will have a naval training school and there will be naval officers' training as well as army."

"You've got it all planned out, eh Rafan?" The general teased. "I assume you mean these officers were in World War II, not one of the regional conflicts since then. That would, indeed, make them pretty old," the general commented. "Of course you know I was a private at the start of the Big One." Umbarik laughed. "That would really make these men old...like me! Age is so subjective," he continued. "But, in any case," the old man beamed, "I know you've done all that. But, who is in charge of this country's navy?"

Rafan blinked with lack of understanding.

"We need a fleet officer. So, you are in charge of your creation, I am happy to say. I've managed to get Sabu and the other ministers to agree to naming you Lieutenant Commander, the ranking officer in the navy!"

Rafan blushed with pride and pleasure. He had already considered himself in charge of the navy, so it was not modesty that made his cheeks turn pink, just surprise.

"You'll answer only to the minister of defense, and of course, Premier Sabu. We will not have a command relationship anymore, since I am of the army, not the navy.

"But, General..."

"Hush, Este. Go claim your reward. You'll need one of those snappy uniforms, one with lots of braids." Umbarik was beaming with pride.

CHAPTER 8

A new era of Malfon history started. The first ship in the navy was christened the *Rafan.* The first cruise took the ship out of the small gulf, around the Arabian Peninsula, through the Red Sea and then back. The expensive trip curtailed any other cruises for several months. But, it gave the men a proud beginning. It also gave the Malfonies exposure. Everyone that Rafan talked to, from his old friend M'hut, to the top of the government, was astounded with the success and positive impact.

"Captain, what do you call the cylindrical thing the ropes are wound around," an excited Rafan had asked during the cruise.

He had no experience, of course, with nautical nomenclature as was true of most Malfonies. Rafan had made sure he didn't miss personally being involved on the ship's first voyage.

"That's called a capstan, sir. The ropes are called hausers," the naval man explained. He was an elderly man who had indeed served in World War II aboard a ship not much different than the *Rafan*. The commander wasn't sure whose ship the skipper had served on, since Malfon hadn't had much of a navy at that time. The seaport hadn't been utilized fully for some years before the U.N. had awarded it to Norova after the war. That, perhaps, had some bearing on the decision on whose port it would be.

"I don't know anything about what's going on here on board," Rafan admitted with rare humility. "But, it looks like everything is going well."

"Yes, sir. Things are going as well as could be expected with an old ship and untrained sailors," the lieutenant replied.

"An obviously uncomfortable Rafan apologized for his ignorance in the current situation. His uncharacteristic humility perhaps surfaced due to his discomfort. "I'm sorry I don't know much about running a ship. But, as fleet commander I find it my duty to learn a lot about it before long. I'm starting now, and will continue to study naval information after the voyage until I feel competent to give orders to you and the other officers."

Even though Rafan felt a twinge of seasickness, even in dock, he was devouring the cruise in detail. He watched cautiously as the ropes, or hausers, were coiled on the deck where men were checking them for weak strands. He wore a smile on his face that he couldn't contain. It was a smile of pride.

"Well, on board you won't need to be giving any commands. You won't have to be knowledgeable on routine things," the officer told him. "The crew and I know what to do."

Of course that was true. The skipper didn't mention that on board, he gave the orders. It was his ship.

When the *Rafan* returned to port on schedule, Este couldn't wait to see the general. The general was the only one with whom he could share his excitement of the voyage. Few had seen Este Rafan as cheerful as he was at that time.

"Well, Commander, did you encounter any difficulties on your shakedown cruise?" The general asked when they met in the capitol shortly after Rafan's return.

"The trip went pretty smoothly, considering the age of the ship, and the inexperience of most of the crew..."

"And the age of the officers?" the general joked.

"Uh, yes." Rafan shared the tease. His excitement was still obvious. "The ship is slow. It took us an entire day to round the tip of the peninsula. Some of that time was spent at anchor, practicing disembarking and re-boarding at sea. That will be important when we start salvage work. We put a small boat over the side and retrieved it without losing anyone. The boat was rowed. We don't have a motor launch yet." Rafan was working hard at controlling his excitement. But, he felt it important to seem professional, even with General Umbarik.

"Yet?" the general interjected. Umbarik tapped Rafan's arm playfully. Rafan enjoyed the touch. He missed his parents.

"I hope we will eventually have one, General. There are a lot of things we are going to need yet."

General Umbarik let that comment ride.

"At least the ship's engines didn't break down. I think that would have been a disaster for morale. The men worked very hard to get those old chunks of metal running as good as they possibly could."

"What other activities did you have while you were gone?"

"Since we didn't put into port anywhere...we didn't have permission from any other government, or our own...we couldn't practice docking procedure 'til we returned home. But, we did some turns and various maneuvers under power. When we got back to Norova, the docking went well. All in all it was a successful trip. The crew and officers were very happy and ready for our next voyage immediately. Unfortunately, the next time the ship leaves the dock will be some distant time in the future. We do have some patching to do, and we haven't been budgeted any money for another excursion."

"I'm sure you're working on a cure for that illness," the general said. "I'm glad things are going well in any case." The general and Rafan parted and went about their separate business.

CHAPTER 9

A neighbor of Malfon, also a landlocked nation, called upon the Malfon navy to ferry its army to a joint maneuver in Eastern Europe. The troops were transported across Malfon and onto the *Rafan* in Norova without incident. Another neighboring nation had lost a ship and requested Malfon's salvage capabilities to recover it.

"Commander Rafan, we have been allies for many years," an ambassador told Este. "How would the Malfon navy like a chance for a taste of real military action?"

"I don't know what you have in mind, Ambassador, but we might be interested. We have prior commitments for a ferrying service, and then we will be doing a recovery for a few weeks early next year. When did you plan to use the Malfon navy's services?" Rafan knew his ship and crew could easily transport the foreign army to its destination. He wasn't all that sure that the necessary equipment for the salvage job was possessed by Malfon and wasn't positive how to acquire it if pieces for the inventory were missing, but he wanted to line up as much work as the navy could possibly handle.

"We wouldn't need your navy until next summer. What we have planned is a beach assault. We would want your ship to bombard the landing site and then our force would take the beach from our own landing craft and wage the mock war inland."

"You're sure this is a mock war, you're not really going to attack someone and take us into the conflict with you are you?" Rafan was not serious, but joking was something not expected from the commander, and the ambassador wasn't sure. Rafan was buying time to think. Malfon's navy didn't have any ammunition, and the guns on board the *Rafan* were untested and quite obviously incapable of firing. Rafan's mind was working on these problems as the ambassador spoke again.

"No," he laughed nervously. We will be assaulting our own beach. But, we do not have any ships capable of shelling the shore. We have only small boats. We want the operation to be as realistic as possible. If we were ever to need a real engagement, hopefully we would have time to prepare a complete navy, or rely on allies. But, with no threat on the horizon, we cannot justify spending the money at this time to create a full navy. Keeping troops at peak training is important, though. The men still need to experience the effects of shelling, get used to the noise, learn to co-ordinate their movements with the actions of the ship or ships that would be involved in a real battle. That is where Malfon's navy comes in."

It must be nice to be able to afford maneuvers like that, Rafan thought. He had never heard of Malfon's army ever doing that sort of thing.

Rafan thought he saw a solution to the ship's status problems.

With the time available, he could request payment in advance for the use of the navy and use the money to buy ammo and repair the guns. The men would have to undergo new training as well, to learn how to fire the guns. The expense would definitely be beyond the scope of the profit brought in from the two projects that were already planned.

"I think we can fulfill your needs at that time, Ambassador. The only requirement I must make is that payment be made in advance. We cannot afford to reserve time and then have a job fall through when we could have had some other action scheduled."

"I am sure that will be no problem, Commander. But, our Minister of Defense will have to work that out with yours, I presume. Incidentally, we will furnish the ammunition. That should be taken into consideration when finalizing the fee."

Rafan didn't let the relief the financial help caused him show to the ambassador. "Yes. Minister Aturk will be advised and awaiting contact. I will inform him of the details personally."

CHAPTER 10

"Thank you, Commander," Aturk said when Rafan relayed the information on the navy project to him. "I will take this under consideration."

"Take it under consideration? Minister, we have to make this work. We have a chance to make a big chunk of money on this. When we add this financial gain to the navy coffers we'll no longer be in deficit."

"Who said the profit would go to the navy? Our country has many needs...Many that most people feel are more important than running a navy."

"I'd like to know who those people are. Everyone knows that if the navy profits it can help feed the nation. It's just the kind of short-sighted thinking you're doing that has gotten our country into its present state. Minister, it is the navy that is making money. Sure, it should contribute to the good of the country as a whole eventually, and it will. But, right now the navy needs to get on its own feet. The cabinet has been granting funds for us to operate, at a minimum level, out of the general treasury. The treasury is being depleted. The navy was designed to contribute to the treasury. Once it is operating at a constant rate, it will."

"The treasury is being depleted more quickly than ever, thanks to your navy," Aturk reminded.

"Let me get the navy healthy. Approve this project. Then I promise you the navy will start earning its budget by providing its own funds, with enough left over to contribute to the general treasury instead of siphoning from it."

"Are you telling me how to do my job?" Aturk asked. It was not the first time Rafan had run into a roadblock furnished by the minister. As always, at those times, Rafan sensed insecurity on the part of Aturk. Where his was grounded, Rafan did not know. But, he had learned in his usual quick up-take that there were ways to get around Minister Aturk. Sometimes it took cajoling, sometimes an end-run, and sometimes it took a lot of help from General Umbarik.

"No, sir. I just respectfully remind the minister that the maneuvers are scheduled for July and we will need your decision before then."

"Thank you, Commander," Aturk said gruffly. "That will be all."

Aturk led a lonely life, much like many Malfony men. In a country where war and industrial accidents didn't result in lopsided losses of male citizens, Malfon found the genders more closely equalized in survival rates. However, with men employed in the army, and now the navy, receiving meals and clothing at work, it was often the women who suffered the worst effects of malnutrition and poverty. Women were generally not allowed to work and there were almost none in the services or in the government.

Aturk had lost his wife in a divorce and thus, like many men, including Rafan, he lived alone without female companionship.

Aturk was close to no one who was married and even Rafan had only one married companion of consequence... Corporal M'hut.

The few available women were uneducated women who were unattractive to most of the men, even though most Malfony women were uneducated. Only the most attractive of these women were sought after and they were quickly engaged at a young age. In this aspect of their lives Aturk and Rafan were more alike than either of them would have admitted. They either had no interest in a woman, or had no opportunity for connecting with one.

CHAPTER 11

The naval ship *Rafan* was finally ready for its military action of shelling a beach in a mock assault after an uneventful cruise to pick up the foreign army. Pressure from Umbarik via Premier Sabu had obtained Aturk's go-ahead. When the ship arrived on station, Este Rafan was on board.

"Captain, turn the ship a little to the left," Rafan ordered. "We're pinching the landing craft against the ship."

"That's the hull of the ship, Commander," the lieutenant commanding the *Rafan* told his ship's namesake and his superior officer. "And, that would be 'to port'," he said with a grin. "And, on board I give the orders, sir."

Rafan eyed the elderly officer swaying with the movement of the sea. "Yes, of course, captain." The ship's motion did not help Rafan contain his irritation, but he knew the lieutenant was right. He knew he didn't even belong on board. He wasn't sure if he should be in control of the navy, but he felt that was the only way to be sure the enterprise succeeded. He knew how to get things done, he told himself with customary confidence; things that mattered, things that helped Malfon and its people. So, he was in charge of the navy. He'd scheduled himself on board for this maneuver. He wanted to be a part of this navy. It was what he'd conjured up when he was still in school. It was right!

Rafan felt a rumble in his belly and steadied himself on the nearby steel rail. "Captain, I will give the responsibility for running our ship to the men of the navy.

Excuse my misguided enthusiasm," Rafan, seemingly swallowing his ego, said with a smile.

The 'landing of troops' was much more of a seagoing test than anything attempted before, and now Rafan saw that he wouldn't be able to take first hand experiences any longer. Not only was he slightly seasick and in the way, but he had other important work to do that required his presence at the palace.

"There goes the last boat ashore," the skipper told the fleet officer. "From here on it's all up to those marines. They'll take their boats for the trip home. They only needed us for the launching and shelling."

"The guns worked satisfactorily," Rafan said, nodding.

"Yes. Number one gun jammed once briefly, but the boys knew how to fix it quickly." The lieutenant turned to Rafan. "It's been an honor to have you aboard, sir."

"A couple of shells cooked," another gray-haired officer mentioned nonchalantly as he joined Rafan and the captain. He was the executive officer.

"Yes, but it wasn't our ammunition. So, that's not our problem, is it?" The skipper reminded the two others on the bridge wing.

"Well, two duds and a brief jam aren't much to complain about," Rafan stated while managing an approximation of a smile. He preferred perfection.

"No, sir," the two older men chimed happily together.

A moment more was spent staring at the shoreline crawling with military personnel. Then the captain clapped his hands together and turned to his XO.

"Let's get out of here. I've got a sweet old gal waiting for me at home."

“Yes, sir,” the XO responded. His skipper was one of the lucky ones, one who had a wonderful wife. The junior lieutenant, being Christian like his captain, could envision that life. To him, the Christian life style seemed so much less constricting than the Muslim one. He pressed a lever on the box at his elbow and yelled.

“All hands, resume sea stations. Duty officer, take us home.”

After the sea voyage Rafan felt more lonely than usual, a feeling he didn’t let himself acknowledge. He also felt a sense of loss. Realizing he could no longer personally oversee his projects was driven home by that voyage. There would be too many projects. He couldn’t be everywhere at one time and he couldn’t do everything himself. His impressive capabilities paled beside some of those of his underlings when operating in their field of expertise.

He grabbed a handful of figs from a bowl on the table in the common room of his house and sat despondently on an overstuffed chair. His parents had scrimped to buy that chair. It was one of Rafan’s favorite spots to be away from the palace, when he wanted to think. It was also his favorite resting place.

Rafan’s mind didn’t stay down for long. Within minutes he was up and moving with motivation. The woman who did his laundry would be there soon and he needed to change clothes.

CHAPTER 12

"It's nice that we have been getting steady work for the navy, Commander. But, it will take a year or so to fully get this outfit running properly," the lieutenant that skippered the battleship told Rafan a few months after the shelling exercise.

"Yes, I believe you are right," Rafan agreed. He had just come from a visit with Corporal M'hut and had shared the same feelings with his only close associate besides General Umbarik.

"Finally the navy is supporting itself, though. The men seem to have no complaint with the work they're doing."

"No. I haven't heard any grumbling about being a merchant marine rather than a 'real navy'," the skipper said as they stood looking out over the rail on board the ship. "Many of these sailors have the first job they've ever had in their lives. They're happy to be feeding their families. Sometimes that's not just wives and children, but parents and aunts and uncles as well. The uniforms are the best clothes they could expect to wear in their entire lives. We've had to keep people in the army from joining up. We can't have one service deplete the other."

"Wouldn't that be a disaster...everyone deserting the army so they could join the navy!" Rafan thought for a moment. "It must be the uniforms...but, it wouldn't be so bad to have a few of those younger officers..."

"Sir!" The naval officer scolded without concern for whom he was addressing.

"Well, the navy is benefiting the entire country, and even the army enlistees are better off because of the navy." Rafan concluded. "The rivalry has ticked efforts up a notch on both sides. As the country benefits, so do the people of the country, including those in the services. Besides, we'll have young naval officers eventually."

The elderly captain cleared his throat but said nothing in response to the clear reference to the age of his officers and himself.

With the navy so successful, Rafan felt it was time to expand.

"Captain, I think it is time to take advantage of the enthusiasm of these young recruits."

"The navy is indeed a merchant marine for the most part. I think the addition of a merchant ship to this command would pay handsome returns. An additional ship would even expedite the efficiency of the service as a whole," Rafan said. "I hunger for the battle to bring that event about. It means back to the arguments with Aturk and maybe asking for more help from Minister Arat and General Umbarik. But, we have to grow as a country, and the navy is the starting point."

"I agree with you, sir," the lieutenant said with a nod.

CHAPTER 13

The Defense Minister watched the naval commander enter the cabinet office. The distaste he felt for Rafan flavored his thoughts.

"Minister Aturk, I'd like to buy a merchant vessel to start more profitable operations for the navy. To accompany the battleship, I'd like a tanker or freighter."

"What?" Rafan's abrupt approach caught the minister off guard. But, directness was often Rafan's way.

"I'd like you to bring the suggestion to the cabinet meeting for me. Since Minister Arat has been out of the country for some time, trying to sew up more business for the battleship, and of course attending to other things, I have been unable to reach him. His blessing is needed, of course. But, I also want your backing. Since Arat is unavailable, I have come to you first." Rafan hoped that a little buttering-up and ego-stroking would pay off at some point along the line. "I would like you to be the one who brings this proposal to the meeting, since my department falls under your ministry."

While the rationale of Rafan approaching Aturk rather than waiting for Arat's return made sense in currying Aturk's favor, the minister obviously saw the ploy of importance and ego building quite clearly.

"Just like that, eh? You make a request of me like I was your servant. You expect to get an okay for anything you want to do. You thought you'd come and see your old buddy Aturk and get my blessing before you told Arat, eh? I'll bet General Umbarik knows all about this plan, and he's not even in the same branch of service as you. You don't need his go-ahead anymore. "What if I don't agree with your idea? In as much as you haven't discussed it with me, I don't see how I could possibly bring it up in the cabinet. I can't see how I can be in favor of it, under the circumstances. I certainly can't be sure I'm not against it. What will you do in that case?"

The minister's tone was testy. Rafan knew Aturk was of nearly pure nomadic blood. He claimed it was pure. As Aturk saw it, Malfon was more his country than those who had controlled it, like Sabu. Rafan realized Aturk could probably have been premier, but he lacked ambition. Perhaps, once he had ambition, as the general had told him, but the title at the top had held little draw for him, and even less now, apparently.

"Why would you rather growl about what is wrong than put out any effort to make it right?" Rafan asked. "You don't like any suggestions that might make things better, especially mine." The minister's disposition better fit as loyal opposition than leader, though he rarely conflicted Sabu, Rafan thought. "I'm trying to discuss this with you now," Rafan tried to explain. He was not surprised at Aturk's response to his request. He had expected nothing less. He was well aware of Aturk's attitude. Rafan knew his approach to Aturk had nothing to do with the minister's bristling. However, this was the route Rafan had chosen to take to achieve his objective.

"Why are you so set on obstructing me?" Rafan asked. "Do you envy my upward movement? You could set your sights higher and achieve and sustain greater power if you wanted. I'm not affecting that, or is it something else?"

"Oh, yes...Rafan, the country's savior. I'd forgotten... No. I hadn't. The need to follow protocol really bothers you, doesn't it Commander? That's what bothers me,

Rafan. I am your immediate supervisor, so you get your ideas cleared by me, not Umbarik, not Arat, not the premier. It doesn't matter who you see first, because without my approval it goes no further. You flatter yourself thinking I am out to deter you from your path to greatness. The country will wear you down. The very people you are working to help will tire you out. I am only looking out to see that you don't force them into false hope before that happens. You cannot grow flowers in the desert, Rafan."

Could a lifetime of frustration result in this antagonistic disposition? Rafan wondered if he would be an Aturk someday.

Rafan knew that co-operation from the defense minister was impossible at the moment. But, now he could say he went to his boss first, before maneuvering around Aturk to accomplish what he knew was in the best interest of his homeland.

"Rafan, your navy is a joke. The temporary success you've had will falter and the old battleship will start to be a drain on the country again. It'll probably sink before long. Malfon will be worse off than it was before you borrowed all that money on the international market to fund your pipe dream.

"I was reluctant to be part of that plan, but Arat and the foreign affairs minister were convinced it was a good idea. I didn't agree with them on that, but I didn't want to be seen as the reason we weren't prospering, so I went along. But, I certainly won't back you in building your merchant marine fleet and put us further at risk. The results thus far will show that it would be another preposterous idea of yours, with an even less likely positive outcome."

"I'm sorry you refuse to discuss this sensibly, Minister. Perhaps another time. You may not have had the time to read the paper I sent you on this project. I encourage you to review it. Others will read it and you won't want to be the only minister who is uninformed. I won't abandon the idea, sir." Rafan's tone was polite and non-offensive. Making enemies, even willing ones, was not to Rafan's benefit. "I'll mention our meeting to the other cabinet members and inform them of my idea. That's necessary, of course."

"Still telling me how to do my job, eh, Rafan?" Aturk sniffed and turned away. He had attained higher rank than any other native Malfony. He was not going to grant permission for Rafan to out maneuver him and deal elsewhere. "I am not going to approve your request. But, I can't stop you from speaking of it to others." Aturk had to be careful not to become the only naysayer in the government. If the others necessary for the plan to go ahead gave their approval, then Aturk had to leave himself room to join in with them, or look the fool.

However, he did not believe it would come to that. Surely the others would see the folly of giving Rafan more financial backing. The solidly built long-time government official slicked back his black hair and sniffed again, a chronic action stemming from a life in a dusty desert. It was growing worse as he aged. He ignored Rafan until the younger man left the minister's office.

True to his word, Rafan did not let the idea go away. He turned to his old friend General Umbarik. "You see, sir, with a slight increase in indebtedness, we could purchase a small tanker and transport crude oil from small producers to the big refineries or storage facilities. Right now, the little guys have a hard time shipping their oil. The supertankers can't afford to dock for small loads, and wouldn't even fit in some of the ports anyway. There aren't many small tankers around anymore because the money is in moving large shipments. Nobody wants to deal with the small producers...except us. "We can afford to use a small tanker. We don't need to make the big money everyone else is after. We'll make plenty as the exclusive provider for the area's small producers. Some of them aren't even pumping right now because they can't ship. We can pick up their crude and take it to the supertanker ports."

The general mused. "Where would you get the small tanker?" he asked.

"There are some old ones, mothballed, out of use. We could operate one profitably on a small scale, and do a service for our friendly neighbors as well."

"Are you sure you're only talking about one tanker? Your words sound ambitious...pipelines, trucking?"

"Sir, just one ship. The other countries have pipelines and such to get the oil to a port. But, I am ambitious," Rafan assured.

"I hope you understand, sir, that we are only able to operate where others could not because our standard of living is so low, any improvement in wages and family income is a godsend. I do not intend for that to always be the case. This expansion will raise our standard of living.

"Yes, I see, and what plans do you have for us when this is no longer the case?" The general laughed at his own question, then went on, "it is true that we're getting along better with some of our neighboring countries, now that we can provide them with something of value. I'm speaking of salvage and transport work. They've always treated us as a poor relative. Now, Malfon is being noticed. I like that, Commander. Perhaps the tanker would improve upon that. By God, I knew we could make that kind of progress with your help. You and I as a team will make bigger changes yet. Right, Este?" Umbarik stroked his bare chin. "It's hard to believe it hasn't been that many years."

"Yes, sir. But, the problem, sir," Rafan reminded, disregarding the general's compliment, "as I have explained, before, is Aturk. Technically, all my ideas have to go through him and he just turns a deaf ear. The other ministers accept his assessment. Inevitably, I have to go around him to gain whatever success I achieve. Only Arat among the other ministers works with me at all. I don't understand why Aturk is like that, sir. What happened to him that has got him so set against me, and progress? It seems a lot like jealousy, but something more."

"It's not so much you as it is him," Umbarik said. "Aturk is mad at himself, and his ancestors. To him, you represent the European despot that bought his homeland. It angers him that his relatives sold out. Then he begrudges the visible improvements your ideas make in Malfon. He asks himself why he couldn't have done that, or at least his people.

"Even in his hungering for the old ways, he realizes Malfon is better off than when the people were nomads. "You are raising Malfon to new heights of respect and stability. Where Prince Sabu spent his money to provide for the country, you've gotten the country to continually provide more and more for itself. Aturk thinks, if anyone should be doing that, it should be him, or someone of nomadic blood," the general explained. "He is mad at himself because he hasn't.

"What's more, he remembers the tales passed down about how the original Prince Sabu's family had tended to madness, which led to their downfall in Europe. He fears that aspect of you. Supposedly, the intermarriages of royalty begat some individuals responsible for atrocities enacted upon the subjects, and faulty judgment in other areas. So, believing all this, Aturk mistrusts all European blooded Malfonies and worries about what it is doing to the mixed-blooded people now populating Malfon. There also is the religious difference. You and I cling to Christian beliefs and Aturk is a Muslim. That bothers him too. He feels all Malfonies should be Muslims."

"I'm not making all the differences by myself. I just start the ball rolling sometimes. Besides, I'm partially native Malfony," Rafan protested.

"False modesty still doesn't become you, Rafan, and I wonder if it has any vestige of reality. To Aturk, you are a European. He won't accept your bloodlines, or your religion. You are the difference, and you know it. You are the only thing driving the country out of its apathy. Before you and I teamed up there was no forward movement or improvement in Malfon. The people know it. You have an immense following among the people. You are the one who got us a navy and jobs for many Malfonies."

Rafan smiled a private smile for his friend. "You're part of it too. You pushed the tandem paper project through Aturk, up to Sabu. You helped me overcome the obstacles in forming the navy."

"You are the one who talks to the people on the streets of Creche about your plans for a better future. The people have heard of the changes you suggested in officers school. You are the face of the changes in this country. They many not know what the tandem paper project was, but they know it was a good thing and you came up with it." The general waved a dismissing hand at Rafan, but the commander went on. "But, Aturk doesn't do anything. Why doesn't he, if he feels the way you say? If he'd make an effort to help improve things, it would be different. I wouldn't feel I have to take on as many things as I do myself. We could be part of a bigger team. He could make a difference.

"The differences in our bloodlines have been blurred by a hundred years of living side-by-side. We're all Malfonies. A hundred years is a long time to hold a grudge," Rafan pointed out.

"Be that as it may, Aturk sees you as threat of some sort," the general told Rafan. "Aturk has been beaten down by years of frustration. Sabu and the people of this nation have taken their toll on him. He no longer cares or, perhaps, is incapable of making an effort on his own. Aturk is not an ambitious person. He never has been. But, he is a somewhat vindictive one, and that is the role he now serves. "However, Sabu likes your ideas. He likes to get the international credit for your work and still be able to duck any blame. You make his country look good, then he looks good internationally. Here at home everyone knows where the credit belongs. But, appearances are all that matters to the vain son-of-a-bitch. Don't let Aturk get to you. But, don't get so aggressive that the premier feels pressured. He doesn't like having to make any effort. As long as you can gingerly slip things past him, the frustration level from him shouldn't get any worse. That's just some friendly advice.

"Now, as far as that problem about the tanker goes...I think there is a solution. Instead of needing him to present your ideas at Cabinet level, I think you've gained enough respect from a majority of the ministers to be accepted as an equal."

"I am not sure what you're saying, general," Rafan stated.

"I am saying that you may never have to get Aturk's approval for anything ever again, if this works out the way I think it will. You'll have to surrender your military rank, but you'll have a direct line to the premier.

"What are you saying...?"

"I am going to propose that we create a cabinet post for you. It may take a little while to get it through, while I do some lobbying. But, I think it will fly.

"Sir, I..."

"I'm not promising a sure thing, but there's only one way to find out." The general rose from his desk and escorted a speechless Rafan from the office.

CHAPTER 14

"I refuse to recognize this upstart, pushy dreamer, as an equal. Only a few years ago he was only an army private! Now, you want to appoint him to the Cabinet?" Aturk's shout could be heard far down the hall from the meeting room. "Umbarik, are you insane?"

Premier Sabu spoke softly. "You seem to forget, Minister Aturk, that only I can appoint cabinet members. You can only confirm or deny that appointment."

"Are you trying to say this proposal was yours and not Umbarik's? I've heard what's been going on behind my back. I will not accept that lie. You cannot seriously be considering this."

"I would watch your accusations, Minister," Sabu warned.

Sabu knew that Aturk was normally his staunchest ally, but he felt no compunction for calling him on the carpet.

"Premier, Minister Aturk," Umbarik began, "it should be acknowledged that, indeed, I did suggest the appointment, but having been officially presented by the premier, we need only to vote on the confirmation to settle the issue."

"That will not satisfy my objections," Aturk screamed.

"Nothing will satisfy you, Aturk. Put aside your personal feelings about Rafan and look at the merits of the appointment," Sabu chastened. "Giving Commander Rafan a Cabinet post will place him in a better position to deal directly with foreign contacts. He will be more able to make decisions on the spot when dealing with international dignitaries. Sometimes that is a very important consideration."

"I am well aware of that, Premier. That is what scares me. Who will restrain Rafan? He will be free to do whatever he thinks is proper, without any supervision. We will all be at his whim's pleasure."

"I will still hold control over Rafan, Minister, and may I remind you that this terrible power you fear Rafan having is the same power you enjoy at the present time," Premier Sabu said.

Aturk was temporarily stunned, fearing some sort of reprisal.

"But," Sabu went on, perhaps sensing that fear and acting on it. "You are an acceptable defense minister, but beyond that, I do not see additional value to your opinions. We will now vote on Rafan's installation."

"Premier," the Commerce Minister interrupted. "I do not wish to upset you, sir. But, regardless of Commander Rafan's performance to this time, and your favorable impression of the young man, I, and perhaps some of the other ministers here, are not sure Rafan is mature enough to handle the power you wish to bestow upon him. I too have a favorable impression, but I feel we are placing too much on this young man's table at once. We might inadvertently derail the very enthusiasm and creativity that we admire by overburdening it."

"I understand your point, Minister. I have had my concerns about Rafan's fast rise to fame. But, let us solve this by the vote."

"I refuse to vote in this matter!" Aturk yelled.

"Aturk abstains," Sabu stated calmly.

"I vote for the creation of the post and installing Rafan," said Umbarik.

"You are not a cabinet member, general," Sabu pointed out.

Aturk fumed and pounded from the room.

"I vote in favor of the appointment," Minister Arat said.

"I don't think Commander Rafan has the experience for a minister's post yet," another minister stated. "I vote, 'no'."

So the vote went, with some ministers having something to say, and others simply voting yea or nay.

From outside the government it seemed Commander Este Rafan got whatever he wanted, and it was always something good for the people of his country. It also seemed that way to many inside the government. But, it was not so. The cabinet position was voted upon and voted down. The majority of the ministers agreed that Rafan was too inexperienced, and even Sabu's support had been lukewarm.

"The matter is settled, gentlemen," the premier acknowledged. "There will be no new cabinet position."

"Don't worry, Rafan," the general told Rafan, who had been sitting quietly inside the chamber while the discussion went on, "I will bring up the appointment again, and with a little more time under your harness, the navy will continue to shine so brightly that opinions will change and your favor will grow even greater than it is now. The passage of time will make you not seem like such an upstart. Once they get more used to having you around, they will start to think of you as one of them."

As they passed out of the room, Rafan turned to the general. "But, I'm not one of them. I don't want to be one of them. They are do-nothing cronies that obstruct the good things Malfon could achieve. That's why they voted me down. I scare them because I do things!"

"Keep that attitude under control and you will progress faster. Remember, for the time being at least, these people are your superiors. You need them. You will need their help from time to time. You need to be one of them, an equal in power, if not in character, if you want to get things done."

"I know, sir. But, just last week I was talking to a European Foreign Secretary and he asked me if we could provide transport of some cargo to an inconvenient little port near here for them, and I had to come back and make the request from Minister Aturk."

Rafan shrugged his shoulders demonstrating helplessness. "By the time I got back to the Foreign Secretary, they had abandoned the idea completely. If I could have just said yes when we were talking, I'm sure we could have had the job." Rafan looked up at the slightly taller general, "I almost did say yes, authority or not."

"I'm glad you didn't. Taking liberties you are not in possession of would short-circuit your eventual rise in stature by fueling the fear that you are out of control. Remember, we are partners and I want what you want. But, let me caution you from time to time. I have the experience you don't have. Where you see a blank wall I may see handwriting," the general advised. "Do you forget that I have to report to Aturk too?" Patting Rafan on the back as they walked down the hall after leaving the meeting, he said, "at least I got you a promotion to full commander," referring to the only real action that had taken place at the meeting.

"Yes, sir. I didn't mean to not be grateful. Thank you."

"Perhaps you should take some time off, get away from business. A rest might let you see things in a better light and help work out the details in some of those other projects you have buzzing around in your head."

The general stopped walking and looked closely at Rafan. "Do you know any ladies you could spend some time with? It might do you some good to broaden your life," Umbarik said with a smirk. "It could even put you in a better light with the other ministers if they could see you outside of solely focusing on your work."

"This country is my life, general. I can't take time off from it."

"Yes. I knew you'd say that."

The two men separated. Rafan was on his way to a celebration of Corporal M'hut's graduation from Officers School. The general would probably show up there later. M'hut was now one of the motivated members of the Malfon military.

CHAPTER 15

Rafan continued to exert his influence over the navy and anywhere else he could get a foothold. Still irked by having to report to Aturk, he managed to make only moderate headway on his projects. But, time passed, and as General Umbarik had promised, the creation of a new cabinet post was brought up again.

"Premier, I still staunchly object to creating a post for Rafan. It is not just a personal vendetta. I just don't see a position he is qualified to fill. All areas of concern are being attended to by the current number of ministers. His military influence is a Defense Ministry concern and I see no experience on his part beyond that realm," Aturk fumed.

He was slightly more under control than he had been the previous time the question of a position for Rafan had come up. Perhaps Aturk was buoyed by the fact that the commander had not been installed the last time, or maybe it had occurred to the Defense Minister that things were changing and a more cerebral approach might be more effective in thwarting the effort this time. Things he had heard in the halls of the palace had alerted Aturk to an even increased respect for Rafan. He knew he couldn't afford to run too strongly against that sentiment and hope to gain his objective...stopping Rafan's appointment.

"Minister Aturk, General Umbarik has addressed that concern. The creation of another cabinet position would allow the commander to fit his expertise into the post," Sabu reminded.

"But we don't need another cabinet post. What expertise are we talking about? Expanding government is not the way to accomplish the betterment of this country. Even Rafan would acknowledge that. It was he who stated that the only business in this country was the government. Now that we've started to grow economically, it is not the time to enlarge the government. We need to privatize and create industry."

"Industry? Now who is the unrealistic dreamer?" Sabu asked. "Besides, we wouldn't be enlarging government. We simply would shift Rafan from naval commander to a cabinet position, leaving the same number of jobs filled."

"You can bet the new position would incur a staff of some sort, and what of the naval command then? Someone would have to fill Rafan's position."

General Umbarik headed off an unproductive argument. "The position that I've proposed to create this time, I don't think you've heard yet, Minister Aturk. I assume that, since you apparently don't read the memos I send to you. I'm suggesting we create a specific ministry that you might be able to condone."

"What are you talking about, Umbarik?"

"I suggest that we install Este Rafan as the Minister of the Navy. He would still be involved with his navy, thus able to exercise his expertise, and he would not be in a position to step on any other ministry's toes, so to speak. The free reign you fear for Rafan would be somewhat reduced."

"But, the Minister of the Navy would still fall under the Defense Ministry," Rafan objected. He hadn't been taken into the general's confidence on this latest veering of direction. He had been quietly awaiting the outcome of a vote until this revelation.

"Precisely. It would be a full cabinet level post, but would share many duties with Aturk's ministry, thus not allowing Rafan to run amok as he feared you would without oversight. The new minister would have the freedom to make decisions independently, but the over-all strategies and intentions would be worked out by both Defense and the Navy, with Defense having the final say," Umbarik explained.

"I think that is an excellent compromise," Minister Arat vocalized. "I suggest we vote."

Aturk's face showed puzzled contemplation. He was unsure how to assess this event.

"But..." Rafan started to protest. The compromise was very unsatisfactory to him. It left him with a job that still ultimately had to answer to the defense ministry, and Aturk. While unsure that a cabinet position was really what he wanted, settling for a cabinet position that didn't solve his problems was certainly not to his advantage, to his mind. A slight shake of the head from General Umbarik stopped Rafan's complaint. Rafan trusted the general, perhaps he had something in mind that Rafan did not know about.

"I suggest an unanimous vote," Malat Sabu encouraged. "Can we all agree with this proposal?"

The room rang with a chorus of yeas, some more enthusiastic than others. The most enthusiastic was Minister Arat, the outspoken opponent of the previous attempt to appoint Rafan a minister. The new proposal apparently met with his approval.

But, perhaps there was more enthusiasm than just his approval of the new proposal provided. The minister approached Rafan as they exited the formal gathering.

The two ministers stepped aside to allow the other officials to pass in the hall.

"Minister Rafan," Commerce Minister Arat began with a smile. "You and I get along well enough. I appreciate the accomplishments that you have achieved. I'm sure you don't think you do it all by yourself, but I like the direction you are trying to move the country. It is all the more amazing, how much success you've had, since you have only been a naval commander. It must be like pushing a rock up a hill with a toy shovel." Arat smiled a little harder. "Your accomplishments give me enthusiasm I hadn't experienced in my entire political life."

Rafan wondered if this was true. It was a little hard to believe that he shared the challenge to pull Rafan up in the same manner the general did.

"I know it bothers you that some of your projects have to be cleared by my ministry, some of which I've refused. I know you were perturbed by my initial resistance to your appointment to cabinet level. But, that's the way this government works. I've done what I felt was right, in every case. Just like now I feel supporting this new position is the right thing to do. I'd like to think that we now share a focus. Perhaps I didn't fully understand your intentions before. But, I still think I've handled our relationship properly. We are parts of a team that includes General Umbarik, you and I. Unfortunately, I cannot include the other ministers as positive components of this team. As a group, we three are achieving things that none of us could have done alone. Perhaps you've never considered me a part of those achievements, but indeed my signature is on the line for many of them."

"You only went along with many of them because everyone else did, or you couldn't find a reason not to sign on," Rafan said.

"While I was not a part of the creative process, as the highest ranking of the three of us, I was the one who put them over the top and got Sabu's acquiescence. It took you two to show me that we can be a better nation than we are." Arat wiped his brow with his robe sleeve. Being a Muslim, he wore traditional desert garb, and the loose sleeve of his robe made a good cloth for wiping the usual day's heat-enduced perspiration from his face. "It took you and the general to show me how it can be done. At times we even prevail over our premier," Arat chuckled. "And it took me to accomplish that." Arat laughed more strongly.

Arat was part nomadic heritage and part European stock. He was second only to Sabu in power, not withstanding Aturk. But, Rafan had difficulty believing the sincerity of this man of arrogance and apparent enlarged ego.

Arat was never seen in the company of women, but he often had an entourage of young men. The Commerce Minister was sophisticated in all things concerning appearance and manners. His private life was a mystery to those in high government positions and they were content to leave it one. His composure under every condition concealed an ambition that apparently was only stagnant, not dead. It was obvious he saw himself as a leader of leaders.

"Thank you for the compliments, Minister," Rafan responded. "I do not feel that you have been unnecessarily skeptical of my projects when I've brought them to you.

I'm glad you think that we can work together. There is much to be done before Malfon can even be considered a third rate nation. It's a pity Aturk is not as willing to work with me." This comment evoked another laugh from Arat.

The two men were still standing in the hall, but everyone else was now gone. Rafan was still not sure what was really on Arat's mind. He had just been appointed to a ministry position that to Rafan's mind was pointless, and this man of power was having the most prolonged conversation he'd ever had with him moments later.

"I've wanted to meet with you, Rafan. I have something in mind. I want you to know that we are together on this, and the general too," Arat said. "I know there are others, like Aturk, who will not be. I will let you in on the details as they are worked out."

"What are you talking about, Minister?"

"For now, suffice to say that we need leadership, not the layabout kind Sabu has been providing. It will take drastic action to bring about any change. I know you want change. We cannot continue at the pace we are presently forced to take, due to Sabu's restrictions. We need faster tracks for things like your great ideas, Rafan. We will have change soon. I will be in touch," Arat finished.

Rafan had always thought the middle-aged Commerce Minister to be a bit stuffy. But, there was a new vibrance to him that Rafan had noticed. The man smelled oddly, prone to using too many bath oils, but Rafan had never disliked him and now he seemed to be asking the navy man for an alliance of some sort. What lay ahead Rafan couldn't guess. But, he would progress cautiously as long as he liked what was being achieved. If the general was involved then what lay ahead could only be good, Rafan felt sure.

Another meeting took place not long after the meeting between Arat and Rafan. It took place in the premier's office.

"Aturk, I feel I need to rely on you to help me balance the Rafan faction in order to maintain control of this country's stability," Sabu pleaded. "His following is getting stronger and stronger."

More and more Sabu sought comfort from Aturk. The premier considered him his main, if only, ally. He was an ally because the minister feared losing his job and a life that was much easier than that of his fellow countrymen.

"I am feeling beset upon from all sides. The people see the improvement that they credit Rafan for producing and wonder why I hadn't done it before he came along. I know the people have no idea what's best for them, so I pay them little mind. But, some of the ministers are blatantly resistant to my wishes as you've surely seen. They see me as desirous of only preventing change. They say I try to maintain my rule by keeping the status quo, that I have no concern for my subjects. That's not true. I know what's best for them, and that's what I do. I can't let a bunch of untested ideas give them false hope and fail miserably. That would cost us financially and spiritually.

"I receive no such grief internationally. But, Este Rafan, General Umbarik, Minister Arat, and now the Foreign Affairs Minister, are belligerently confronting me at every opportunity. You even confront me at times."

Aturk felt his confrontations were justified for the poor treatment Sabu gave him when the Defense Minister needed support. But, he kept his thoughts to himself. He understood the points Sabu was making and didn't want to be included as part of the problem.

"I will certainly stand by your side, Premier. Although, I am not sure what I can do for you in stemming this tide of dissension." To the Defense Minister, the premier was part of the problem that caused those like Rafan to rock the boat. Sabu was just another spoiler of Aturk's homeland...an undeserving, unimpressive one. Any assistance Aturk would give out would be for his own self-interest and would be handed out on a situation by situation basis. Of course, he wouldn't tell the premier that.

"If the need should arise to put a stop to the efforts of Rafan, you can count on me," Aturk chanted convincingly with his posture representing an impressive image of a loyal man in uniform.

CHAPTER 16

Rafan was very comforted by what he saw in the streets of Creche. Where once there had been empty streets or poor people squatting on the sidewalks Prince Sabu had built decades ago, now there were people walking with a purpose. Many of them were in uniform and uniformed or not, they had places to go, jobs to reach, something to do in their lives. In just the short period of time that Rafan had risen from an army private to Minister of the Navy, the attitudes of the people had noticeably changed. Malfonies were starting to dare to hope for a better future. That attitude change was even evident in many members of government. M'hut was quickly gaining power of his own by exhibiting ambition he had never before shown. Willingly playing subordinate to Rafan, M'hut reinforced the new minister's confidence in his ability to handle any situation that should occur. Thus buoyed, Rafan returned to work only to find Arat waiting for him in his office.

"Rafan," Arat told his newly recruited protégé, "come with me. It is time to act for the improvement of our country. I hope I am not amiss in assuming that I have your support in this action."

General Umbarik and Rafan had not spoken since the meeting where the Minister of the Navy had been installed, so Rafan had not been able to sound out the general's stand on whatever Arat had planned. "Minister Arat, what action are you talking about? What are you planning to do? We haven't discussed any plan, or even what we want to accomplish specifically. Is the General here?"

They walked along in silence for a moment. "Just stand by my side. That's all I ask," Arat finally said. They reached Premier Sabu's office. "It is time for action," Arat repeated.

Inside his office, Arat approached the premier. "Premier Sabu," Arat said loudly enough to be heard by the others present in the office. "It seems to many of us that you are obstructing all the gains that we seek in making Malfon into a homeland we can be proud of. We feel that you are happy to take credit for the successes of others, but not to lead this country to progress," Arat went on boldly. "My supporters and I demand more of a leader than just following the trail blazed by others. You know as well as I do that Este Rafan, General Umbarik, myself, and a few others, are the only ones making a difference in this nation of ours. You take no responsibility for a false step, but lay it at the feet of others. You take no initiative on your own, of any kind. You restrict the progress we attempt."

Fear of where this was leading showed on Sabu's face.

"You vetoed the merchant marine tanker project, for example..." Arat continued.

"Minister Aturk convinced me that enlarging the seagoing capabilities of a landlocked nation would be folly," Sabu interrupted. "His okay was needed for me to even consider it." He gestured to Aturk on his right. "I am not sure these plans you speak of are the ones that should be followed..."

"What other plans are there?" Arat asked. "Have you come up with a plan to employ more of our people? Have you figured out a way to feed them better? Has Aturk established himself as a foolproof advisor? Can you trust

Aturk to come up with the right answers for our future? Can either of you offer anything? Hah! One of you is as bad as the other."

"Aturk has had no plans, I agree, but without my approval, neither do you," Sabu stated with authority he did not feel at the moment. Aturk's face took on a frown. Rafan could not help but notice that the premier began to wring his hands. His nerve was failing before this onslaught.

"You rule by default, Sabu," Arat spat out.

"What is it you want me to do?" Sabu asked. But, he already knew. What little control he'd ever had over the situation was slipping away.

Rafan had never seen Arat speak or act so aggressively.

"Minister, Arat," Rafan inserted, "I am sure you have good intentions, sir, but perhaps we should be more respectful..." He was looking around the room for General Umbarik and found him. "Perhaps we should all talk about the situation calmly."

Rafan looked to General Umbarik to see if he was truly backing Arat's actions and attacking attitude.

The general seemed prepared for the moment, showing no signs of trying to restrain Arat. Rafan wondered if the general had kept his part in this planned confrontation from him for a reason.

Perhaps Umbarik thought that Arat's intentions wouldn't coincide with Rafan's and descension in the unified front would temper any action and result in diluting initiative to the point of failure. Arat apparently felt the right time was now, and it appeared the general did as well.

"Besides the merchant marine proposal, you've stood in the way of every major improvement we've tried to make for this country," Arat continued, ignoring Rafan's interruption.

"By 'we', I assume you mean you and Rafan," Sabu said. He was trying to salvage something from the impending deterioration of his power.

"And others," Arat assured.

Nodding at Rafan, who was standing slightly behind Arat, taking in the events unfolding before him with unbelieving eyes, Sabu continued. "I'm sorry you see things this way, Minister. But, I must remind you that you and Rafan are not the leaders of this government." His bravado didn't sound convincing. He was clinging to hope that he could keep the damage to his regime to an acceptable level, but knowing that hope was a small one. But, to his credit, he wasn't ready to give up yet.

"Ah, but we ministers, in a majority, are," Arat countered. "You cannot rule without us supporting you."

Sabu's mind sought a safe harbor as his skin began to show beads of sweat. He knew what Arat said was true. His mind drifted to a long forgotten meal on the roof of the palace with his wife. He was being served graciously by admiring waiters proud to be selected to serve the premier. Was this all a thing of the past? He feared it was. The refuge of his unfocused mental wandering could not stand up to his fear of what was occurring in the present. He would miss the trappings of luxury that he had enjoyed. He didn't want to lose them.

Sabu gathered his moxie and addressed the Commerce Minister forcefully. "I remind you that I am the premier. You will live with the system as it is, or you will be replaced. You are my advisors, not the other way around. Malfon will move forward at a pace of my choosing.

"I appointed each and every one of you. You do not decide how Malfon is run. You should be quite satisfied." Sabu tried a new ploy. "You enjoy a very influential position, with lots of personal benefits. I allow you considerable sway in all matters." Sabu hoped reminding the minister and his supporters of how well off they were compared to their countrymen would make them pause a moment to at least reconsider their actions.

"That is not good enough for our country," Arat said. "For years I have lacked the energy to confront the ennui Malfonies share. Now, thanks to Rafan, I am willing to take action. I will no longer stand by and watch opportunities be missed. I want better for everyone."

"What? Have you no limit to your need for glory? How dare you talk to me like this!"

Rafan railed to speak, but only managed to cut off the premier so that Arat kept the floor.

Arat did not alter his stance. He pointed a deliberate finger at Sabu. "It is not for glory. I need nothing more for myself. It is the people of Malfon that I am trying to help." Arat motioned toward the doorway. "The guards have already been instructed to remove you to your private quarters. They are with us, if you resist..."

"What are you doing, Arat?" Rafan finally got out.

"Arat, you are making a mistake!" Sabu yelled. He knew it was over, but continued to fight.

"I have warned you, Sabu, the guards are with us. They are loyal to Rafan."

"But, I'm not..." Rafan attempted to deny his involvement.

Arat turned to Aturk. "Minister, we are prepared to keep you as head of defense, if you don't jeopardize that," Arat informed his associate. "You've done an acceptable job, Aturk. You show no initiative and you're obstructive. But, perhaps that will change, and maybe we've needed that anchor at times. The defense ministry requires no more of you than you are capable of. We are not a military power. You have done nothing to actually shame our country that I know of and you may be counted as one of us, if you choose to be," Arat suggested.

Aturk quickly summed up the situation and stepped back.

The general continued to be quiet and only moved his gaze from one participant to another. This was Arat's show.

"Malat, don't resist," Arat continued. "You know that you've only remained in power this long because no one had the ambition to unseat you. But, we now have that drive. We cannot let you stand in our way. We have a vision of the future, and you are not in it. Don't let your ego make you incautious. I warn you, we are serious." Arat's voice verged on being pompous.

Sabu looked over at the guards now stationed near the entrance to the premier's office. "You mean Rafan has the drive!" Sabu spat back with more spine than he had shown in years. "You can't do this. I am of royal blood. The international community will condemn you."

"I am also of royal blood," Arat countered. "The international community has probably wondered why this hasn't happened before. I think we will be accepted. Rafan is being recognized as a positive influence around the Middle East. That will win us respect. Now, will you exit on your own, or shall I have the guards escort you?"

"Arat is right, Sabu," General Umbarik said. You might even be better off with us running the country. If you stop and think about it, any benefits we bring about, you will share in with the rest of our people. There were no benefits coming the way things have been going, at least not very soon."

Rafan, sensing that the deed was done, once the general spoke, tried to emphasize the positives. "I am sure you will be treated with due respect in your, uh, retirement. We'll see to it that you retain the privileges of a former ruler." Rafan saw a need to reassert himself, and for the first time since the confrontation had started, he sounded less like a young man watching his elders in awe and more like the motivated leader he had become.

"Does he speak for you, Arat?" Sabu asked.

"Of course. General Umbarik, Rafan, the others, and I, speak with one voice."

"I knew it would come to this, that ambitious son of a bitch..."

"Don't make it hard on yourself, Malat," Arat suggested. "It's over."

"I warn you, it's not. I pose no threat, but watch yourself, Arat. The danger will come, not from me, but from Rafan. I have sensed it from the moment I met him. He will not stop until his dreams of glory are fulfilled, and you are in his way. It may seem he is only looking out for Malfon, but he is really interested in his own destiny."

"This was my idea, Malat. Rafan has only given me the hope of success that made me go ahead. Rafan will be a most valuable part of the team that will bring Malfon into the modern world. Together we will see to it that no one in this place will live in poverty and squaller any longer."

Only then did Rafan realize that he now occupied a position of power superior to General Umbarik. There were few in the country who held a higher position than he did. Arat was counting on him, not the general, to be the kingpin of his new regime. The other ministers were only his equals now, except the newly contrite Aturk. Now, things could really get done! A smile crept across Rafan's lips.

CHAPTER 17

Rafan had long since noticed that the lax military courtesy he had been surrounded by as a palace guard and an army officer was a thing of the past. No one had been replaced. The result of Rafan's enthusiasm had infected even those who had been slovenly.

Over the years Malfon's army had evolved into a reasonably presentable military force, and of course, the navy had started that way. There were no more guards missing from their posts. There were no more personal conversations with feet on the desk.

Rafan was very proud of all this. It was his updating of manuals, his tandem paper processing, his creation of the navy, his personal charisma in public and among the military, that had changed things for the better, and he knew it. Malfon was on its way to respectableness.

***

"Este, how nice to see you," M'hut said. "Or should I say, Minister?"

"Este is fine, Mahumud." This man and the general were the only two people to whom he would have said that. "I don't suppose this is a social visit."

"Really, it is," Rafan replied. The two men were standing in the doorway of M'hut's home, both of them in uniform. Rafan had yet to give his up, but would soon have to as a civilian minister.

"Well, come on in," M'hut welcomed. "Pardon my poor hospitality."

"Where is your wife, Mahumud?" The naval man asked.

"She is with her mother. She is quite pregnant if you don't know. You haven't seen her in a long while. I think she seeks out her mother to share condemnation of the man who put her in that condition."

Both men laughed. It was obviously a joke. The laughter felt good to Rafan. He hadn't felt much like laughing at any time during his life. But, now, with Arat's coup, laughter was usually well beyond Rafan's reach. Perhaps things would be better, but for now they were just more tense. He hadn't eased into his new cabinet post yet, but he was anxious to do so. Then he would see how things would be.

"How are things going in the army?" Rafan asked. "I don't know what's happening there now that I'm in charge of the navy."

"Don't try to tell me the general doesn't keep you posted. I know better."

"I want to know what you're up to, Mahumud. How are you doing? I want to know what you think."

M'hut had trouble believing that Rafan actually cared about his life. There was another reason he was asking questions, M'hut knew. "Nothing has changed much in the army. We still guard the palace. We have a couple of soldiers helping your sailors guard the port in Norova, as you know. Once in a while someone resigns or finishes his hitch and goes and joins the navy so they can wear one of those fancy uniforms."

"And we have to retrain them," Rafan said with a grin. The easy laughter came again.

"At least the defections help me move up the power ladder sometimes." M'hut looked across the room at a bare wall. "I can't help but be amazed that the goofy dream you had all those years ago about a navy for a landlocked nation has actually come true. It is as you told me it would be. People have pride in their navy. The sailors are proud of themselves. The guys in the army see that the navy is providing income for Malfon, just like you said it would, and respect that. You've made me believe, Este. The navy is an answer to some of our problems."

"Yes, some of them. But, Mahumud, I am concerned about how the army is taking the events at the palace," Rafan asked, once again somber.

"Actually, I think most of the army is relieved. Everyone knew Sabu was a deterrent to a better future. The troops and everyone I've talked to outside the military are confident things will get better now, faster," M'hut answered.

"That's comforting to know," Rafan stated. "I don't see Aturk or the general leading a counter coup or anything, but there might have been some upstart lieutenant looking to take matters into his own hands."

"You don't need to worry about the army," M'hut said. "I trust you have those crazy wave jockeys of yours under control."

"Yes." Rafan allowed himself a little smile. "But, I'm just not sure where we're headed. I think we're headed in the right direction, but only time will tell." Rafan had reservations about fussy Arat. In truth, the only person he was sure he could trust was himself.

The two men shared a cup of tea and discussed the old days of army duty together, and their childhoods.

"Remember the time Private Hoya thought the dust storm was a distraction for an attack by Norova?" M'hut asked.

"Yes. He had too much to drink that night to be coming on duty, that's for sure," Rafan shared. "But, you didn't courtmartial him."

"No. He was obviously more than drunk. We had to relieve him of duty and put him into psychiatric care. We took care of his family, my wife and I. The army couldn't afford to offer any help."

"Yes, that care couldn't have been gotten if he'd been court-martialed and dishonorably discharged. You did well by him. You're a good man, Mahumud." There was more chatting, then it was time for Rafan to go.

"There's a place for you in this future, I'm sure," Rafan told M'hut.

"I hope there is. I should tell you, I'm up for a promotion next week. So watch your heels. You gave me the desire, now I'm acting on that motivation. See what your enthusiasm has done?"

"Congratulations, Mahumud. I know you deserve it." Rafan gave one last handshake and left.

After the navy man disappeared down his doorway path, M'hut returned to the project he had been pondering when Rafan had appeared at his home. He indeed would be promoted the next week, but he had an agenda that went well beyond that which he didn't want to share with Rafan just yet. His desire to make something of himself had been sparked by Rafan. But, now roadblocks to his goal had started to turn up, beginning with his wife and unborn child.

M'hut's new drive made him define his goals for the future after much brainstorming with his wife, Anna. He decided he would apply himself to becoming Premier Arat's personal aide. He had been working on a resume and presentation when his guest had arrived. However, the result of the family brainstorming was not agreeable to all his intentions.

Within minutes of returning to his task, M'hut's wife came back from her mother's and demonstrated the problem she presented to his cause.

"You're still working on that resume? Anna asked. "You agreed to drop it."

"No, you decided it should be dropped, I didn't," M'hut responded. It was at times like this that he rued the enlightened lifestyle he allowed his wife. Most of the women in his country would not have raised an objection to their husband's plans, no matter what they were. But, Anna was steeped in her European ancestors' beliefs that a married couple share their life plans and refused the traditional Muslim woman's role in a family. She had been raised in that unusual freedom. Mahumud had married her knowing and approving of her aggressiveness. But, now, for the first time, it was galling to him.

"Anna, I want to make something of myself..."

"You are something, Mahumud," she interrupted. "You are an important member of our army. Many men would love to have your position."

"Fewer and fewer, Anna, now that there are better opportunities on the horizon. I can be a man of real importance. If I become Arat's aide, I'll have money and power."

"Yes, men and their power," she scoffed. "You would also have danger. Sabu's overturn was quiet, but things are changing in Malfon. The next coup might not be so peaceful and you would be caught in the middle of it."

"There won't be another coup. Everyone is happy with Arat at the top. Este Rafan is at his side and the country is better off than it ever has been. Why would there be a coup?"

Anna M'hut glared at her husband. Her unusual level of education did not help her to express her concerns.

"I want our baby to have a father," she said.

"He, or she, will have one."

"You will be involved with the government, Mahumud. You won't have time for a family, just like Rafan."

"Anna, I will go ahead with my plan, whether you like it or not."

"Yes, I know you will," Anna replied.

"I would like your support," Mahumud called after her retreating figure as she left the room.

CHAPTER 18

As a result of the coup, when Arat became the leader of Malfon, there was a vacancy left in the commerce ministry. The post went to Rafan. Thus, he consolidated the positions in the commerce and the navy ministries.

"Once again you have proved yourself capable of foresight, Rafan," Arat said. "The merchant marine proposal for another ship has worked beautifully."

"Shifting the project to the Commerce Ministry was a very important move, sir. I kept direct control and Aturk was not in the chain of command to obstruct me, though I doubt Aturk would have put up much of a fuss this time."

"Yes, Aturk knows where the power lies, and that is where he lines up," Arat agreed.

"The second ship is much newer than the old battleship, and more seaworthy. It will take much less time and money to prepare the tanker fully than it did to get the battleship ready. As you know, it is already functioning, but it will be more effective soon. It has a capacity of 10,000 gallons of crude oil. That's just right for what our purposes are. Our oil producing neighbors are already lining up for the service we can provide...and they so direly need."

"Yes. I am aware that small shipments by water to the large oil ports where the supertankers can pick it up with the larger quantities stored there will be much better for the small producers in the area. The haphazard methods they've been using were very frustrating for them."

Malfon began to show signs of the wealth the merchant marine/navy was bringing. More sailors were recruited to service, thus more people had jobs and money to spend on imported food that Malfon could not grow in its desert land. Starvation was becoming a thing of the past, as was malnutrition. Those who still could not afford what they needed were gladly cared for by those who were experiencing a relative overwhelming surplus. A few individuals found that they could bring in the fruits and vegetables needed from Norova and elsewhere and make a small profit selling them at home. This start to private enterprise was drawing off the need of working for some facet of the government or working on foreign soil to survive.

Rafan was still not satisfied. "Even Norova and our other neighbors are benefiting from our prosperity, such as it is. Norova gets rental money from us for the port space and our merchants are buying foodstuffs from them in greater quantities than when they were only feeding themselves. I understand there is even a transport concern traversing the trail into the mountains to the East to carry anything that our neighbors there need transported."

***

Rafan was addressing a group of his countrymen from a dais in the center of Creche. "The population of Malfon is more heavily employed than at any time since World War II. True, there are still too few jobs, but with the revenues from current projects, the government is able to help the unfortunate ones that are unable to stand on their own yet. The military is growing, and with its growth comes prosperity. Our ships not only provide work for seamen, but dockside workers and ship re-fitters with specialty training such as welding, clerking, and engine repair. And, now, with private sector jobs occurring, I promise more prosperity and more achievements. Together we will make Malfon a great country!"

"What is he campaigning for?" Arat asked General Umbarik, both of whom happened to be nearby in a street market. "I'm not sure I approve of his stirring up the citizens. It's enough that he just continues to do his job as well as he has and not take bows for it."

"Well, for Rafan, perhaps it is not. You know, Rafan is ambitious, and he's still young. Give him a little room to glow. If he gets to exercise his ego, perhaps his creativity will increase as well. He doesn't have any outlets but what he does in government. We certainly don't want to restrain him. We need his youthful vigor and keen mind to go the next step. There is much yet to be done in this country," Umbarik told the new premier.

"Yes, of course. I just hope we don't regret what the next step is," Arat concluded as the two older men passed through the wildly cheering crowd. The Commerce Minister's star was still rising. His sojourns to the town center dais were becoming ever more frequent. It seemed he wanted to make sure the people of Malfon knew he was behind the improvements in their lives, and of course, they did know it.

***

The navy was becoming larger and required a new top leader.

Rafan, as minister of the navy, without objection from the Minister of Defense, chose the man for the job.

"Mahumud M'hut, I know you are in the middle of your own endeavors to become a ranking officer in the army, but how would it be if I pulled strings and was able to appoint you a lieutenant commander in the navy? You are experienced enough in military service. General Umbarik never went through any officer's training. It would not be an unprecedented occurrence."

Rafan had surprised M'hut at his army post at the palace and now was adding to the army man's surprise. "But, Este...Minister, there are others..." M'hut tried to protest.

"Mahumud, you are my man. You are now the leader of the navy, effective as of this minute." M'hut could only stare at the minister in silence. So it was done.

***

Due to the age of the fleet, often more of the auxiliary work was necessary than the actual at-sea activities, M'hut soon found. Rather than view this with resolve to live with the status quo, Rafan urged M'hut to view this as an opportunity. Rafan promptly pressed for the need to buy another ship.

"A newer cruiser is a logical next step. Something of the World War II vintage again would do just fine. I want this one fully armed."

Arat raised his eyebrows when approached by Rafan with this statement merely months later.

"General Umbarik and I have discussed my plan and he thinks it holds merit. I also envision an air force, or at least an air branch of the army or navy. Every first class nation has an air force of some sort. We can't consider ourselves up-to-date without an air force." Arat looked at General Umbarik, who was accompanying Rafan, but sat quietly to Arat's left.

"My old friend, Corporal M'hut, once of the Palace Guards, has been doing a great job in his position as Commander of the Navy. Without so much as a complaint from Defense Minister Aturk, I was able to dispense with trivialities and obtain the appointment for him. His years in the army have given him all he needed to be in the top position of the navy. I don't feel anything has lacked in that post since my transfer from that post to the cabinet. As you probably know, there are some who grumbled that having friends in high places sure paid off, and that he was jumping over more senior men. But, any grumbling was done by those who were not fit for the position themselves, in my opinion."

"Fine, fine. We know all this, Rafan. But, what's all this about an air force, or a new cruiser, for that matter? M'hut is doing a fine job. But, do we have the money or really have the need for all this new stuff?" Arat asked.

"We have the need for the same reason we need an armed navy," General Umbarik answered.

Arat was a bit confused, but he left the need for that explanation alone for the moment. "Perhaps we should slow down a little. We don't want to make our neighbors nervous. A cruiser? Wouldn't a freighter or another tanker be more practical? Buying warships is certainly going to draw some attention."

"But, we need a warship, a cruiser!" Rafan exploded.

Arat recoiled slightly. He had noticed that Rafan's fuse had been getting shorter and shorter, his explosions more and more frequent. "The people want other things, Rafan. They think we might be getting too militaristic. Some want to know if it wouldn't be better to sell the battleship and get a freighter of some kind. Even junking the *Rafan* and buying a freighter might not be a bad idea," Arat explained.

"By 'some people' I presume you mean Aturk. 'The people have lost sight of what has brought them this new prosperity. It was the navy, and me!"

"The people, and I mean more than Aturk, have not forgotten that. Yes, Rafan, it was you and the navy idea. But, let's not lose sight of what's good for the country now. Perhaps things have changed enough that there is a better direction to go now. Remember, it has been a very few years since you were just an army private. You've come a long way, and yes, thanks mostly to you, so has the country. Perhaps maturity is lacking enough to see beyond a single goal. Experience will open your eyes to more opportunities if you'll be patient."

"You want to return to Sabu's pace?" Rafan fired back at Arat.

"Rafan, There are still those who are unemployed, unskilled, or over-specialized, who grouse and wonder if you know what you're doing. We need training schools. We need more opportunities outside the military sphere. We don't want to get stuck doing the things we've already done and lose the greater opportunities now that we can start down that road."

"Those people don't know what they're talking about. How can they complain when they are so much better off, even if they're among those least benefiting from my improvements? It takes time and we need to expand, to continue to do better. Patience will only lose us the inertia we've gotten. Gaining experience and being aware of opportunities can happen along the way. But, we need to keep the ball rolling with an expanding navy!" Rafan ranted.

The general was strangely silent again. Rafan's staunch ally was staying as neutral as he could in this conflict.

"Perhaps, Rafan. But, expand in what direction? Maybe, to be blunt, you need more experience, let us say, more seasoning, to understand what is best for the people. You cannot be aware of everything that is going on, and the rest of us have ideas too. I don't want to deter you. But once in a while we have to stop and take stock rather than just constantly running headlong into the next situation over the existing path." Arat was finding it hard to be diplomatic with this young man. "As you grow older you will be more prepared for the future. You'll see that."

"Grow older? Like you and the general, and Aturk? When I become senile, then I will be able to see and think more clearly? Is that what you mean?"

"I think we'd better discuss this another day, Rafan," Arat concluded. He started playing with the cuffs of his somewhat frilly shirt, a sure sign that his ire was rising. The general shooed Rafan from the room. The general was still the only one that could herd Rafan away from confrontation.

***

"Well, now are you satisfied, Mahumud?" Anna M'hut asked her husband. "Or do you desire still more power?"

The surprise appointment as Rafan's replacement as the naval commandant had derailed M'hut's planned path, but he wasn't sure if that was a good thing or not.

"I would still like to go higher in the government, if that's what you mean. I want to make as much of a difference as I can. Look at what Rafan has done. I want things to be as good as they can for my family."

"You are no Este Rafan," Anna cautioned in a not unfriendly tone of voice.

"You should be happy that I'm not likely to be in the way of the next coup you seem certain is coming." M'hut ignored her comment and laughed a mirthless laugh. "I'll either be leading the military in a coup, or be overrun and pushed out of the way in the rush to depose Arat."

"Dear husband, you wouldn't be where you are if it wasn't for Rafan. Your plan of reaching greatness was planted by Rafan.

"You told me that yourself. Your dreams of being able to make a difference, as you put it, of being at the seat of primary power, were fathered by Rafan's enthusiasm."

"And his accomplishments, Anna. What's wrong with that?"

"I think you should be realistic and be satisfied as the head of the navy. If Rafan gets you pondering another appointment, turn it down."

"I could have turned my current position down, but I didn't want to, nor would I want to turn down any other post Este offers me. What have you heard?"

"Nothing. But, I know Este Rafan. He'll want to keep his closest allies near him. You're the closest thing to a friend he has."

Anna, of course, had known both Rafan and her husband when they were in school. Anna was not at school; just the boys went to school. Girls were not sent to school. She had gotten her education at home from her parents with additional tutoring, and informally, from Rafan, the star student. But, Anna had hung around the school playground and, of course, mixed with the other kids her age. "You get a bitter look every time the subject turns to Rafan. What has he ever done to you?" M'hut commented.

"Nothing," she mumbled, suddenly disturbed by a kick from the baby she carried. "Nothing at all."

"Well, I, for one, am very pleased with this navy he has turned over to me, and everything he has done for me. Do you remember him telling us about wanting a navy for Malfon when we were kids? We thought he was crazy. But, here I am, commandant of the Malfon navy...thanks to Este. The navy is the most prosperous business in the country. Este has done a great job. We're giving people jobs they want and providing income for the country just like Este used to say he would."

"Yes, I remember his childhood dream," Anna told her husband. She closed her eyes and made her waddling way to the bathroom.

CHAPTER 19

Despite little confrontations such as the one with the new premier, things continued to roll rapidly in Rafan's direction. No one was worried about Premier Arat's intentions, but there was growing concern over Rafan's ambition. This concern was both in the government and in the citizenry, but the public was generally more content to let things continue as they were progressing. Things were good, but it seemed each day there was more and more powerful rhetoric from the Commerce Minister. He was certainly more visible than anyone else in the country.

"'Rafan plans to help Rafan, not the country," Aturk grumbled gently to Arat. "There will come a time when his plans will displease people. He has a need to be fulfilled, regardless of other consequences. It is already approaching the point where his support is weakening. Many people are not happy with the taxes Rafan has pushed through. They complain that their prosperity is being drained away to support the government programs Rafan has come up with, like the welfare fund. They don't like the military spending. It seems counterproductive. The navy was making money. Why should the new jobs that are now available be taxed to support it, to buy more ships?"

Rafan's future for the country cost money. The zlots came from taxing the non-government businesses. Rafan felt it was a fair request for the things the government did for them, like obtaining lower fuel prices under contracts with the producers that used Malfon's tanker. There were many things the businesses couldn't do for themselves that the government took care of for them. Just keeping good relations with the oil producers was a full time job. Fuel for vehicles was no small item, but necessary to keep commerce running.

Ultimately, even Arat had to worry. “Yes, now Rafan wants another warship. He still hasn’t put together a proposal, but we know that he wants an air force as well. The people who have benefited from his programs don’t want to pay for any more. But, there are still those who are waiting for their ship to come in, so to speak, and they want more of Rafan’s dreams. It’s quite a problem.”

“Remember what Sabu said,” Aturk said quietly. “I think he was right. Rafan is dangerous.”

“Perhaps. I think it is time to trim Este Rafan’s wings, or his hulls, if you will.” The always elegantly attired premier shooed Aturk away just as one of Arat’s equally impeccably dressed aides entered the premier’s office. Arat arose with a smile spreading across his face.

CHAPTER 20

"What on Earth, or sea, do you need another warship for?" Premier Arat asked Rafan when next they met formally. "Are you planning to go to war?" He was trying to be humorous, difficult for the stuffy premier, especially when dealing with his young Commerce and Navy Minister.

"No, sir," Rafan answered respectfully, without any attempt at humor in return. "But, you see, right now we are at Norova's whim. We lease our home port from Norova, and if that lease is broken, we have no place to house our ships. Our merchant marine couldn't function and our economy would go back to what it was, or worse. For that matter, our ships are at risk wherever they go."

"So you intend to arm us to suggest to Norova, and the rest of the world, that they'd better not displease us or else?" Arat interpreted Rafan's intent as bullying, though he was not sure Malfon would ever be in a position to follow through on the threat.

"No, sir. But, I think we ought to be prepared. What recourse would we have if something happened?"Rafan asked.

"We couldn't raise a strong force quickly enough to make a difference," Arat scoffed.

"It would be too late to do anything if we had to raise a military deterrent after something had already happened. But, a standing military, a true military, with naval capabilities, could make a difference."

"Are you suggesting conscription? A draft?" Arat asked in surprise, making a drastic jump in his mind.

"No. If we have another ship, we'll get enough volunteers for our purposes. We always have, and we still will. Even with private employment improving all the time."

A somewhat relieved Arat continued. "But, the ports are Norova's. If they want to take them back, that's their right."

"They should be our ports..." Rafan started, then returned to his pragmatic pleas for another ship. "Our ships spend a lot of time overseas, not just in port in Norova. We are currently powerless to protect ourselves if some foreign power should decide to commandeer our ships, or sink them."

"Are you expecting someone to do this?" Arat asked seriously. Then in afterthought, "Sink them, I should think. Who would want our creaky old tubs?"

"While I don't think anyone would attack Malfon itself, there is the possibility of a shuffling of government power in a host country. That could result in seizing ships in their harbor.

"Maybe a conflict between us and another country could flare up while our ships were moored in that country's port. If, for any reason, an act of aggression against us should take place it would be a deathblow to us. We would be completely at the mercy of whatever came next."

"Are you concerned that our recent gains in standard of living would make us a target? I remind you that we are still well below average in per capita income. We are not so well off that we are a threat to anyone. Why would anyone strike out against us?" Arat questioned.

"We have no position to deal from to maintain our gains," Rafan insisted.

"I wouldn't call a battleship defenseless," Arat commented with pride.

"Ours is. It is a relic, and we've converted it for salvage work. There is virtually no armament left on it."

"But, why would any nation attack our ships?" Arat asked again.

"Maybe not a nation, but an act of piracy, or terrorism! We're in the league of oil now, even if we don't produce it ourselves."

"There have been supertankers hi-jacked on the high seas. We would be a safe target."

"With little return for their effort. Rafan, we could fall back on the United Nations if we have any international problems," Arat reminded.

"How could we expect justice from the United Nations when the likely aggressors would have more control over its actions than we would? We're not very important to the U.N. I don't want our country's future in someone else's hands," Rafan preached.

"Not even mine, it would seem," Arat mumbled to himself. "Remember, it was the U.N. that gave our ports to Norova. We were basically neutral in World War II, but we lost territory."

"But, Norova is friendly to us and lets us use the ports. We share ethnic heritage. The national border is just an imaginary line."

"Norova is very friendly with us. They like the income from the port lease. They weren't using the capacity, so now they don't have to leave it unused," Rafan continued. "If that imaginary line is so unimportant, why are you so set on leading this country? We could just share with Norova. We could just be one country. We wouldn't need a premier. Don't tell me the people outside on the street don't have any national pride."

"Just a minute..."

"Maybe we were all once borderless nomads, but today's generations didn't know that time." Rafan stopped talking and Arat sat silently for a moment.

"Este, what happened to that compatibility we shared not so long ago?" Arat said informally. "We both want the same things. We want what's best for Malfon. I have always respected you. I hope you still respect me."

"Let me have the new cruiser, Premier," Rafan said defiantly.

"Ahh, very well," Arat announced reluctantly. "We'll see. But, you realize that a warship involves the defense ministry, don't you? Minister Aturk should be handling this."

"I'll do everything within proper channels," Rafan assured his leader. He knew Arat was taking an easy way out of telling him 'no'. "I just wanted to make sure you were behind me before I approach Aturk. We cannot depend on him to solve our problems. But, hopefully, we can trust him to be loyal. If I can tell him this has your approval beforehand he will not stand in the way."

"I hope such thinking is not always foremost in your mind, Este," Arat admonished. Rafan bristled at the familiarity Arat was attempting to establish between them. "There are things we do depend on Minister Aturk for, and you and I have other concerns beyond the military. His recommendations need to be heeded."

As Rafan left the premier he not only was setting out to gain a cruiser for the navy, but already had other schemes on his mind. He would not let an obstacle like Aturk derail him.

CHAPTER 21

The battle of wills at the M'hut home continued to rage.

Whenever Mahumud would mention something positive that had been achieved by Rafan, Anna would launch into a tirade.

"Why are you so antagonistic about Este?" Mahumud asked his wife. "What is it about him that makes you so set against him and all he is doing?"

"I'm not against what he has done. But, I think he has done enough. It is time to let natural events follow and take the place of his grand schemes," Anna replied.

"What?"

Anna paused and gave her husband a searching look. "But, yes, I do hate Rafan."

"I don't understand it. When we were kids we were all friends. Este and you and I used to play together nearly all the time. We were inseparable. Then we became adolescents and you wanted nothing more to do with him. I thought you were just growing apart like kids do as they get older. But, now you hate him. Maybe it was something more. You seem to hate him more each day."

"I do."

"But, why?" Mahumud asked. "I remember now, you didn't even want to invite him to our wedding."

"He didn't come."

"He was on duty," Mahumud said defensively. "Now, you're so upset that he might drag me up the government ladder with him..."

"I'm glad he got you appointed naval commander. That kept you away from Arat's side."

“But, you’re still worried Rafan will get me in harm’s way...that he’ll make me too big a target.”

“Yes. I love you, dear husband. I don’t want to lose you. I don’t want our child to be fatherless.”

“Would you stop worrying about that. There won’t be any danger. Malfon is becoming calmer every day. People are happy.”

“So Rafan tells you. Listen with your own ears. Things are not as settled as you think. Don’t put unbridled trust in Rafan,” Anna finished.

CHAPTER 22

Fortuitously, perhaps, the elderly interior administrator passed away, and Rafan took the opportunity to pull the interior affairs under his ministry. Indeed, he claimed, what was more to do with interior than commerce? No other minister opposed that point of view.

"It bothers me that so many of our countrymen must leave our land to seek employment. Even in these improved days, there is not enough work at home. Malfon is still a dry uncultivated desert. We are unable to produce enough food to feed ourselves, let alone market any for profit. One of our strongest private interests is transporting foodstuffs from Norova and elsewhere. While I applaud these efforts, it hurts me to know that it must be done." Rafan was again addressing a crowd at the town center.

The crowd murmured and milled. The people still listened to Rafan, but they were growing weary of his promises. Things were improving, but at an increasingly higher cost. More and more of his countrymen saw Rafan as an unrealistic dreamer. "If we could produce sufficient food, we could take another major step toward being a contributing member of the world community. True, there are many other things we need to tackle, but none of them is more urgent than trying to feed Malfon."

"Disband the navy and we'll have a lot more food for everyone," someone in the back of the crowd yelled. "The sailors eat twice their share!" It was a well known fact that one of the draws to naval service was the quality rations it consumed.

"But, the navy is what gave us this better life!" Someone else yelled back. But, it was at best, a tentative support of Rafan.

Before the shouting got out of hand, Rafan got attention back on his speech.

"We'll never be able to feed ourselves, or stop paying outrageous prices for what we bring in, let alone build up a varied economy, unless we attack the problem of how to grow more here in our dust bowl. I know it can be done. I only ask your support. I promise you we will make the desert bloom!"

CHAPTER 23

"But, Rafan, we can't move our country. We live in a desert. How do you propose to change that?" Minister Aturk asked when the Commerce Minister brought his idea to the Cabinet. While no longer openly antagonistic, fearing reprisal from Rafan's apparent supporter, Premier Arat, Aturk still continued to chide Rafan for his visions of Malfon greatness.

"The heat and the sunshine are fine," Rafan responded with a laugh shared with the others in the chambers.

Laughing was becoming a less common event as Rafan gained power. Rafan's sense of humor had diminished through the years. It was only nine years since Este Rafan's duty as a palace guard. But, Rafan's dedication constantly increased and made the time seem much longer as his importance grew. It was stunning to realize that so little time had transpired in his climb toward the top. On this occasion the other ministers were glad to see a smile on Rafan's face. They hoped it might be a preview of a saner time in the mind of their Commerce, Interior, and Navy Minister.

"What we need is water," Rafan continued. In the spirit of what seemed to be a lighter moment, one of the other ministers brought Rafan a full drinking glass. Amid the laughter, Rafan pushed forward.

"I am committed to the ultimate goal for Malfon. I have let nothing overshadow my desire to improve our plight as much as possible."

The cabinet settled into a more somber mood. It was true no one had ever seen Rafan with a woman, involved in a soccer game, or in any way occupied with anything other than the work he did for his country. It was difficult to question his dedication, or his successes.

"There are many things on my mind, but the one I want to share with you today is my vision of how to turn our desert into a garden. I want to talk to the leaders of Talon, our eastern neighbors. In their mountains there is a higher rainfall than here on the flat desert land. They do not have much more water than we do, but I want to talk to them and see if they would enter into an agreement to pipe water to our undeveloped areas for irrigation. If they will agree, we can start growing our own food."

"What's in it for Talon, Rafan?" asked Premier Arat. "Why would they want to help us?" The stirring among those present quieted down while they waited for Rafan's answer.

"I know you're all skeptical, but Talon is looking for prosperity too. They could use the revenues we'd provide for the water. Perhaps we could even increase our trade by selling them produce that they don't grow for themselves. Simply put though, initially we would just pay them for the water," Rafan explained.

"And I suppose the money to pay them will come from more taxes," Aturk said with a smirk.

"Can you just cut back on the navy and use the money from that to pay for this?" another minister asked.

"No. No. The money would come from the crops we'd raise and sell."

Several ministers chuckled nervously. "Rafan, isn't that getting the cart a little in front of the horse? We don't have any crops yet. We don't even know if your idea would work...if we would ever have crops. What if we succeed only in growing enough for our own need?" Arat asked.

"Like you said, maybe we could increase trade by selling them produce, but initially we would have to just pay them for the water," Arat threw out. "Where will that money come from? Will the government own the farms that use the water? Is government supposed to pay for the water and give it to the farmers for free? How would this work? It sounds to me like more taxes would have to be involved."

"I think the Talonites will work with us. I think they'll help us build a watershed in their country so that we both can profit from it."

"You're talking like we've already decided to do this," Aturk interrupted. "Who have you been talking to without our knowledge?"

"No one!" Rafan fired back.

"Just a minute. Just a minute," Arat refereed. "I feel that I should overrule you on this one, Rafan. I think you have overstepped your bounds. But, it would be nice to have that irrigation." The smile on Arat's face could have been a reflection of a vision of his favorite melon sliced and placed upon his after dinner plate.

"What harm can it do for me to talk to them," Rafan asked.

"All right. Talk to them, presuming you haven't already. I know you have the right to make decisions on your own on some matters, but if the costs on this are out of line, or if there are any other problems I want to hear about them before any agreement is made," Arat ordered. "That goes for any involvement outside your ministries, as well."

"It won't do any good to talk to them," said Aturk. "The Talonites will not be interested in spending their money to help us be more productive. We won't be productive so we could pay them off and they know it. They'd have to put up the money...for what? To take a chance on Rafan's plan working, eventually? Why would they do that? They won't be willing to wait for some future pipe dream payoff." There was tittering laughter at Aturk's choice of words.

"Whatever, Rafan, make sure you report back to us before you finalize anything," Arat finished.

Once again, Rafan was off to work his magic for the good of his country, a more difficult endeavor was hard to imagine.

Talon was not historically on great terms with Malfon. There was a high probability the idea wouldn't work if he got agreement from Malfon's neighbor, and an even more likely probability that there would be no such agreement. The lack of firm support from his own government didn't help either. Nevertheless, Rafan was undaunted.

CHAPTER 24

As it turned out, the Talonites weren't interested in sharing their water, even without cost to them and additional income in the long run.

"The rainfall in Talon isn't much more than it is in Malfon," the Talonite Ambassador told Rafan. "What if we draw water off for Malfon and create a shortage for ourselves? What if there is less rainfall than usual? Who decides, and how is it decided, where the cuts come in usage? Does Malfon do without, or do we?"

"Those are things our foreign ministers would have to work out, sir," Rafan assured the ambassador.

"No. Any income we would get from this would not make up the difference in losses to a crop failure caused by sharing too much of the water unknowingly. Our country could not afford that. Our only gain would be from that income, and we could lose enough of our ability to grow our own food to make it worthless to us."

"But, the project would increase the ability for both our countries to grow more efficiently. That would be another plus for Talon," Rafan assured.

"It would encourage us to try to grow more, yes. But, when there was a problem, the failure would be more disastrous."

"If that is the way you feel about it, sir," Rafan conceded temporarily, "then I will take that message back to my premier.

"But, I can tell you, Mr. Ambassador that I will be back again. I will have another proposal. I will see this project completed."

"I admire your confidence, Minister. But, I am leery of your words. They take on the sound of a challenge, a warning."

"So be it," Rafan said. "Good day, sir."

CHAPTER 25

"That damn ambassador," Rafan ranted to General Umbarik. "If I could have talked to the president I could have gotten the deal done."

"Rafan, you don't know that," Umbarik replied. "Let it go."

Rafan had barely reached Creche on his return from Talon before he was in the general's office.

Slightly calmed, Rafan told the general, "I'll go home and rest a bit. But, I'm not letting this go, General. I'll see you tomorrow. The trip was dusty. I could use a bath."

***

Anna M'hut couldn't help but sweat, standing in the direct sunlight on another of the consistently hot days of Malfon. There was no winter in Malfon, or spring, or fall, just summer. She and Mahumud were having a fight nearly as heated as the outdoor temperature. Their arguments had become a daily event.

"Why are you so upset that Rafan got turned down for once?"

Anna screamed. "So Talon won't share their precious water!" We've never had that water, so how can it be such a big deal that we won't have it now?"

"That water would go a long ways to making it possible to grow more of the crops we need to improve our lives even more. It would lessen malnutrition. Wouldn't that be great for our baby? Our population is starting to grow, we need more water. The water might let

Malfon grow enough food to sell to other countries. Our figs are recognized as among the best in the world. We might finally be able to grow enough to ship them abroad."

"So now you want to be a farmer? The navy isn't good enough for you? Did Rafan put you up to this?" Anna fumed.

"What are you talking about?" Was all Mahumud could say. "Arghh!" He yelled once he found his voice. "Why are you always going on against Este? What is the problem? What can bother you about this plan to bring more water to Malfon? He must have done something to you somehow for you to hate him so much. You hate him so much you can't even stand the things he does that can't be denied are good for us. God, I wish you weren't so liberated. A nice quiet submissive wife would be a blessing right now."

"You think I should be just all happy all the time?" Anna rubbed her extended belly, "you should try carrying this around all the time, husband dear. I'm sorry, I'm not in such a good mood that I can put up with all your mourning for Rafan's hardships."

Mahumud's words had the established effect on Anna. Even though she fought back, whenever her husband asked why she hated Rafan so much, she immediately went silent and slipped away.

Mahumud was nearly curious enough to ask Rafan his side of the falling out, years before that had alienated Anna and Este. But, he didn't want his friend to find him antagonistic like his wife, so he never asked. He also didn't want to do anything that would anger Rafan and hinder his chances of clinging to Rafan's rising star.

CHAPTER 26

Rafan's anger festered for weeks after the setback with Talon. He was treated to the taunts of Aturk and others who had told him he would not succeed. But, soon the youngest minister in Malfon was again at the premier's door. He would not accept Talon's refusal as final, but in the meantime his mind was working on alternatives.

"Premier Arat," the resourceful Minister of Commerce began, "it would seem I've suffered my first major defeat. But, we can still have the water we need for irrigation."

"Unless I've been dreaming, we still live in a desert, Este," the premier joked in his haughty manner. His smile was remembrance that Rafan hadn't gotten his cruiser either. This was his second setback. He couldn't know that Rafan didn't consider that project dead yet.

"I've been silent these few weeks, but I have not been idle. Instead of succumbing to the slings and arrows of those who would rather ridicule me than find an answer to any of our problems, I have been working out the details of other ways to make our meager rainfall work more to our advantage."

The premier sat back and relaxed. He knew that what Rafan had to say would be worth listening to, his ideas always were worth at least that.

"Malfon isn't perfectly flat. So, terracing would work. If lots are terraced so that all that small amount of water we have collects at the lowest point, that area will have enough moisture for some crops. We wouldn't be able to plant large amounts of land, but it would be better use of the land than the haphazard method we use now. We could also build concrete catch basins to store water."

"Would there really be a significant improvement?" Arat asked.

"Yes. As it is now, when rain does fall, the water soaks into the soil so rapidly that we can't use it. With catch basins the water would not all soak into the soil, it would be stored until we want to use it. The collected water would only be transferred to the lowest segments of the terraces. The basins would be covered to slow evaporation and to catch condensation."

Arat shook himself from the daze Rafan's dream-painting had put him into momentarily. "What about the costs?"

"How can you worry about that when there is so much to gain?"

"And this is all we have needed all this time to improve our ability to feed our people?" Arat set aside his concerns about expenses for a moment, enthralled that there was hope here for a major improvement in Malfony lifestyle. "Rafan, I am ashamed that neither you nor I thought of this before now, to say nothing of our predecessors. But, if the basins are covered, how will the rain get in?" Arat asked. His immaculately clad aide entered Arat's office and stood quietly off to the side.

"Mostly from runoff that doesn't soak into the immediate surrounding area. But, we could have retractable roofs, too. That way, when it rains the roof is open and when the sun shines we close it to block out some of the heat and catch the evaporation.

"There will be considerable expense, Premier. I'm sorry to tell you. Terracing the ground, and building the basins will cost. It will be difficult to come up with the money, even without the retractable roofs. Full support among the ministers is unlikely."

Rafan thought for a moment. "I don't think we really need the retractable roofs. That was just something that I thought up to answer your question. After all, it only rains a few days a year. There's enough of an expense without them. The money can be drawn from the profits the navy is now bringing in, even though it will mean a little less for other needs. This is the most important thing for Malfon right now. Feeding ourselves has always been a drain on our economy. The short term loss of funds will create rewards many times over. As for the ministers...are you not the premier? Are you not the supreme leader? What you say is what goes. The ministers' approval is only window dressing. If you press for this, they will not resist you."

Arat looked over at his aide and sat forward in his chair. "I have only your word that this will work. I trust you implicitly, but I must have the details if I am to ramrod this through the cabinet."

"You will have the details. But, there is one more thing I want to discuss with you."

"What is that?" Arat asked warily.

"There is more we must do to turn a great deal of Malfon into a salad bowl rather than leaving it as a dust bowl. To achieve that goal we need seawater conversion."

"Rafan..."

Rafan cut the premier off. "Seawater conversion," Rafan quickly repeated. "We could set up..."

"Rafan, we don't have any seawater! We are landlocked!"

"Yes, sir. But, we can set up conversion systems, at our piers in Norova. They would turn seawater into steam, condense the fresh water and pipe or truck it here to Malfon."

"I am aware of the technology, Rafan. But, the cost would be prohibitive, even if all the other details fell in line," Arat objected. Arat assumed an aristocratic air.

"The steam we create could lessen our need for outside electricity to run the operation. It wouldn't eliminate it, of course, but with an efficient enough system, we might be able to use some of the energy for other needs here, even. I realize the pipeline may have to come in the future, but trucking water can work beautifully in the meantime. Think of all the irrigated crops we can grow!"

"What about the cost of the gasoline for the trucks?"

"Yes, that's an expense. But, we can't eat gasoline. Call it a cost of producing vegetables rather than a cost of desalination, if that helps. Isn't it worth a little expense to feed more of our people?"

"Rafan, you've got to be delirious. This will never work! Where would we get the start-up money? You want the terracing and catch basins, and now this? Come on, Este, we can't spend the same money twice! Don't you think you're asking for just a little too much?"

Arat had been wearying of Rafan's projects for some time, but still looking for the gems that occurred among them so he gave some freedom to pitch his ideas. But, this was pushing Arat to his limit. He could not reject the creativity that was benefiting the country so greatly. But, more and more of the ideas from the young minister's mind approached lunacy.

Arat's initial opinion was that this was another one; however he had to admit the other seemingly crazy ideas often worked out. This seemed to have merit, along with the lunacy. The navy/merchant marine was a smashing success, and who would have dreamed that in a landlocked country...only Rafan. The army was more appealing than ever. As a result, the people of Malfon were eating better and living longer, more comfortable lives in measurable terms, even in just the short time Rafan had wielded his power.

"We can scale the system to our budget capabilities," Rafan defended undaunted. "If we could spend one million zlots and bring in one million gallons of fresh water, it would be tremendous and worthwhile. But, if we can only spend one zlot and bring in one gallon of water, then we would still be better off than we are now." Rafan, as always, was extremely convincing. "Norova can buy food it can't grow because it has other resources. We can't. We need to produce our food."

"But, surely, there is a minimum necessary to even start such a project. Do you think we actually could come up with enough money for all this? Perhaps we should just begin with the terracing and the catch basins, and save the seawater conversion for later, for when the basins pay off enough to afford the rest," Arat bargained. The fact that he was bargaining instead presenting an edict indicated that the weaker side of his nature was prevailing under duress.

"Consider this, Premier," Rafan pitched again. "We can sell the by-product salt overseas. That will help pay for the costs of the terracing and catch basins as well. If we do this all at once, the returns will come more quickly.

We would have income from the salt, we would have electricity made by the power plant running the desalination system, provided by fuel bought with maritime profits, and we would have more water to grow crops and not only feed our people, but to sell as well."

"Rafan, I can't believe you're seriously planning all this! You know I've been in your support all along. I haven't forgotten that it was you who started the fire under me to take action to get Malfon out of the morass we were in, but this is too much! The initial outlay in zlots would be immense, no matter what level of production we choose. It would break the treasury. The fuel for trucking would demand an enormous commitment just to be efficient. We'd be in way over our heads."

The premier's haughty manner was slipping more and more as it sometimes did when he was dealing with Rafan.

"Premier Arat," Rafan began formally. "I have studied this. I assure you that it is plausible. It will cost us 100,000 zlots to get started at the level required to overcome losses. We have been so successful with our seafaring enterprises that getting financing for the project should be no problem. That would prevent depleting the treasury. The figures will sell the project to an investor."

Arat's reluctance was ebbing. His resistance to Rafan's pressure was being overcome. "You're sure there's a market for the salt as well?"

"Yes. I've covered every facet. There are countries with livestock in need of greater salt production than they possess. We can provide for that need. There are other uses as well, all over the world."

"It would be nice to have irrigation," Arat admitted.

Rafan's enthusiasm was contagious and his arguments were plausible. His pressuring was relentless. The premier mused silently for a moment.

"All right. See to the arrangements with Norova and get started. If everything looks like it will work the way you say it will," Arat instructed, "we will go through with it. But it still seems to me that there are a lot of things that could go wrong. Norova may not cooperate, for one."

"It will work, sir."

Arat paused again, lost in thought. Then he spoke one final thought. "By God, Rafan, we'll make something out of this country yet." The premier was experiencing a moment of egocentric pride. "But, I'll need those details," he reasserted.

CHAPTER 27

"Minister, we are hoping Norova will be as excited about our plan as we are. While there will be no immediate advantages to your country, increased prosperity for the area can't help but improve prospects for future gains for Norova," Rafan told the Norovan commerce minister.

"Word of your plan has preceded you, Minister, through our ambassadors. I can't say that we are at all excited about it, at least in a positive way," the Norovan said. "Norova does not share your goals of modernization and progress. We are content to remain as we are. We granted your country port facilities, that is all. We did that, not out of our concern for Malfon's need, but for the income it provides. We are not without need for finances to maintain our way of life. With this project you propose, Malfon's involvement within our borders would be increased. That is not to our liking. As you said, there is no benefit to us. Why should we not be upset at your plan to use the facilities granted to you for maritime purposes for other uses? What gives you the right to do as you please in our nation without consulting us?"

Rafan noted that the minister did not mention that Norova's notorious greed was part of the port deal. Nor was there any mention of the many Malfonies working in Norova. Norova was indeed concerned with modernization and progress, just not as aggressively as Malfon.

"I am consulting you now. The ambassadors have been discussing this, as you said. We are not making changes without your consent. We are seeking your consent." Rafan was having trouble controlling his irritation at the pointless obstruction by the petty official. He was fully prepared to go ahead with the project without Norova's permission, let the pieces fall where they may.

"Yes, we are discussing it. The leaders of Norova have already discussed it. It occurs to us that Malfon is becoming more aggressive as it becomes stronger economically."

"You would prefer a weak Malfon?" Rafan's rage at this affront came to the surface. "You fear us?"

"Relax, Minister. We are not pleased with your proposal. But, we are quite convinced you will proceed with or without our approval. We can find no good reason to stand in your way. There is no legal defense. Our contract for the use of the piers is vague. It does not specify what use or uses the piers can be put to, and to deny what the world will perceive as a wonderful undertaking for the people of Malfon would surely damage our standing in the global community."

"You could find some reason to take away our port facilities, or issue a new contract that constricts the use of them. It could be done in a way to not harm Norova's good name," Rafan spit out.

"We could. But, would you stand for that? We might lose that income you provide us. Besides, as you implied, there might be some future good in the situation for Norova that we cannot yet see. You can build your desalination plant. You have Norova's permission."

CHAPTER 28

"Now, Rafan has his desalination plant up and running in Norova. There are no bounds to his ambition," Anna M'hut wailed to her husband.

"It's Malfon's desalination plant, and what is wrong with that? Surely, you can't be against improvements like that. It's not military or political. What harm can it do?" The beleaguered Mahumud asked in desperation.

"It is political!" Anna raged. "I've been meeting with some people who know what's going on better than you, my blind husband. Rafan is going to get us into a war, or bankrupt us, or..."

"Who have you been meeting with?" Again, his wife's education and freedom was galling Mahumud even though he thought he believed in equality of the sexes.

"For one, Minister Aturk." Anna dropped the name like a bombshell.

"Aturk!" Mahumud shrieked. "He is the obstruction that keeps us from achieving more. He is the only leftover from Sabu's administration of ennui!"

"It's a good thing he does slow you down. He says these projects of Rafan's are putting our nation's finances in the red. The taxes people have to pay now to underwrite his big dreams take away most of the improvements the projects have made in peoples' lives..."

"I don't believe that. We pay taxes and we're much better off than we used to be. We could never have afforded a baby before..."

"And you're in Rafan's precious navy. You get benefits everyone doesn't share."

"It's Malfon's navy, and mine," Mahumud said while realizing it really was Rafan's navy.

"Why are you so protective of Rafan? You wonder why I hate him. You've looked up to him since we were kids. Is it because he protects you, or is there more? I wonder why you idolize him."

"Is there more to why you hate Rafan so much?" Mahumud fired back.

"Perhaps there is," Anna spat, then turned away and left the room. The baby was due in a very short time and the eminent delivery hadn't improved Anna's disposition.

Mahumud was stopped dead. Was there some problem Anna had with Rafan he didn't know about? If she was secretly meeting with Aturk, anything was possible. Was she so mad these days because she thought he should know, and was fighting an internal battle over her options? He wondered...or was it just the pregnancy?

There were people meeting with Minister Aturk? That was news to M'hut. If Aturk was consolidating power, maybe there would be another coup as Anna had feared. Maybe she knew something he didn't indeed. But, he found it hard to believe Aturk would have that kind of ambition. Malat Sabu was living quietly out of power and would not be behind a ploy to return to politics. He was enjoying all his previous privileges without the headaches of dealing with the country's troubles. He, too, would not be any more ambitious than he ever had been. He was benefiting from Arat's rule as much as anyone. M'hut couldn't think of anyone else who would have the ambition and complaints to confront the premier's authority. Perhaps there was someone who didn't think the premier was exercising enough control over the country's future, and over Rafan. But, he had no idea who.

M'hut's mind considered his wife, but discarded the idea. But, nevertheless, the meetings with Aturk bothered M'hut seriously. Anna...?

CHAPTER 29

Not much time passed before Rafan's dissatisfaction with the existing agreement with Norova erupted in another demand for the expansion of his plans.

"It is time to build the pipeline," Rafan announced one day to the assembled cabinet and Malfon's premier. "Any other means of getting the water to the desert is limited." Only a few weeks had gone by since the seawater project had first sprinkled the dust bowl and already begun to turn the desert green. Now, Rafan was pushing ahead.

"Minister Rafan," Aturk began, "we are having difficulty paying for the plan as it is. We cannot afford to add on more expense."

"But, Minister Aturk, the project is paying for itself. It will be able to sustain added expense by just extending the period of indebtedness, with no increase in payments on our loan. The project will become more efficient."

"I see that the minister has been working on this behind our backs again," Aturk carped.

The sentiment was overwhelmingly in favor of Rafan. At this point most Malfonies were enthralled with the seawater project. There was no increase in tax complaints since most of the terracing had been done by hand by the landowners themselves without much cost to the government. The landowners needed only instruction and a few pieces of equipment. This avoided putting a strain on the treasury. So, the pressure the payments for the seawater put on the farmers was not as severe as had been anticipated, and was paying high dividends in agricultural production.

"Crops are growing where they have never grown before. The three pronged water project of terracing, catch basins, and seawater conversion is so successful that for the first time Malfon farmers are able to sell produce to neighboring countries in profitable amounts," Rafan reminded Aturk. "Can we afford not to expand our capabilities?"

It was obvious to the members of the cabinet, and indeed, to Premier Arat himself, that standing against Rafan would not sit well with the people who fed their nation. At least that realization occurred to all but one cabinet member. Aware of national sentiment or not, Minister Aturk dragged his heels.

"I know all this, Rafan, and I don't think the success merits jeopardizing everything to take on a still more ambitious project. With farmers growing more than enough crops for themselves, no one in Malfon can be considered starving. I know the variety of crops that can be grown is still limited. Only arid crops will flourish and not enough of those can be sold abroad to purchase supplemental nutrition. That is something I think we can live with. As might be expected, there is no way to assure that everyone gets a fair share. That is more of a concern to me than growing more. This condition of greed will continue, and even now the benefits of the project expenses are not equal and will be more lopsided with increased distribution."

If there was more money to be made by selling dates overseas, then that is where they would go, rather than to the neighbor scraping by on an army private's salary to feed a family of four. If there had been an absurd amount of produce grown, perhaps this condition would not have been a problem, though Aturk obviously thought it would have been. But, with just slight overproduction this imbalance surely did exist. The discussion in the cabinet ended with no action being taken. But, Rafan had served notice of his intentions.

At another cabinet meeting just a short time later, the cause of the inequity in distribution and other problems stemming from newly acquired prosperity were discussed.

"The catch basins are working splendidly," Rafan crowed. "The terracing is doing its job as well. The Talonites can keep their rainwater. The new pipeline will more than make up for the water we didn't get from them. Incidentally there is news about that from Talon. They seem to be having a change of heart."

The pipeline from Norova to Creche, to carry the converted seawater had been approved eventually and work was underway on its construction.

"We are becoming a nation of farmers," Aturk grumbled.

"There is no wealth in farming. Our country is still poor. Where are the great dreams you have told us of Rafan? Are we not to join the elite of the world...to be admired, respected, and honored? Ha!"

"Ah, but we are farming! Our survival is assured. But, once the pipeline is performing we can turn our attention to other prospects. Perhaps we can start some manufacturing," Rafan argued.

"Now, you're going to get the population excited about another pipe dream," Aturk smirked amid laughter of the other members of the cabinet, albeit subdued in deference to Rafan's recognized power. The respect that had been unanimous was diminishing and being replaced by discomfort and sometimes fear, as it became clear to those near to him that what Rafan wanted, Rafan got. There was no direction but Rafan's direction and one way or the other the objective was reached. The fact that Arat let it be that way was eroding Arat's popularity as well.

Rafan's wish fulfillment was becoming truer all the time.

Not everyone was convinced that everything Rafan wanted was best for the country any more. His priorities seemed to have less and less to do with the needs of his countrymen and their wishes than with the needs of Rafan's ego. It was hard to fault the irrigation projects, but there were those who even wondered if giving up a nomadic lifestyle decades before had been a good idea. Solidarity of Rafan's support around the country was becoming fragmented. Some opposing factions were lunatic fringe, but some were well meaning individuals of propriety.

"Manufacturing?" Aturk asked incredulously. "The confidence of the Malfony people is so high they will question nothing that comes from your mouth, but I will. They do not hear what we hear from you. They would be shocked at your attitude at times, Rafan."

"As they would yours, Aturk," Rafan retorted. "The population is growing. Families are now starting to have children again. In just the last few years more children have been born than in the last fifty years. The people have hope. They are optimistic that things will get even better."

"Then they haven't been looking at the tax bill you've given them," Aturk groused. "Who decides what is the best life? Is the way to insure the future to make us pay dearly now? I think the public would not be happy to see the way you respond to our premier. They expect the premier to be respected, not manipulated..."

"The taxes they pay are only possible for them to pay because of the economy that money creates. The taxes make it possible for everyone to benefit." Rafan paused and took a deep breath. "Minister, the point is, people who have been afraid to bring children into their poverty-stricken world suddenly feel comfortable to have two, or even three offspring to share Malfon's future. The premier and I have a good working relationship. I merely point out aspects he may miss without my oversight. The people wouldn't be upset about that, if they saw it happening. The people are happy. That's what comes after survival...happiness."

"Then perhaps we should leave well enough alone," Arat interposed.

"No. There will need to be more than agriculture as a basis to our economy...more than the military. As we said, Minister Aturk, we are becoming a nation of farmers. We cannot all be farmers. We need to provide jobs for the growing population's labor pool, for ten, twenty, thirty years down the road. Only the government can make that growth fair and equal."

Aturk could only moan, and the other ministers randomly nodded ascension or grumbled discontent and uncertainty, depending on their personal perceptions. Many eyes turned on Premier Arat.

"Minister Rafan," the premier said. "We were aware that the increase in water supply was not your sole intention, and while we thank you for that gift, I cannot condone moving forward on something so drastic as industrialization for our country. We do indeed, you and I, have a good working relationship and because of that, and the fact that I am premier, I expect you will respect my decision."

"Hear me out, Premier," Rafan pleaded, with no pleading in his voice.

"You got your pipeline, Rafan. Enjoy that victory for a while. I fear we are moving too fast with changes."

"But, sir," Rafan tried again with a little more humility.

"Este, let it rest. Perhaps in time..."

"Yes, sir," Rafan submitted for the first time in many months.

It was obvious he did so with great distaste and no intention of giving in permanently. "Incidentally, sir, I've recently had a communication from the Talon ambassador on that watershed proposal of mine. It seems they've had a change of heart." Rafan could not help but fire this final shot to soothe his feelings.

"Really?" Arat inquired with interest and raised eyebrows.

"Yes, sir. It seems Talon is rather impressed with our success on the seawater project and convinced that we are capable of following through on our endeavors successfully. I sense that they want to be on the best possible terms with a country that is going to progress with or without their help."

"Well, I knew that they had adapted some of our terracing methods to coincide with their hillier terrain. So now they think they can afford to share their water, eh? Ha!" Aturk acknowledged. "Well, I'm surprised."

"They want to build a dam on one of their mountain streams. It is dry half the year, but it's much sounder technology than catch basins. They want us to help them. I imagine that means pay half the bill or something," Rafan finished.

"How much does Talon want us to pay for the construction of the dam?" Aturk asked.

"I haven't talked to them about it yet," Rafan answered. "I only heard from the ambassador that they wanted to get together with me about it."

"You mean you haven't been holding private talks behind our backs? That's a first," Aturk mumbled.

"Minister," Arat hissed at Aturk.

"Rafan," Arat continued, "do you agree that we need the Talon project?"

"Yes, sir," Rafan told the premier. "The Talon project will be more productive and less costly to maintain than desalination. I don't want to put all of our eggs in one basket. Norova could shut down our pipeline or our plant. We would be foolish to overlook a better source of vital water such as the one Talon offers. With two pipelines we have insurance against any action against us by either supplier. Besides, as has been pointed out, more water can only help our situation."

"Would Norova terminate our lease?" Arat asked. "What would become of our navy?"

"They took our port away from us once, after the war," Rafan said bitterly, then brightened. "I warned of being at the mercy of foreign powers. But, I have not heard of anything like that in the offing. Norova has been very gracious to us the last few years. If there were a threat of loss of the port we would have to address that action in a very serious manner. But, let's concentrate on the new water project."

"Perhaps we should voluntarily shut down the Norova project," Arat suggested. "We might be creating a sore spot by appearing greedy. What's more, by shutting down the more expensive seawater project we could still have more water without the cost. We would still be better off than we are with just the Talon project. If we don't antagonize the Norovans they would be less likely to consider taking the port for our navy away."

"The seawater plant doesn't antagonize the Norovans. Closing it down wouldn't have any effect on whether we'd lose our port," Rafan assured.

"Premier," Aturk began, "are you aware that there is a exodus problem in this country? I think sometimes you are as blind as Sabu was inambitious."

"Norova won't have a problem with anything we do at our piers as long as they make a profit from it. Remember, Norova is greedy. We don't need to give up the desalination," Rafan interrupted.

Arat went on as if Rafan and Aturk hadn't spoken. Not even taking note of Aturk's callous remark. "I have reports from the guards that there are people moving across our borders in search of better conditions." Aturk looked at Arat in disbelief as the premier acted like the subject had come from his own mind.

"But, this has always been the case." Arat's response and the ignoring of their comments irked Rafan and Aturk. The premier went on without giving either man additional attention.

"This is different," Aturk forced Arat to take note of him. "Not only are people assuming things are better job-wise and living condition-wise, but they are fleeing the high taxation rates that are now being inflicted upon them by our commerce minister to fund his projects. They think they will be better off in Norova or Talon." Aturk intentionally avoided pointing a finger at Rafan directly by calling him by name. But, he disregarded the fact that Rafan was even there. He was not about to lose his momentum by conceding anything to the young minister. Aturk was well aware of Rafan's standing with the people. He would only push so far.

"We aren't able to finance all our advances. The navy cannot provide enough; private enterprise consists almost solely of farming, or trucking farm products. So we depend on taxes to make sure everyone is benefiting from our gains. These deserters didn't choose these improvements in the infrastructure and want out. We have international emigrants. We always have, but now there is no need for it. Maintaining the status quo now would slowly allow sustenance to everyone without any expansion of the tax structure needed to create more projects. There will eventually be more navy positions, more farming opportunities, more need for truck drivers, without more input from our commerce minister.

"Taxation makes it seem like there must be a better life outside Malfon. The neighboring countries are taking it well so far. Many of them need to add to their work force. Really, things are not better in Norova and Talon, and they won't be happy about a drain on their resources to pay emigrant Malfonies once the need is met. Housing is already a problem in Norova, and job depletion is starting to occur there. Ironically, we are better off than the countries our people are immigrating to for a better life.

"Even in the old days, some of these people would cross back into Malfon each night to benefit from whatever we could offer, then take the trip back across the border the next day. They still do this now to avoid taxes, because they don't work or technically live here. What have you got to say about this, Rafan?" Arat, finally acknowledging the commerce minister again, demanded.

"I am aware of the problem, Premier. We are going to do something about it," Rafan asserted.

Aturk cut in politely, "I bring this up, Premier, because it indicates the feelings of many of our people. Cutting the costs of a project would enable us to lower the tax rate, or at least stabilize it. That might lessen the urge for the people to leave Malfon. For that reason I believe closing down the seawater plant would be a good idea."

"Nonsense," Rafan shouted. "We will need that revenue for future projects!"

"Not if there aren't any," Aturk threw back.

"There has to be. We can't be stagnant!"

"Enough, gentlemen," Arat interrupted.

"I said I will take care of the deserter problem, Premier," Rafan restated.

"Then you admit I'm right," Aturk smirked.

"I admit there is a problem. But, I don't agree with you on the cause of it, nor on how to solve it," Rafan finished.

"Premier, I am concerned that increases in national revenue raising could cause a revolt that would force me to bring my armed forces into conflict with our own people in order to keep order," Aturk told Arat.

"Maybe that is just what's needed," Rafan offered. "We still do not have enough jobs in this country. That is why these people are crossing our borders. That's one more reason to keep both water projects and search for more projects that provide jobs. They are jobs that cost the government money, but put money into the coffers from the salt sales, from the taxes collected on the produce sold that we would not have were it not for the water projects, and again I stress, allow us the ability to branch out into manufacturing.

"Once the private sector is solidified the government will be out of the business market and our only source of funding will be those taxes. The marine salvage business can be turned into a private enterprise. The farmers will own the land they farm, and their crops. The truckers will have more merchandise to transport. Isn't that a worthy goal? Yes, we'll still need those taxes for moving forward and paying the expenses of running the government and providing services. But, they won't be a burden to a vibrant economy."

"Rafan, I have heard enough of that," Arat scolded, fully aware that he was the premier and that the rest of the room was slack-eyed at the spectacle of these two ministers going at it against the premier's wishes.

"Manufacturing would create other jobs...more trucking, and marketing, for example," Rafan started up again, ignoring the premier's admonition.

"I tell you, the people are on the edge of doing something about the spending they see the government doing with their incomes. They don't like paying taxes to fund more big idea projects," Aturk insisted.

"Our people are better off than they've been at any time in their lives. They know that. I refuse to believe we are suffering from my taxation policies, which I remind you are ratified by this group as a whole. The grumblers are the few who do not yet have jobs, or perhaps the highly paid who bear the brunt of the tax load. They have no reason to complain, or know we're trying to work out some way to help them, at least. You, of all people, know we are doing better and better at taking care of all Malfonies," Rafan stated proudly to Aturk.

"I will not say it again, Rafan. That is enough. Some day when we have all calmed down, perhaps we can bring this subject up again, but for now that is all!" Arat shouted loudly. Murmurs came from around the room. The premier's tone indicated there would not be any more business discussed. There was none of the premier's stuffiness in his voice, only command.

The cabinet began to disband. Negative notes prevailed in the comments of the ministers. Arat had clearly had enough of both Rafan and Aturk.

"Sir, one more thing," Rafan tried again, refusing to let up. "I have not heard anything more about my request for the cruiser for the navy, or about the army air corps."

"Take it up with Minister Aturk and Commander M'hut. Now get out!" Arat shouted.

CHAPTER 30

Mahumud M'hut was recalling the day a couple of months earlier when his family had enlarged by one nine pound bundle.

"Your beautiful baby boy is still doing fine," the doctor said interrupting M'hut's reverie.

"Another good citizen for Rafan's little paradise," Anna said with a mixture of anger and awe at her new son.

"Enough of that!" Mahumud quietly spit out. "We have a son that will benefit from all that Rafan has done. Besides, some of the credit for a better future for him should go to our premier. Arat is the leader of our country."

The couple finished with the doctor and passed through the doorway into the bright sunlight.

"No, it is Este Rafan." Anna insisted. "It is Rafan's country."

"All right. That's the last time I will hear of this scorn for my friend. Unless you can tell me a reason why I shouldn't stand by him and be thankful he is my benefactor, I will not tolerate any more of this divisiveness from my wife!" Mahumud's voice strained to control his anger while staying soft to avoid frightening the baby.

"Your friend and benefactor. All right. I'll tell you the source of my hatred. I think Rafan thinks more of himself than he does of the country." Anna's anger was soaring beyond the control she'd held throughout the arguments with her husband. "Apparently only someone who has known him since he was a child and is not blinded by devotion can really see that. So, most of the country still supports him as you do. His taxes make marvelous 'improvements' that nobody asked for, and making Malfonies able to eat better has only started a population explosion that will make us have to continue to spiral production upward to maintain that standard, at the cost of even more taxation," Anna continued to boil. Her pent up rage surged to the forefront. "But, there is more than that...more than the antagonistic posture he shows the other countries of the region that will surely get us into a war." Anna took a deep breath before going on, "just before you and I got married Rafan and I were talking of getting married ourselves."

Mahumud's shock showed in the paling of his face, and in his verbal response. "What?"

"That's right. While you thought our little three way friendship was drifting apart, Este and I were secretly meeting out of your sight. It was an attempt to avoid hurting you...to avoid letting you see our relationship as the reason for our drifting apart as a threesome.

"I guess it was almost entirely my idea. I hate to admit it. I thought up the idea of marriage. Este didn't have much to say..."

"But, you and I were seeing each other..."

"Yes. Rafan eventually turned me away. That's when I realized it had all been my idea. He was just being friends like we'd always been. He had no idea we were being secretive. When I forced him to see what I was aiming at, he told me to go to you. He thought it was just coincidence when we ended up alone together. He knew you loved me, although you and I weren't that seriously involved then. It's surprising, looking back on it now, as naive as he was, that he didn't say anything to you about our meetings."

"He did. He even joked about those coincidental meetings," said a disheartened Mahumud.

"He's still that naive, at least when it comes to women. Este and I never got too far along the romance trail, if you're wondering. He said he had no time for that kind of thing in his life. He was already thinking of the future. Remember, he'd had the landlocked navy idea long before then.

"But, I just couldn't give up on him. He told me to marry you. Even then he was trying to help you. I cornered him alone at his home one night and tried to seduce him. He got violent." Anna let the memory play across her mind. Her face showed emotional pain. "I thought he was going to rape me, but that wasn't what was on his mind. He beat me and told me he never wanted to see me again. He told me to marry you and to never hurt you. The humiliation and the physical pain of that night were the beginning of my change of thinking on Rafan...and it's still with me!"

"But, I don't remember seeing you bruised or..."

"I kept them covered. Remember, I was a proper Muslim girl until we were married...burka, veil, the whole works."

"You said you wanted to be a virgin at your wedding."

"I was. But, I wanted to be sure the bruises were gone before you saw me."

They arrived home.

Mahumud's emotions were torn. His friend had beaten his wife and humiliated her. But, Rafan had allowed him to marry the woman he loved. Was that a sacrifice for a friend?

Rafan had hidden the nature of his meetings with their mutual friend from him...or more correctly, his wife had hidden an attempted affair with his friend. No matter what anger he could conjure up for any possible wrongs done him by Rafan, he couldn't deny that his friend seemed to have been looking out for him even then.

"Then I was your second choice," Mahumud asked his wife in a flat statement.

Anna's tone softened and she reached for her husband's hand. "Not really," she said. "It was just that damned forceful presence of his that attracted me. I realized quickly that it hid something less appealing. I love you, my husband, and always will."

Mahumud brooded quietly and finally reversed roles on Anna and started down the hall to the bedroom.

CHAPTER 31

Brought to the present by a shout from someone down the street where he was walking, Mahumud was carrying his son to one of the parks that Rafan's water projects had allowed. M'hut still wondered what other secrets were being withheld from him.

Was Anna's apparent hatred a shield for some additional guilt? Was Rafan playing him for a fool? He was looking out for M'hut, it seemed. But, was that a diversion from some other Rafan ploy?

Rafan stood not far away from M'hut in the new green area of vegetation. Both men were unaware of the other's proximity. Not far from the palace, Rafan inhaled the scent of the mint growing there. He enjoyed looking over this new landscape, so different than the one he had viewed from the rooftop guard post less than a decade earlier. His joy at this accomplishment was tempered by the vision he had of still greater achievements. He rubbed his hand through his short cropped hair.

There were a few people nearby who saw Rafan. Some waved at a man they admired. Some avoided him in a way that could not be construed to be anything but displeasure at recognizing him.

He turned and walked back to the palace. The heat felt good. He chose to only remember the people who had waved. He noted to himself that all those people were better dressed than they would have been just ten or fifteen years earlier. None of them appeared to be undernourished either. He took solace in that.

Whether or not they had all waved, everyone had benefited from his efforts. He wondered how any of the people in the park could not have cheered for him.

Rafan rarely saw his home. The changing image of Malfon was his life. If he was not in a field enjoying the heat and smells, he was usually at his desk in the ministry, whether asleep or awake.

***

"Minister Aturk, have you had any success preventing Rafan from influencing Premier Arat to allow him to buy the naval cruiser?" Anna M'hut asked the defense minister.

"Arat is giving your husband and I a little leverage on that proposition," Aturk answered. "Rafan hasn't gotten his cruiser. But, I'm not sure we can hold him off forever."

"But, wasting money on a military project is so wrong when there is much to do elsewhere," Anna continued. "How can Arat even consider it?"

"Not to mention the taxes we would have to pay to buy such a thing as a ship," another woman in the group said. "It's not necessary to keep expanding and increasing expenses. Why can't Rafan just let things progress on their own without any more big plans?"

"You don't know Este Rafan," Anna told her. "He's always got something bigger and better on his mind."

"Ladies," Aturk addressed his small group. "We are all agreed that Rafan has to be controlled. Let's not waste time discussing that." The group, entirely women except for Aturk, was meeting in a small office room at the new school. As the women squirmed in their seats trying to get comfortable on the wooden chairs, Aturk continued.

"Today, I want to set the priorities on the projects we oppose..."

"The ship!" Anna shouted. "That's number one! I don't want my son to go to war! That's what will happen if Rafan keeps building the military!"

"Yes, the ship is number one right now," Aturk agreed. "But, we have to look down the road at Rafan's future plans. Premier Arat looks favorably on most of Rafan's projects."

"Well, he has done a lot of good things," another woman spoke up for the first time.

"But, the costs are getting too great!" Anna reminded. "Is Arat as bad as Rafan, or Sabu?"

"Ladies. We are not revolutionists. We are only trying to influence the government to act reasonably. We are trying to keep minister Rafan from running away with our country. I give you an audience with that government. You give the calm voice of the people a hearing in public," Aturk explained. "We're unified in what we wish for."

"We want Rafan removed from power!" Anna shouted again.

"Anna M'hut!" Aturk shouted chidingly back. "You seem to have a particularly strong revilement for our commerce and interior minister. Loosing that will not serve our purpose. We need to stay respectful to avoid outward conflict. We need to work together quietly toward our goals. The goals of what is best for our country are not necessarily what is worst for Rafan. Our goal is not to give Anna M'hut what would give her the most pleasure."

"We still have no idea of how to control Rafan, after all these meetings," Anna complained, but calmed down.

The meeting returned to a thoughtful discussion on setting priorities and then adjourned an hour later, while Anna controlled her feelings, but not her comments.

***

Rafan frequently visited his old friend General Umbarik. The old man had retired a couple of years after Rafan had taken the cabinet position and was obviously in failing health. It saddened Rafan to see the old man wending his way to the grave. Umbarik, however, was always chipper on Rafan's visits.

"You've done miracles, my boy. One day you'll be premier. Mark my words. I wish I could be around to see that."

"Don't talk like that, general."

"Like what? Are you denying your ambition?"

"No, sir. I mean about dying."

"We're all dying, Rafan. You should be glad of that. That's how you'll get to be premier. Arat's not much younger than I am, you know. His lifestyle is not exactly a healthy one, as well."

"General!"

"Pish!"

"You think that I will be the next premier?" Rafan let the general's statement sink in.

Umbarik nodded. "Come to think of it, you'll probably change the title, just to show your independence," the general laughed.

He ignored Rafan's admonishment. "Or maybe you'll do what Arat did and just overthrow him!"

"General! General, why are you saying these things?"

"I'm just saying what I think. Old men can get away with that. Everyone thinks we don't know what we're saying and just shakes their head, like you're doing." The general laughed again. "Good on you, Este. Well, what's on your mind for today's visit?"

"I'm frustrated with all the delays. The water projects are still not complete. We still don't have that cruiser for the navy..."

"The cruiser is not your concern any more, Rafan. You have other things to worry about, like jobs, and the economy. Let M'hut and Aturk worry about the navy," the general advised.

"I know. But, I feel like I need to be in control of everything or it won't get done."

"You're not premier yet, Rafan."

"There are so many things that we need to do yet, and all I get is foot dragging from the top on down," Rafan complained. "It's almost as bad as it was under Sabu. Even Aturk is getting bolder in his obstructing again. He acts like he's got support from Arat, or somewhere. Arat has tried to put a permanent 'no' on my industrialization plan..."

"Rafan, you have been like a son to me..."

"And you like a father to me."

"...I've enjoyed these last few years of my life living vicariously through you. You sought my expertise in maneuvering the halls of politics early on. You've sought my advice at all times. There is no more help I can give you to achieve your goals...our goals. You are accomplishing what you and I set out to do since the first day you reported to my office to be my aide. It is up to you to carry on. You cannot let the difficulties you experience get you down. I only ask that you be careful to be sure what you do is essential for the betterment of Malfon. Do not lose sight of that. Don't let your emotions cloud your judgment. You can put up roadblocks for yourself by taking a poor approach to a problem. Remember that."

"Yes, sir," Rafan promised. "Let me give you the details of the most recent things I'm working on, general." Rafan seemingly brushed aside the general's remarks. "Since Arat and Aturk have put the naval expansion and air force projects on hold, and as you stated, they are not directly my concerns any more, I have been trying to find a less offensive way of industrializing under another name."

"Just out of curiosity, Rafan, what does your old friend M'hut think of the cruiser idea?"

"I guess he's not sure it's necessary," Rafan answered.

"So it is not just Aturk holding things up, eh? M'hut is not pushing the idea whole heartedly?"

"I don't think Commander M'hut shares the same ambitions that you and I do. I believe he is content with the status quo."

"Perhaps there is something more to his lack of enthusiasm for your project. Perhaps his ambitions lie elsewhere. Or, perhaps your project is not the boon you think it is."

"I don't know what other ambitions he would have, or what other reasons he might have for not supporting me more strongly."

"If M'hut believes that the cruiser is not a good idea, can you accept the fact that he may be right? Are you willing to accept that you might not be the best judge in that respect? He is more directly involved now than you are. He might have a clearer view of the project than you have. Remember, this is your old friend, the man you picked to be naval commandant. Do you not still have faith in him, Rafan?"

"I refuse to believe that expansion of our military is not a natural progression of our growth as a nation, and the cruiser is essential."

"Oh, well, if you're that sure..."

"Don't pish-posh me, general." Rafan was slightly miffed at the old man's attitude. "I remember who M'hut is..."

Rafan stopped talking in mid-sentence and looked queryingly at his mentor. "Listen to what I want to do to get around Aturk and Arat on the industrialization," Rafan redirected. "We can talk about the military another time. Aturk and Arat seem offended by the term industrialization. So, I'm going to propose a geological exploration to explore the feasibility of oil drilling!"

"What?"

"Yes!"

"But, surveys were done in the early 50s and nothing was found," the general informed Rafan.

"I know that, sir. But, I don't believe those surveys were thorough enough. In these days of high demand and potentially higher prices, deposits that might have been ignored as insignificant back then could be seen as worthwhile and profitable today. Both Talon and Norova have mineral deposits and oil. I cannot believe we have neither. All the countries around the Arabian Gulf have oil, and some have valuable minerals. How can we not have anything?"

"Perhaps we do, Este, but it still might not be practical to exploit it. Oil has to be exported to be valuable. We don't have the capability to distribute it easily. We are landlocked."

"We have a port in Norova," Rafan countered.

"It doesn't have the capability to handle exporting oil. The seawater plant and the naval and merchant marine activities are almost more than can be handled, and we don't want to jeopardize those capabilities on the chance of financial gain from oil," the general croaked in a weak voice.

"I think the potential is great enough to work at overcoming those problems. The records of the previous geological surveys have disappeared. There is nothing on file. We need to find out what is out there.

"I think there was an attempt to belittle our resources to prevent plunder by outside influences, or perhaps Malat Sabu had a secret agenda with foreign investors but was overthrown and died before he could benefit from it. He couldn't have foreseen his recent death or his overthrow and made no arrangements for those contingencies. The foreign investors could still be wondering how to approach Arat about the issue. In the last couple of years, in the time since Sabu's removal from office until his death, he would not have been of a mind to reveal his plan to his successor."

"What will you do?" Umbarik asked, growing weary.

"I can't see how I could find out about any secret plot, so I will initiate new research. My hope is that this will not smack of industrialization to Arat and will not be blocked."

"Well, good luck, my friend," General Umbarik said. "But, I'm sure Aturk will say that you're spending money for nothing. Now, I am tired. Go now and let an old man rest."

"Are you sure you're all right, general? You look pale."

"Go, Rafan. I am fine."

It was to be the last time Rafan saw the general. Before Rafan was able to act on his newest plan, Umbarik died of a massive heart failure. It was on an uncharacteristically wintry desert evening. He was at the palace where he was visiting former coworkers.

CHAPTER 32

"I lost my parents at too early an age. Though it was a few years ago now, I still feel that loss. Now, I have lost General Umbarik, my best friend and a second father to me. My sadness is huge, not just for my loss, but for Malfon. We have lost Malfon's best friend and my best friend as well," Rafan told the massive turnout of mourners at the graveside.

The terse Christian service brought tears to Rafan's eyes, and those present at the funeral were already aware of the change that seemed to come over the minister. His face had changed. He seemed sad, but somehow more manic, more intense, more resolved. Resolved to the loss of the general, yes, but perhaps resolved to something else too. His voice was solid, his demeanor forceful, as if daring anyone to contest his words. He didn't make a political statement at the time, his speech was about his old friend. But, the face that looked out at the other mourners was not the old Este Rafan. That man would never be seen again.

"General Umbarik had confidence in me. He knew I had abilities no one in Malfon had shown in decades. He said he had lost his competitive spirit and energy and I gave them back to him. He gave me support and guidance when I wasn't sure which way to go to accomplish my goals.

"To Malfon the general gave his life. As long as he was capable, he strived to do what he thought was right and best for this country of ours. He never had to convince me that his actions were always in the best interest of our citizens. I vow to not let any of the devotion perish from the leadership of this nation, if I have to spend twenty-four hours a day working for that purpose. You know me. You know that I also live for our country. I cannot take a wife or raise a family and allow those things to take from me the energy I need to improve our country and the lives of you people, my fellow Malfonies. I have no regrets that this is the path I have chosen."

Anna M'hut looked at her husband and said, "I see his devotion at the exclusion of everything else hasn't changed. He continues to have to exclude women. Beware any woman who could distract him," Anna smirked.

"I know that our premier shares the appreciation of General Umbarik's dedication and supports mine," Rafan went on. "On this day of mourning the passing of a great man, I vow to you and all the world that nothing will stand in the way of continuing toward his goal of making Malfon a greater country than she already is. I vow to never stop the work the general did, to make each and every man able to work at a job that fulfills his needs. He will be able to feed himself and his loved ones and be proud of his homeland. We will pay tribute to the general in that success. We owe that dedication to the general's memory."

The strong female voice at the back of the gathering yelled disrespectfully, "What about each and every woman? How about reducing military spending? Who made you king?"

She was quickly and quietly quelled. It was not Anna, but someone she knew well.

CHAPTER 33

In an unbelievable turn of events, only a few hours after General Umbarik's burial, Premier Arat died. The cancer that only a few were aware of felled Malfon's leader. Scuffling for a successor was limited. Most ministers lacked ambition or backed Rafan. Aturk would not be tolerated. The observant knew what to expect. Over expected token objections from Aturk, Este Rafan became Malfon's new premier. Umbarik's prophecy had come true. The event's only shock was that of Arat's actual death. The succession was totally without surprise.

Rafan quickly took the reins under his control, shocking many in Malfon further in his apparent lack of consideration of the events of the previous days.

"I am sad that General Umbarik will not be around to experience the future we gentlemen will create," Rafan told his cabinet. "I am sad that Arat was suddenly taken from us as well. But, we can let nothing distract us from renewing our zeal to move Malfon forward."

"Premier Arat told me to make us all aware of the need for caution as we move forward," Minister Deusein told the group. Deusein was the newest member of the cabinet, but had obviously had at least one conversation with Arat before he died.

"Arat believed that Rafan would take his place some day and that we should give him our respect as leader of our country. But, he stressed that we use caution in our actions as a group."

"All very well," Rafan said, not the least offended. "But, we must, indeed, move forward."

The changes from Rafan began occurring within hours of his swearing-in. Minister Aturk stood as the main obstacle to all of Rafan's ideas and it was evident that the new attitude of the premier-designate would condone none of that obstructionism.

The actual swearing in was done by a Christian priest, which did not sit well with Aturk.

"What does all this ritual mean to the rest of us," Aturk asked. "I don't accept any vow of this sort with any seriousness."

"There is only one holdover in this cabinet from the group that served under Malat Sabu. If Minister Aturk is not comfortable with the current situation, he is free to step down. Minister Aturk has been a constant foot dragger. It is my intentions to have Aturk relinquish his position with this government anyway."

Aturk blanched only slightly. A personal affront such as this was unheard of in a cabinet session, let alone at a swearing in ceremony. An argument might happen at a meeting, but not direct insults of this sort. A private meeting with Aturk to make the request, or demand, was the correct manner to handle this matter. It was just one more thing that was different with Rafan in charge.

"Premier Rafan," one of the ministers spoke up as the ceremony concluded, "we need traditional carry over. We need a counterbalance of the old and the new. Minister Aturk should stay."

"We will have carryover without Aturk. The rest of us have all been cabinet members under the previous government."

"But, Aturk is the only cabinet member who preceded Premier Arat. That gives him a longer point of view from which to appraise our activities."

"I wouldn't trust his appraisal." Rafan took a deep breath and exhaled. "Very well," he intoned carefully. A new calmness seemed to come over him. "There is merit in what you say."

Perhaps Rafan was not yet sure he could hold sway over the entire cabinet if they opposed his will. He knew to pick his battles. "Aturk will stay. But, if there is any obstruction for the sake of obstruction alone, it will not be tolerated. There will be no personal vendettas allowed by Minister Aturk."

Aturk wondered if vendettas by the new premier were allowed. He felt sure he knew the answer. The minister of defense only replied to Rafan's stare by saying, "I swear my allegiance to Malfon, my home." It seemed age was robbing Aturk of what little ambition he had ever shown.

CHAPTER 34

"The group of us who fear Rafan is concerned that no one is going to prevent him from leading us to destruction," Anna M'hut told her husband.

"Where do you see evidence of that?" Mahumud asked incredulously. "Everything he has done has helped Malfon."

"Not women," Anna stated flatly. "And our neighboring countries are nervous about all of Rafan's rhetorically ambitious intentions. Minister Aturk was quite clear about that."

"I suppose you're right about that. There is some growing dissatisfaction among the populace. I can't believe it's that large a group of detractors. Surely it's a small minority. I can't believe anyone would take some kind of forceful action against Rafan. Women are benefiting from his works to a great extent. "Don't expect me to take action. I'm just a naval commander, not a leader of government opposition. I'm not going to lead a faction against my friend, understand that."

"No, my dear husband. I don't want you to. I don't want you as a target, in harm's way. I ask no more of you than your support."

Anna held back a comment about Mahumud's desire to be at the seat of power with Arat, but expressing no such desire when it came to Rafan. Este had not asked Mahumud to be at his side.

But, apparently Mahumud didn't consider that a slight. In fact, he was denying any desire for more power, declaring he would not lead an opposition faction. If it became the only answer for Mahumud's wishes to be at the head of power that would not be his chosen path.

"I know Este treated you badly before we were married. But, that was a long time ago. I cannot hold that against him. Don't you think it's time to forgive? If Rafan chooses not to elevate me on his coattails any longer, so be it. He has done so much for me already. I owe everything that is good in my life, even you and our son, to Este. I am satisfied with my life." Mahumud avoided his wife's glare.

Anna saw that her activities would have to be shielded from her husband's eyes. In Mahumud's mind Rafan's assistance in gaining position and prestige had already been sufficient to deserve his undying loyalty and appreciation. It was only the second time she would keep something from her husband. Anna realized she and her group were fortunate that Mahumud had kept still about them so far. It was apparent that Rafan was not aware of any anti-government campaign, possible only if Mahumud had not tattled.

"Very well, my husband. You've made it clear how you feel. But, I cannot forgive Rafan. More importantly, even though a large proportion of our people are Muslims, women want to peel away traditions. Many men are starting to assert themselves on behalf of the women. They are asking for changes and restrictions on Rafan's plans. People are chafing at the tax burden. We are scared that there will be violence."

Again Anna walked away after making her statement, leaving Mahumud staring after her, still unsure of the path of action he should follow.

Rafan had been the only one who could see that the navy was the best entity for forcing progress in Malfon's economy. It had brought in foreign currency. It gave the people of Malfon pride and resources no other route could have provided as well, as quickly, or as inexpensively. The military model had been in place, only an international venture of a respected and prestigious entity could have gotten the results the navy did, because Malfonies knew the military and supported it.

Rafan had also been the only one who apparently saw Mahumud's value, for only he had seen to it that Mahumud had progressed along the road that brought him to his current place at the head of the navy. But, perhaps now was the time to let things find their own level rather than continuing to force projects for the desired result. Mahumud wished he knew for sure. Maybe Anna was right!

CHAPTER 35

Ironically, Aturk's importance was increased soon after Rafan assumed the ultimate power in Malfon. Rafan's long awaited expansion of the navy and army came about quickly.

"The notice circulated for men to join the army air corps has been received favorably," Rafan informed his ministers.

"Yes, sir," one minister agreed. "But, there has been some agitation among the women of our country."

"I know. They're always worried about their men in the service," Rafan acknowledged.

"No, sir. These are women who want to be in the service. They say they want jobs too. They want to be able to determine the course of their own lives."

"What? Women have no place in business, or in the military. That is the way it has always been."

"Yes, sir. But you have to be aware of this sentiment."

"What is the matter, Premier?" Aturk asked. "Do you fear that women being used in the military will see me as their champion instead of you?" The older man smirked. Aturk had always been recognized as a dignified woman's man, even if a loner.

"Aturk, you may think I fear you. But, I never have and will not start now. Your prowess with women doesn't impress me. It is you who fear my power. You are already trying to impair my authority," Rafan spoke with rancor. "There will be no women in our military. That is settled. Now, go about your business."

Each of the members of the cabinet wondered if the day would come when they would be confronted with Rafan's power.

If there were no limits, he could easily oust each of them as he wished. Their only strength was a unified position, solidifying their tenure against him.

Before the cabinet dispersed, Rafan had one more shot for Aturk's ego. "While Aturk has done nothing to distinguish himself, he has done nothing to shame himself or his country. I am grateful for his good sense in making this so. Therefore I am sure my orders will be carried out."

Aturk's ears burned. It was enough to have been passed over for the Premiership in preference to this inexperienced young man, but insults of this sort were almost unbearable for the Defense Minister.

It would have been easy for Aturk to take out his pain on M'hut, Rafan's old friend and commander of the navy, or to provoke the secret group to which Anna belonged into action. But, Aturk was not the dangerous blackard Rafan tried to paint him. Not only did Aturk not desire to punish the career officer who was doing a good job, but he knew such an act would only force Rafan into a tougher stance.

M'hut was already showing signs of stress since his friend had become premier. Aturk knew not to attempt to use one man against the other. Their mutual support was long established. But, it seemed M'hut was beginning to see Rafan in a different light, rather than in the loyalty-blinded glow he had always used to view his friend. Aturk was content to let that change of perspective grow naturally. No nudge was needed, Aturk hoped.

CHAPTER 36

The death of General Umbarik not only grieved Premier Rafan, but also accelerated the change in the young man that the general had been mentoring. Though his influence had been growing throughout his life, Rafan's loss caused him to grieve everyone involved in his life more than ever before, by removing the only major constraint to that influence...General Umbarik.

"I don't care if there are a hundred people who think taxes are too high," he told the newest member of the cabinet, the Foreign Minister, Aman Deusein. "There are things that need to be done, and we need the revenue from the taxes to do them. The people don't understand how costly it is to maintain the things they have become accustomed to benefiting from, or how much is still lacking from their lives. They do not have the dream that I do which shows what Malfon could be like if we keep moving forward."

"But, sir, these things do not need to all be done at once. If we could take them a little more slowly, the treasury could stand the burden without more taxes." Deusein's squeaky voice annoyed Rafan, and the minister's habit of shuffling his feet when walking, or even when standing still, reminded the premier of a slow moving sloth.

"I told you I don't care what anyone thinks, including you. These projects are important, whether anyone but me knows it or not. We need to get them done...now!"

"Perhaps you could speak to the public about this and let them know, make them understand," another minister offered.

"They cannot understand. They don't know what's in their best interests. Maybe the next generation, educated in my schools will be smart enough to understand. But, these people today, cannot. It is up to you, my ministers, to bring the needed situations about so we can move forward. The public be damned. Get that cruiser, build and maintain the water pipelines, do the oil exploration, create an air force. Get these things done! I can't do it all by myself! I want no more objections from any of you!"

The formerly polite Rafan was gone. The new bullying Premier Rafan had taken his place. He was glaring at Aturk. "We have to act in the best interests of the people in spite of themselves."

"But, if the people themselves don't want..." Deusein tried to reason. Deusein was only slightly older than Rafan and a newcomer to government and had guts belying his squeaky voice and nervous shuffle. He had grown up with parents who commuted to jobs in Norova. His adult years had been spent farming and trucking. Eventually he had found himself working in Rafan's desalination plant, where Rafan had received glowing reports on him. This led to Deusein being appointed to the cabinet. His varied experience gave him a point of view that he was not afraid to share with their monomaniacal premier, somewhat to Rafan's chagrin.

"If you cannot do it, then I will find new ministers who can."

Rafan had already been condensing the cabinet. He was not only the premier, but he was also still the Commerce Minister and if Aturk should falter, he would certainly not replace him with another man. The post of Navy Minister was basically a nonentity. The other ministers knew that their positions were tentative. Even though Deusein was personally appointed by Rafan, the newcomer was wise enough to avoid deliberately crossing his benefactor. Especially, being new, he knew it was most important for him not to push the premier too hard.

Deusein gave up trying to make his point.

"These people, who are complaining about the taxes and whatever else, are a very small minority who make too much noise. It may become necessary to quiet them to keep them from spreading their discontent to everyone else and sabotaging our efforts. As I'm sure you're aware, most of our people are happy to see a leader of royal blood who is doing something for them for a change."

It was true. Rafan still enjoyed a great deal of support from the people of Malfon. Even the majority of the dissenters didn't directly blame the premier. They tended to worship him. The people of Malfon were, indeed, living lives much better than any they could have dreamed of ten years earlier. Rafan's only worry was that he, like General Umbarik, would perish before his work was completed. Whether or not there was a finite point of completion, he never asked himself.

It did, however, hurt him that he was not worshiped as he once was, just a few years earlier. There hadn't been any dissenters then, other than Aturk.

CHAPTER 37

Rafan stood watching the movements outside, on the streets of Creche. It was not the bustle of a New York or London, but it was a far cry from the apathy commerce had experienced for decades under former rulers.

Rafan felt proud that Malfon was prospering. When he took time to ask himself if he was really responsible for all this, he answered himself with a resounding, 'yes!'

The fools that thought he didn't know what he was doing, or what's best for Malfon, like Aturk, and maybe even that new Deusein, were the clueless ones. Only he, the premier, had the ability and the ambition to bring about the needed changes. He was sure about that.

The phenomenal skyrocket his life had been riding, from poor undernourished orphan to young leader of his country, confirmed his belief in himself.

Some thought he'd lost sight of what was best for the country, that his ego was guiding him for personal fulfillment. That was nonsense, he knew, after all he was Este Rafan, the implementer of the tandem paper processing principle, the founder of the Malfon navy, the star pupil of the army officer school, and...and, how could they doubt him?

His hurt for not being universally loved vacillated with anger at the ignorant ones he felt responsible for that lack of appreciation and adoration.

Some of those people thought he needed some time off, a holiday. Hah! How could the needs of the country be put on hold? Surely nothing would get done in his absence. Maybe they just wanted him out of the country for a while so they could take control. Well, he wasn't about to let that happen.

There had even been talk of his need for a woman. Someone like M'hut's wife? Oh, how she had tried to distract him from his focus on the future with her vile body, her putrid femininity.

She had been the only one able to provoke him to violence. Sure he had arguments, but there was no physical involvement. They knew better than to obstruct Premier Rafan! Only Anna had been bold enough to get the best of him. That was long ago. More power to Mahumud for putting up with her. He could understand why some people needed what she offered. But, he didn't need it. Anna. He was happy for his friend Mahumud, the new father. But, why were there no self-sacrificing women like his mother anymore? His mother had known her place. She had given Este everything she could, to get him a chance to be where he now was.

No, there was nothing wrong with him, he was sure. Only the fools like Anna and Aturk didn't understand. He and Malfon would continue to go forward to bigger goals. He didn't need to listen to the others, didn't need a holiday. He didn't need a woman.

CHAPTER 38

M'hut and Anna talked about her feelings for Rafan. "There was more than just a rejection, Mahumud. I loved Rafan. I'd spent five years dreaming of finally being old enough to marry him and have his children. Then he rejected me," Anna told her husband.

"But, it's been over for years. It's a long time to hold a grudge," Mahumud responded.

"You don't understand, do you? That slap in the face sent my self-esteem in a whole new direction. I had to fight hard to handle it. Thanks to Allah that you were what I needed and you were there. You helped me get myself back. But, that feeling I had for Este was gone, replaced by hatred. Hatred for what he made me feel. Yes, you've heard me right. I do think Rafan has gone overboard with his plans for Malfon. But, mainly I just hate Este Rafan."

Mahumud didn't know what to say. He said nothing, and finally made his way to Naval Command to put in a day's work. He sensed a new barrier being raised between his wife and himself.

CHAPTER 39

"Citizens of Malfon," Rafan began. He was addressing a crowd from a balcony in the palace not far from where he had patrolled as a palace guard not so many years before. "We have come a long way in the past decade or so. Many of you are in our army, our navy, or are working at one of our water projects. Some of you are selling the produce you grow to those who do these other jobs, and even to foreign buyers. Malfon has no starving people any more. Our diets are balanced and nutritional. What we cannot grow, we can buy. Now, I am going to tell you something that will make an even more miraculous change in all our lives. After extensive months in the desert, a research team has found oil in Malfon! Malfon, at last, will be wealthy!"

The cheers had barely died, it seemed, before the oil fields were paying off. The earnings from the oil allowed the diversification of the economy. Malfon's economy defied description in normal terms. It was not a socialist concern, even though the government was the primary business and owned most of the income in the country. Malfon was not a traditional monarchy. There was no king per se. Capitalism was only just starting to appear. But, everyone knew that oil meant that the whole population would benefit in some way.

CHAPTER 40

"Sometimes I wish we didn't live in a desert, Premier," the oil foreman told Malfon's leader. "I'd just like to have a day when it wasn't 120 degrees, and the sweat wasn't pouring out of my body."

"Take a trip to the mountains in Talon," the premier advised with a smile. "Surely you can afford it."

"That is true sir, the value of the zlot is increasing and I am well paid."

Rafan nodded. He was so happy that his belief in oil was justified. Whether there had been a conspiracy earlier in history or not, somehow the missing geological reports could only have been a cover up of some sort. The new findings showed substantial deposits. They couldn't have been missed by earlier surveys.

A lizard skittered past the two men. Rafan spoke again. "Now, tell me how we're doing, Hans."

"Well, the first two wells didn't take long to reach the deposit. The sand is easy drilling. Back fill was our only problem. But with the experience we gained from the other oil producing countries in the Middle East, we had no problem overcoming that. "Now, we have a new well coming in just about every week."

"And no outside international company is involved. The initial expense has already been offset by production?" Rafan knew it had. "I don't know why some of these other countries have let their oil out of their control."

"Yes, sir." Hans replied. Then he continued his report on the status of Malfon's oil industry "We should have the fields completely tapped by the end of the year. Then I see us producing steadily for the next century, at least."

Rafan could smell oil. Since the well they were at was not yet producing, he assumed it was from the machinery or perhaps another nearby well. It could also have been from the foreman himself.

"Is there any chance we've missed locating some deposits?" Rafan asked the oil man.

"Not unless they're under the palace or the streets of Creche, sir."

Rafan laughed. The sound was unfamiliar to him. They were not going to mess with his palace. The thought sobered him quickly.

"Do any of the deposits run near our borders? I mean, could one of our neighbors start drawing off the same oil field?" Rafan asked.

"That is a possibility, sir," Hans answered warily. "One of the deposits runs near the Talon border. Of course we don't know what they've found on their side."

"Thank you, Hans. Keep up the good work. You can feel proud that you are part of the effort that is making progress for our country and helping to make each Malfony a rich future."

Rafan liked the mechanical sound the drilling rig made. So different from the silence of the desert he had known as a child.

CHAPTER 41

The oil revenues provided for the expansion of the industrial base that Rafan wanted. Agricultural need for sustenance was no longer paramount in Rafan's mind. Aturk's worry about Malfon becoming a nation of farmers was no longer merited.

By the time markets were secured for the oil, pipelines were pumping crude to the port in Norova, where ships besides their own tanker hauled it to the buyers who sometimes were only middlemen for the large concerns using the larger tankers in other ports. It was amazing how much easier it was to implement an oil pipeline than one for water. An oil pipeline also snaked its way north to a more prosperous nation that allowed passage for a minimal fee, and bulked Malfon's oil with its own to make large shipments possible. This made calling the supertankers to their port feasible and efficient.

The first priority Rafan placed on his country's plate now, was electricity. Any industry beyond the oil would require electricity.

Throughout the twentieth century when nearly every country employed electricity for cooling, cooking, heating, refrigeration, and lighting, Malfon was only sporadically in possession of those luxuries. Those few who could afford it, such as the government, bought propane, fuel oil, or kerosene, to accomplish fulfilling their needs. Those without money ate only food not requiring refrigeration or cooking, unless it was immediately consumed after being obtained. Wooden things, dung, old clothing, and other combustibles were used when necessary and available, sometimes with dire results from toxic fumes.

The poor suffered through the stifling heat without relief and shivered on a cool desert night. In a land where the days were nearly twelve hours long all year round, lighting was often unnecessary, even though desirable, except for in the kinds of buildings only the government owned.

Though no one was starving in Malfon, there were still a good number who could be counted as poor. It was with these people in mind that Rafan decided to electrify.

The first electric lines were laid underground to bring power from an oil fired generation plant, not far from Creche, into the government buildings. Along with those lines came telephone wires. Previous communication facilities had been primitive at best. But, with cellular transmission still unfounded, the land lines at last gave a chance for modern technology to bloom. The required construction and disruption, to accomplish these advances, gave work to many Malfonies. The salaries were paid partly by the government and partly by the new private corporation that was set up to electrify Malfon.

However, the task proved to be monumental. There was little skilled labor and Rafan insisted on domestic employment.

Additionally, those few people who lived outside Creche could see no gain for themselves and were unwilling to work on the projects, and even protested against any costs that the projects brought them. Disruptions outside Creche were minimal, but resistance was strong. Among these people were those who tended to cling to the old nomadic ways as much as possible.

Nevertheless Rafan foresaw a future with towns popping up all over the desert. Indeed, it would possibly be reality if Rafan had his way and the power lines were put into place. But, if he could have foreseen any other 'future picture', he would have known the grid would not be in place for years. Several oil-fired generation plants were functioning, but there was a gigantic amount of work still to be done.

The sole refinery ran at peak capacity, but water availability was still a problem for new settlements, so without new water pipelines and a few high tech water facilities, the hydro-carbon riches were of little use for development. The huge amount of cash flow required was denied at every opportunity and Rafan found he had less power with the private corporation than he did with the government he ran. The resulting cash flow was too low to expedite a completion of the electrification of Malfon.

CHAPTER 42

"Premier," a minister said to Rafan, "a computer company wants to build a manufacturing installation in Creche."

"Of course," Rafan answered matter-of-factly. "We have invested in the power grid to provide electricity for such an endeavor, and now with our labor costs so low, we present a very attractive picture for any kind of manufacturing. But, we must be careful not to bring in pollution and contaminating side effects."

"But, our electricity is from oil fired generators. They pollute..."

Rafan ignored the interruption. "We must be selective in the kinds of business we allow to set up here."

"Yes, sir," the minister acquiesced. "But, is it all right for this computer company to come in?"

"By all means. Computers are the future and we need to get ready for the future. We definitely want to be involved with that. That should be a nice clean commercial enterprise, not even a true industry in the old sense."

"But, there is silicon..."

"We need foreign investment. Tell the corporation representatives to meet with our ambassador. I'm sure something can be worked out that will be to both our advantages."

"I have to admit, Rafan," Aturk told the premier, "this is one project that had very few drawbacks. The money that was diverted to fund the oil exploration and drilling was paid back quickly and many times over, though there is still objection to the power and telephone line work. I think the computer manufacturing company and those to follow will put the power grid costs and complaints aside just as quickly."

Aturk was not buddying up to Rafan, but he was a fair man and gave credit where it was due.

"I thought industrialization of Malfon was a joke." He couldn't say the words, I was wrong.

"Why didn't any of my predecessors accomplish this? It was just sitting there...if only they'd made the effort."

"There were rumors that Malat Sabut had something going for his own benefit," Aturk said.

Rafan heard the comforting new sound of telephones ringing down the hall and smiled inwardly. He wondered if Aturk had been included in Sabu's plans in any way.

"Yes, I heard those rumors. But, more than anything, I think no one saw the potential. No one believed Malfon could be a great country. It took me to change all that," Rafan bragged.

Aturk cringed. "But, we still must win the respect of the rest of the world. It will take more than full employment and per capita wealth."

"But, why should we care, Premier?" asked Minister Deusein.

The squeaky voice caused Rafan to involuntarily step away from him. "Why do we need to become a world leader? The people would be content with the lives that are now possible. We are all living a better life. Will being respected as a first class nation make our lives any better?"

Rafan's only answer was, "We don't even have the respect of all of our citizens." He turned back to Aturk. "As long as you're here, there is something that has come to my attention that falls under the defense department, as I see it."

"Yes? What is it Rafan?" Aturk avoided calling their leader 'Premier' whenever possible and got away with it.

"I understand there is a group of dissenters plotting against me. They are biding their time while deciding what they wish to do. I hear they have some inside connections," Rafan stated as Aturk blanched. "We can't have our progress obstructed. See to it that this group is disassembled and see if you can find out their inside connection. See to that, please." Aturk wasn't sure what Rafan knew, or how he found out about the group. He was sure his was the only one in the country. He had no choice but to do as he was ordered. Rafan's source would no doubt tell the premier if Aturk shirked his duty.

Only in time would Aturk find out if Rafan already knew he was the inside connection. If he did know, or found out later, what would become of him, Aturk worried.

CHAPTER 43

"Aturk, I want to enlarge our navy again, and the army as well. They are your responsibility, so you will see to it," Rafan told his defense minister a few months later. "Recruit the people that will be needed and purchase another, smaller, faster ship."

"But, Rafan," Aturk objected, still refusing to call him Premier, "we would have to persuade people to leave private sector jobs to swell the military ranks. Is that what you want to do? I thought you wanted to use the military to get our country on its feet, so that it could stand with more than just the government as an employer. That has happened. There is an ever dwindling unemployment core, if you don't count the many women who want to work. Have you lost sight of your own goals?"

Aturk was smirking. "The pull of recruitment for the army and navy is gone. In addition to depleting our civilian work force we would have to incur additional expenses by offering incentives to entice enlistment. People are too well off to need to enlist in sufficient numbers otherwise. Unless you want to use more women than we already have in the military."

"You know how I feel about that, Aturk!" Rafan fired back. "I am very upset about your use of women in the army and navy as it is. I do not want you to resort to enlisting women to fill the quota."

"The women in the military are just doing clerical jobs, Rafan. You can hardly say they are in the military at all. But, there is agitation against spending more money for the military in any form. Another ship, incentives, increased payroll...that won't sit well with public opinion."

"That's the trouble with educating people. They get a little knowledge and they think they know what's best for them. The school has hardly graduated a class, but the radio station keeps people informed. So, they think they know what's what. Who was it that said, 'a little knowledge is a dangerous thing'? What do they think paid for the schooling and started our ability to have a radio station? It was the military, then the industry it fostered! They overlook the details if they don't want to accept them."

Rafan's hurt feelings had been completely overtaken by anger.

"Rafan, I don't think this is a positive step..."

"I don't care what you think, Aturk. Do as you're ordered."

CHAPTER 44

"You know, M'hut, there are those among us who have never believed that Rafan has always been concerned with improving the lives of his fellow Malfonies," Minister Aturk told the naval commander. "Do you believe that developing a navy was the only way to create the impetus to get our country moving on the road to prosperity? Couldn't the army have found a way to benefit our neighboring countries like the navy began doing with salvage and transport?"

"I don't know..." M'hut stuttered and paused.

"Couldn't the army have provided a guard service for Norova or Talon...sort of mercenaries for hire? Could the army have done the work of drilling wells or giving land transportation to those who needed trucking, for a fee?"

"Well, I suppose..."

"Yes, those things were possible. There were other ways to go about building up our country without a navy, even without building up a military of any sort," Aturk finished.

"Well, Este always had this dream of a Malfon navy, even when we were kids," M'hut supplied. "That was his way of doing it. Someone else might have done it another way. But no one did."

"Didn't you ever wonder what was behind that dream?" Aturk asked.

"No. I didn't."

"There is a reason Rafan wanted a navy, Commander. Rafan's grandfather had been trying to move his family to the gulf shore before he died. He thought it would be better for the health of his wife and future children. Rafan's father was one of those.

"When the UN redrew the map of the area in the '40s, that could no longer happen. The shore belonged to Norova. Emigration was not an option for a proud Malfony. So Rafan's parents, his grandfather's son and his wife, were forced to grow up in the desert. Their malnutrition led to their early deaths. Rafan has always been sore about Malfon's loss of the coast. This is a big part of the reason," Aturk explained.

"I don't believe that," M'hut finally found a strong voice to use in countering Aturk's assertion. "Rafan's one concern is doing what is best for Malfon, even at the cost of a wife and family for himself." M'hut thought about Anna's rejection by the premier when they were teens and his heart was gripped by tightness.

"Rafan only wanted the navy because he saw it, even as a kid, as the fastest, easiest, and most economical way to do what he has done. The fact that we had no seaport was only an irritation in completing that plan. Rafan has no ambition but to improve Malfon."

"Believe whatever you will, M'hut. But, I don't think you're allowing yourself to see the entire picture, the complete Este Rafan."

CHAPTER 45

Indeed, the schools, which now numbered two, had been paid for by the monies raised from the foreign investors bringing in clean commercial enterprises and the oil industry itself. Circulating domestic zlots could only do so much. But, once the military got Malfon headed on a profitable track, the oil exploration became feasible, and that brought industry. Malfon's own business base fared well, supplying services, transportation and such, for the foreign investors who brought dollars, pounds, euros, and other currency into the international coffers of Malfon's banking system.

Few of the adult Malfonies of Rafan's generation or older had much formal education. Traditional family teaching was the norm. Some individuals were able to attend school from time to time in Norova and elsewhere while their parents worked there.

There was no language barrier involved in nearby countries and the host countries were willing to teach the Malfony students with the stipulation that a few of the domestic monies being paid the parents would be siphoned off for the privilege. In Malfon, education was considered an unnecessary expense and effort for most. That had been true since the country had been formed in the 1940s.

Rafan, and the M'hut's, were a few of the luckiest ones of their generation. There was opportunity offered in recognition of aptitude and sacrifice. They got full time schooling in Malfon.

This was especially unusual in Anna's case. Rafan believed luck had nothing to do with it. Anna's parents refused to accept ‘no’ for an answer. It had eventually become clear that letting her attend school would cause less trouble than denying her. So, she became almost the only girl to receive schooling in her home country. Home schooling and tutoring, with some on-grounds classes were approved. Mahumud M’hut would not be likely to agree that this course for Anna had been the best since his marriage to the feisty, intelligent woman. Rafan felt his parents had sacrificed themselves for his education. He was committed to making their sacrifices not go to waste. He had gotten the best of the family’s food, and the most. What’s more, money that could have been spent on food was spent getting him anything he needed to thrive and exceed in life and accomplishments. Thus his parents suffered malnutrition, but not Rafan.

With the advent of surplus budgets, Rafan ordered a new brick school built for Creche. It was air-conditioned, electrically lighted, and plumbed with the new sewer and water system that had sprung from the original water projects. Everything deemed logical to encourage the ability to learn was included in the construction package, including technology.

Rafan believed in investing in the future, Malfon’s future, and of course it was Rafan who decided what was indeed important to that future. Perhaps he also remembered tutoring Anna, when he made his education decisions.

CHAPTER 46

"Minister Aturk," Anna called out, "when are we going to do something?" She was at another meeting of the group of dissidents. This time they were at the home of one of the other women in the group.

The odors of the 'treat' the homemaker was preparing for the group made it seem more like a social event, which angered Anna. She was irritable and eager to get to the meat of their purpose and get the meeting over.

"This is not a social gathering," she declared, glaring at the woman stirring a pot in an adjacent room. The main area opened to a door-less archway. The adobe-like brick interior walls were bare, unlike hers at home, and they depressed Anna. She was used to much better housing than this and this level of semi-poverty insulted her. She saw no irony that the disparity between her own standard of living, allowed by Mahumud being navy commandant, and her present discomfort, was the very thing Rafan was trying to eradicate. In some ways she removed herself from other Malfonies. The lack of any guilt for her prosperity did nothing to improve her mood.

"All we do is sit and talk. We share information, but we don't do anything!"

"Gathering that information is the most important thing we can do, Anna," Aturk assured her. "You have information I don't have, gathered from Mahumud. I have information you don't have, garnered from my position in government. Others here had information on what is being felt on the streets. Putting it together puts us all on the same page. We are able to see the entire picture. That will help us decide how to go about making the changes we want. It will help us decide what those changes should be. “Besides, we have a problem concerning these meetings,” Aturk continued.

“What do you mean?” one of the other women asked.

“The premier is aware of them,” Aturk answered simply.

“So?” Anna asked. “There is no law against meetings. At least not yet.”

“With Rafan, you can’t be sure,” Aturk reminded. “It may well be against the law by now. But, the point is, he knows the purpose of these meetings and even the names of those of us attending them. He cannot allow us to go on plotting against him, so I warn you all that we must disband, for our own sakes.”

“No!” Anna shouted. “Then Rafan would win! I won’t let him scare me off!”

“Me either,” another woman said.

“We’ll just have to keep the meeting locations secret. We’ll move them around. There won’t be any way for Rafan to find out where we’re meeting, or when,” a third woman said.

“Won’t there?” Aturk asked glaring at Anna. “He already knows some of your names. He won’t have to find the meetings to find us.”

“Has someone in the group defected?” Anna glared right back at Aturk.

“I tell you, the only safe thing to do is to disband. If Rafan somehow finds out we’re still meeting, any portion of us, he will see to it personally that we’re disbanded. He won’t be gentle, I assure you.” Aturk was pleading for an easy way to carry out the orders Rafan had given him.

"No!" Anna said again, amid a chorus of nodding heads and agreement.

Aturk had never worn a sadder look on his face. He was responsible for bringing these women together in the first place.

He left the women talking among themselves and made his way back to the palace.

CHAPTER 47

"His majesty Este Rafan wants another destroyer," Aturk told Commander M'hut.

"Minister!" M'hut responded. "I'm sure the premier knows what he's doing! He is undoubtedly working for the best interests of our country."

"You know," Aturk began, "you should be a full cabinet minister by now. But, your old buddy, Rafan, has done away with the position of Minister of the Navy. He's now Premier, Minister of Commerce, Minister of the Navy...Ad hoc...And who knows what else?"

"Shall we get down to business, Minister?" M'hut directed.

There was a new animosity between the two, just below the surface. M'hut was uncomfortable knowing Aturk was part of the group he had told Rafan about. He had not given his friend any names, because his wife was part of that group. But, dealing with Aturk while being aware of his duplicity toward their leader didn't sit well with M'hut.

"I think our navy could use a new ship this time. A guided missile destroyer would fit the purpose. I know where we can find one almost new...it's only five years old. One of the more belligerent members of the world community was forced to renege on the production order at a late stage by an alliance of its foes. We can make a thrifty purchase. Our own computer company can contract to outfit the electronics."

"What purpose would this fit, M'hut?" Aturk nudged.

M'hut ignored the question and shuffled some papers in his hands.

Aturk went on, "Rafan hasn't even offered you a promotion and you're still blindly loyal. I guess there is something to be said for that. You're a good man, M'hut."

"Thank you, sir." M'hut didn't feel the same about Aturk, but it was apparent Aturk didn't know from whom the tip on the dissenter group had come. He knew from Anna that Aturk had been informed by Rafan. Aturk could figure it out if he tried, but it seemed he hadn't bothered. M'hut was waiting to hear from his wife what action was expected to follow. Would Aturk act against the group? Would Rafan take action on his own and include Aturk in the proceedings, whatever there would be? Rafan had not given M'hut a hint of his intentions, but surely the group would not be allowed to continue to exist.

"I am going to put you in for Commodore, M'hut. I think I still have the authority to do that. I don't think anyone will object."

M'hut wondered if Aturk was trying to line him up on his side of some future conflict. "Thank you very much sir," M'hut acknowledged with embarrassment. "I believe that the premier will eventually want to be able to use our two small planes at sea. So, I have been on the look-out for a small aircraft carrier or some such vessel."

"My God! We're becoming a military power in spite of the wishes of the citizens of our country to the contrary! Doesn't that bother you, M'hut?"

"The premier and I are still good friends and I believe in him. I try to do my job for the good of the country and at the will of Rafan..."

"And of course, you answer only to Rafan himself."

"And you, sir."

"Hmph!" Aturk commented. "Of course." Aturk took a trip around M'hut's desk in the office at the palace. "The international community wonders why we need to arm so heavily...and there is a good deal of descension in the cabinet, such as it is. There aren't many of us left there with Rafan assuming all the offices for himself. There is not much of a capability to restrain Rafan. Whatever he wants, he usually gets now-a-days. The idea of the cabinet used to be to advise and consent. We even took votes on things in the past and could use our majority opinion to override the premier's intentions. No more." He sounded out the depth of M'hut's loyalty to Rafan. With the tension the militarizing was causing in the neighboring countries and the cabinet, Aturk wanted to know what to expect of the Commodore of the Navy.

He wanted to know how M'hut felt about his wife's involvement in those tensions. How far would M'hut go against his wife for his old friend, Aturk wondered.

"The premier is only enlarging the army and navy to keep it in perspective with the size of the country's interests. As our economy grows, so does the threat to it..."

"But, don't you see the sudden out-of-context surge in military spending? Where is the increasing threat to Malfon?"

Aturk sat down in a spare wooden chair in the office. "M'hut, what if I ordered you, as your superior, to not buy this destroyer? What would you do?"

"I would advise the premier and ask for further direction."

"Which, of course, would be to ignore me and go ahead with the purchase."

"I would assume so, sir. But, I can't read the premier's mind. It can't be denied that the navy is the best thing to happen to this country, ever. So, I have no problem in believing that keeping it up to date is a good thing."

"Even knowing that it might take a draft to find the manpower to operate that ship? Even knowing that your own relatives, even your own son someday, could be coerced to participate in the military? Don't forget the Air Corps needs manpower too!"

Aturk was preaching. "This would not be the palatial guard duty you grew up on, no. This could become a conflict participating armed force."

"I think we should stay with the details on the purchase of this ship, Minister."

"Yes, of course," the deflated Aturk agreed.

There was no use badgering M'hut. Aturk's adversary was Rafan, and he had the upper hand. He was the premier. He had wanted an air force, so he gets two new planes. He wants a new ship so he'll get a ship. Aturk knew that was how it was. M'hut was a good man, but he was loyal to Rafan, no matter what. Aturk also knew he'd have to deal with dismantling the group of dissenters.

CHAPTER 48

"Este!" An excited M'hut called out to his friend, the premier. "Anna is missing!"

The commodore was ignoring the group of people clustered around Rafan.

"She said she was going to her mother's last night and she never returned. We had a little fight. Her mother said she hasn't seen her! She left the baby and she just disappeared! I'm afraid something has happened to her!" M'hut feared her disappearance had to do with her secret meetings. What else would explain her mysterious absence? He had come to ask his friend, the man who might be in danger from the group she met with, for information and hope.

"I'm sorry to hear of your distress," Rafan responded calmly.

M'hut's excitement was lost on Este.

"What should I do, Este?" M'hut couldn't believe Rafan didn't understand his fears. He knew Anna was a part of the opposition group. M'hut had told him personally. Did Rafan know that her disappearance had nothing to do with that, or did he know that it had everything to do with it?

"I don't know what to tell you, old friend. If something indeed has happened to Anna, perhaps you should go to the mosque and pray."

"That is not how it is done. We do not ask for personal favors or for help from Allah. We offer obedience and praise."

"I've never understood your religion, Mahumud. But, that has not stood between us all these years. I am grateful for that. But, as for helping you with your problem with Anna, I don't know what I can offer you. Perhaps you could dispatch some sailors to look for her. Aturk might lend you some army men as well."

M'hut stared incomprehensibly.

"If Anna has left you for whatever reason, I know I can count on your continued efforts on behalf of your country, regardless."

"Of course, Este, but..." M'hut was confused and annoyed with Rafan's lack of concern for Anna's well being. He feared what that meant. "She wouldn't have left the baby if she was leaving me. Besides, it was just a little argument. We haven't been having that much domestic trouble lately. You know about the trouble she may be causing..."

Rafan cut Mahumud off and effectively shielded the conversation from his companions.

"What will be, will be, Mahumud," Rafan stated flatly. "I cannot get involved in your personal problems, old friend. I have business to attend to, do you not also?" Rafan turned back to the bystanders who were watching with interest as the conversation took place.

"Now, gentlemen, as I was saying..." Rafan walked down the hall with his entourage.

A few steps later Minister Aturk approached the premier and pulled him aside from the group.

"Rafan," Aturk began in a somber tone, "the dissident group has been disbanded."

"I thought as much," Rafan added with a nod. "Good work, Aturk."

"There was a little bloodshed." Aturk did not inform the premier that the violence had been necessary to prevent word of his own complicity from reaching Rafan's ears if it hadn't already. If any of the dissident group had been left alive they would have implicated him. Aturk was crushed at having to eliminate the members of his own group, a group he felt might have eventually saved Malfon from Rafan. Self-preservation came first, even to someone with little self-motivation.

Hope had to be served. The time for that group to take action had not yet come. It had to be a choice of not carrying out his orders and sacrificing future opportunities, or sacrificing the group.

Aturk didn't know if Rafan already knew, but a little insurance had seemed a good idea, just in case. Aturk was pretty sure the link to the group had run from Anna to M'hut, to Rafan.

But he didn't let on, and Aturk had yet to name a scapegoat as a plausible connection inside the government. But, with the group truly disbanded Aturk hoped his standing in the government would not suffer. He could only hope that Anna had kept the group secret, or that M'hut would keep it to himself if she had told, for whatever his own reasons might be. If Rafan didn't know of Aturk's part in the activities, it would be better for his sake. Rafan would certainly have to have known that Anna was part of the group Mahumud was reporting on, but perhaps his name hadn't been passed along, Aturk hoped.

"It is a shame Malfonies must resort to violence against each other...without even a good cause for conflict. But, so be it."

The blank stare Rafan gave Aturk said nothing and the Defense Minister went on his way still wondering what Rafan knew.

"Have you heard Commodore M'hut's wife has disappeared?" Rafan called after the minister.

Aturk just continued to amble down the hall away from Rafan's group, but a grimace crossed his face.

CHAPTER 49

From a newly constructed radio station, Premier Este Rafan of Malfon addressed his citizens, and the world. The address would do nothing to relax those who were experiencing uncertainty and fears about Malfon. Rafan only knew that General Umbarik had never doubted him, and Rafan had never doubted the general's dedication to Malfon. Belief in the man who cared for him like a son, and those few he trusted implicitly, like M'hut, gave him little cause to doubt his level of support. That envisioned backing enabled Rafan to disallow any fear he might have had of failure. He feared no assault of a serious nature. He knew he was always right in his thinking, and the people who counted had always encouraged him to let nothing deter him from his goals. That had been true since his parents had preached that when he was a child.

Any appearances to the contrary, his supporters had always told him, were mere smoke screens made by envious do-nothings who were jealous of Rafan's achievements. Only they warned of failure or danger. This confidence made it possible for Rafan to address his countrymen with a message he knew some might find distressing.

"I have the blood right to rule this monarchy. Yes, a monarchy. I am not a president. There is no senate or other house of legislature. I am not a prime minister. So why not call this great country of ours what it is, a monarchy? As in days of old, and even in some parts of the world today, the right to rule is passed through blood lines. Sadly, I have no heirs. But, during my lifetime, the honor of blood right is mine, and for this I will henceforth be known by a monarchical title. You are listening to the voice of the first king of Malfon. I am King Rafan!"

CHAPTER 50

"Yes, it was amazing. It's too bad you missed it," the man at the cafe was telling the group around him. "We all knew Rafan, King Rafan excuse me, was going to give an address on the radio. But, we had no idea it was going to be such a shocker." The man was obviously a little drunk, one indication of a non-muslim background in a country of mostly non-drinkers.

"Everyone was gathered around a radio, wherever there was one. There were a few people who were so fed up with Rafan already that they didn't bother to listen. But, they soon got the message anyway."

The other men listening to the drunk were all sailors in Malfon's navy. They'd been just arriving back from Norova and the docks when the speech was aired. They, too, had heard there was going to be a speech, but had no opportunity to listen while in transit. They were now getting filled in at the cafe.

"So, everybody in the country is listening to the radio to see what their premier has got up his sleeve this time, and he comes out and announces himself king!"

"Yeah, yeah. We know that much, everyone is talking about it. But, what was the immediate reaction of people listening to the radio?" One of the sailors asked. They, too, were drinking. But, the tale teller had a head start on them. He was one of the few unemployed Malfonies, possibly due to a drinking problem. But, even he was taken care of by the government.

"You should have seen it," Freidrick the drunk told the others. "It's only been a few hours, but the people I was with when we heard the announcement turned white, red, and green. Then they began jabbering about what it means. Were things going to be different? How? But, over these few hours everyone seems to be living okay with the idea. Look around you."

They did and noticed that what few people were eating or drinking in the recently built cafe were behaving much the same as they would have any other day.

"It seems that once the shock from the bombshell wore off, which it did very quickly, people couldn't find any real reason to condemn the event of the crowning of the king, so they relaxed. Perhaps everyone is used to shocks from Rafan, uh King Rafan," he laughed, "and getting immune to them. At least that's the way everyone I've been around seems to feel."

"Yeah. Some lady on the way in here was telling her husband that it seemed unpatriotic not to support the change. After all, it was just a title and Rafan was the leader of the country either way," one of the sailors volunteered.

"Of course, if things take a turn for the worse," Freidrick offered, "support could be revoked."

The door to the cafe opened and Defense Minister Aturk entered with a small squad of armed soldiers. There was no police force as such in Creche, or anywhere in Malfon, for that matter, and the army filled the function of police duty when needed. Aside from old age, diseases, and accidental deaths the demise of the members of the dissident group was about the only loss of life experienced in Malfon in decades. It bothered Aturk that this ironic up-tick in violent deaths was of his own doing. It caused him to question himself. But, once again he found action necessary.

"Freidrick Lock?" Aturk asked as he approached the group.

"Yes," Freidrick answered easily. This was not Nazi Germany where everyone feared a uniform.

"You are under arrest for subversive activity against the king." The word 'king' came out of Aturk's mouth with difficulty.

"What?" Freidrick squealed. "I haven't done anything! I just forgot to call him 'king' a couple of times, that's all." Freidrick's alcoholic daze was overcome by fear.

"You are a former employee of the government?"

"Yes. Almost everyone is."

"You have been giving inside information to a group of plotters dedicated to overthrowing King Rafan," again Aturk nearly swallowed the word 'king'.

"What? These fellows had no idea..."

But, Freidrick was already being dragged from the cafe and his companions, who were all too eager to be disassociated from him.

Aturk had found out about an alcoholic, unemployed, former government worker that no one would miss. He had no close relatives, no wife, and no children. He was a perfect patsy for Aturk's needed scapegoat. It was necessary to throw off suspicion about himself being involved with the dissidents if possible. He still wasn't sure what Rafan knew. He had to be sure. Rafan knew there was an inside man. Now he would have a plausible choice for that blame. It was important to Aturk to retain his position of power. It was not just for personal preservation, but he also believed it was mandatory that he have a connection to keep an eye on Rafan's activities, for the good of Malfon.

***

Later, in a small room at the palace, Aturk addressed a gathering that had listened to the shocking speech together.

"Deusein, M'hut, the rest of you, do you doubt the actions of our leader have gone beyond sanity? Can we afford to not worry about his intentions and attitudes any longer?"

"But he still works in the interests of our country. Regardless of his title or his rationalizations, he's done wonderful things for Malfon and he still continues to do them." This was M'hut, ever loyal to his onetime Private of the Guard and long time friend.

M'hut had accepted the loss of Anna, the mother of his son. He had held out hope for her reappearance with self-satisfying explanations as long as he could. But, accepting the fact she must be dead didn't lift the cloud from over his head. Indeed, quite the contrary, the cloudiness deepened to heavy depression at times. It interfered with his functioning, but he knew he would overcome the grief in time. In truth his feelings for Anna had diminished constantly due to her resistance to Rafan, and the revelation that Rafan had been Anna's first choice as a mate. He didn't miss the stress she had been causing in his life, and he was adjusting to raising their son on his own...with help from Anna's mother.

But, his life definitely had a hole in it. He had loved Anna and she was gone. There was nothing he could do about that. Searching for her had not turned up even one lead. But, of course, he had his suspicions. Regardless, that part of his life was over. Rafan's leadership spurred him on enthusiastically, and helped to move M'hut's mind and heart on to other things like more achievements of his own. M'hut's support for Rafan was unwaivering.

Even with Rafan's cavalier attitude about Anna's disappearance, M'hut didn't find any blame to place on Rafan for that event. His suspicions lay with Aturk solely. M'hut couldn't believe his childhood friend would have anything to do with hurting Anna. Even though he knew of their earlier conflicts, Rafan had applauded Anna's ability to make M'hut happy. Rafan knew Anna had made M'hut's life worthwhile. Surely, he would not want to change that. It had to be Aturk protecting himself from Rafan knowing that he was a part of the same group. Aturk was responsible for Anna's disappearance, M'hut was sure.

CHAPTER 51

"There is reason to fear Malfon and King Rafan," the ruler of Talon told his closest aide. "That is enough to justify increased recruitment for our army. I will not go so far as mandatory service at this point, but we must keep our eyes on developments."

"Perhaps the meeting coming up next month will help to soothe nervous anxiety," the aide replied hopefully.

Around the area, governments were holding meetings to discuss the changes in Malfon. Talon, Norova, and the neighboring country to the north, Amena, through which Malfon pumped oil, were all worried about Malfon...and King Rafan.

"Perhaps we should launch a pre-emptive military strike on Creche," the aide suggested.

"Achbar, that's a little bit of an over-reaction, isn't it?"

President Balthasar answered. "Maybe not. If attacking is Rafan's ultimate intention, we may eventually have to attack anyway. A pre-emptive attack would increase our chances of success and spare our country much worry and loss of life in the long run."

"No, I think we'll not go that route at present, if ever, Achbar."

"Unless the other leaders you're meeting with think as I do. We really don't know Malfon's military strength, but it is obviously growing. If we don't act now, Malfon may be too strong for us to defeat."

"I doubt that is the case, Achbar. But, we'll see. Sanctions like limiting the water supplied to Malfon, both from us and Norova, are more likely to be the gist of our talks. That even, will only be the case if the consensus is that Rafan has actually caused his neighbors harm and will not comply with correcting the situation," the president said.

"Norova could revoke the contract for the naval port," the aide added.

"Yes, it could," the president agreed. "That will be up to Norova. That would not only cause Malfon economic damage, but it would damage their navy's options and weaken their military. That's our whole object isn't it?" Achbar was obviously pushing an aggressive agenda.

"Is it? I think it's best to wait until we have some meeting time to see where opinions on action, or proposed action lie. Aggression on our part could provoke a stronger response from Rafan. At present we are only concerned about his military buildup. We haven't had any actual incidents. Talon definitely will not be taking any independent course of action," Balthasar stated.

The finality of his tone conveyed the message to Achbar that the discussion was over.

At the same time President Balthasar of Talon and his aide were having their discussion, another talk was taking place in Norova.

"Cutting their pipeline access would be the most drastic blow to Rafan," the Norovan ambassador told his country's leader.

"Are you speaking of the water pipeline, or the oil pipeline?"

"Sir, I was speaking of the oil. But, both would cripple Malfon," the ambassador clarified.

"Don't you think crippling Malfon would be just the thing to set Rafan off on a retaliation binge?"

"Perhaps..."

"No. We enjoy financial support from Malfon's use of the piers. We've had good relations for a decade or more now. The internal workings of Malfon are no business of ours. We haven't been threatened and we're not going to give Rafan a reason to feel threatened. You are going to meet with Rafan soon to renegotiate the terms of the agreement on the port and saline plant. I intend to co-ordinate that negotiation with Amena and Talon at our meeting next month."

"But, sir, Rafan is unstable. We can't depend on him keeping his part of any deal he makes. If he takes a whim at expansion he may move his army to annex our borderland or something. Then all bets are off. We need to take action."

"You would prefer we start a war?" The leader roared. "No one knows what to expect of Rafan. But, we have more to gain financially, by cooperating with Rafan than we have to gain in any way by making Rafan an enemy."

"He's already our enemy," the ambassador mumbled.

"Enough! Now, go prepare for the negotiations. You have only a few weeks until you meet with King Rafan."

The ambassador bowed and turned away from the leader and made his way to his office in the Norovan Capitol building.

"Besides, there's an oil pipeline in Amena, it could service Malfon's needs without ours, and it's none of our business."

CHAPTER 52

Along the borders, over the next few months, Norova and Talon stiffened their defenses. The outcome of the meeting among the leaders of Malfon's neighbors was more planned meetings and the increased defensive stance. Those countries and other neighbors sought to build their nearly non-existent armies. They also sought to hold comforting talks with King Rafan. Even nearby countries that didn't border Malfon were concerned, due to Malfon's newly acquired air power, such as it was.

Most of the nations of the area didn't have any air force or defense against one. The thought of two planes bombing or strafing their country terrified anyone informed enough to know of the potential advent. Attempts at appeasing any concerns Malfon might have were seriously offered. Since the neighbors could not acquire a consensus, every avenue was traveled, to some extent, to accomplish an agreement with Malfon that would ease tensions.

"I assume the new arrangements for the desalination plant in Norova are satisfactory," the Norovan ambassador asked the king directly at a meeting in Creche. "With the improved situation in our country, we are not so much in need of a great deal of money from outside sources." He didn't mention that not having to cope with the daily Malfony commuters that used to work in his country's labor force was the primary reason for that improvement. There had been no new oil sources, or other breakthroughs in Norova. But, the income from Malfon since the inception of Rafan's navy and other endeavors in Norova had allowed that country to expand its domestic worth and now

Norovans replaced the Malfonies in Norova in the work place. The Malfonies no longer had the need to cross the border for work.

More income in their home country had given Norovans the peace of mind to begin larger families and take on more adventurous undertakings in business. While only a few years hadn't raised the younger Norovans to working age, the new approach to women in the market place adequately filled the holes that the growing economy created. Seeing that even in a country like Malfon, where the king resisted women in the workplace, the society had benefited from their employment, Norovan women were doing their part to improve the economy in their own country.

"The arrangements are satisfactory, for now," the king answered. The Norovan ambassador shuddered at the added phrase. He didn't know what more his country could do to appease this man. "We have become so proficient at piping water from Talon, damming rivers there, and terracing our growing regions where the catch basins exist, that we may not need the desalination plant much longer."

Loss of the income from the ancillary businesses that benefited from the presence of the plant would be a problem for both countries, the ambassador knew, but not a huge one. But, with less shared enterprises with the Malfonies, the greater the odds for enmity, he thought. If the people of the two countries were working together they would be less likely to fight along nationalistic lines. If there was less common ground, there would be less to lose from a falling out. Nevertheless, the Norovan's tension eased at this non-threatening explanation. If the plant didn't mean that much to Rafan, he would have less motivation to upset the apple cart concerning it, perhaps by military means.

But, still leery of the intentions of the young man in front of him, he tried to insert a new idea to soften any concern there might be of Norova's good intentions. Any change in the relationship was an unknown and worrisome, and the ambassador wished he could somehow have foreseen this situation and prepared for it.

It was better to initiate any change and erase the unknown than to sit as unwary prey while the aggressor took charge. "Perhaps we could simply take over the operation for Malfon and supply the water to you." This seemed a possible offer that Norova could live with and from which Malfon would benefit. "We could use the additional employment opportunities and you would be able to call your engineers and such home to work on projects there."

"And leave the supply of life-sustaining water in the control of a foreign entity? Never!" Rafan erupted.

"But, we would not allow anything to jeopardize the water supply." The ambassador was caught off guard by Rafan's irrational explosion. He was fast tracking backwards to atone for his apparent misconception of Rafan's approval of the plan.

"That would cut off a source of income for us...a lesser source of income than you even now pay under the new contract," the ambassador pointed, out, "but, a major source of income for us just the same. We wouldn't do that."

"I will not discuss such a thing," Rafan told the dignitary in a loud voice. "Now," he said with finality,

"What about the troops you're massing on our border? I can see this in no other way than as a threat to Malfon security."

This was something the ambassador was not authorized to discuss in any detail. "Uh, your highness, it is only a reaction to Malfon's growing might." That was the most he thought he could say. He had no idea how incendiary it sounded. He began to smell his own odor as sweat wetted his armpits. He didn't want to provoke this man and create the very eventualities the Norovans feared. But, he had to say something. King Rafan toyed calmly with a pencil on his desk seemingly completely removed from his outburst. Rafan seemed unaware of the tension he was creating.

The ambassador felt he had to stand up for Norova. That was his job and patriotic Norovan duty. But, before he could find a way to express a less threatening reason for Norova's military activity, the Malfon king broke the short silence.

"Ha!" Rafan broke out laughing. He continued to laugh so strongly and at such a length that the ambassador grew uncomfortable at his proximity to the ruler and silently slinked away, not knowing what to make of the episode, except that the king was indeed crazy. Apparently Rafan did not notice the ambassador leaving.

CHAPTER 53

"There is no appeasing that man," the Talon president shouted.

"I quite agree," the Norovan ambassador assured his host.

"The only pertinent thing to do is form a military alliance. We must protect ourselves from Malfon. Other neighboring countries are ready to join us as well."

"Fine. A military alliance was the last thing on my mind, just a short time ago. Now, it seems a necessity. After relating that discussion between Rafan and yourself, we can see he is quite out of his mind. A mad man is an unpredictable danger. Let us hope nothing comes of King Rafan's blustering. But, we will be prepared if it does, even to the point of actual armed conflict."

"Yes. Negotiating cannot resolve a situation involving a man like Rafan. Any agreement could not be trusted. He will always want more of whatever he can expunge from us," the Talonite concurred. The president put his head in his hands and rested while the small group gathered in his office dispersed. "It is a shame people in Malfon have to be subjected to this tension. They alone have the power to curtail King Rafan's mania," he called after the group. Nodding heads were all that was returned as a comment.

CHAPTER 54

The Talonite president was enjoying an increased level of international and domestic popularity as Rafan's support coincidentally began to fragment. The water projects that Malfon had co-produced with him were highly successful. His people liked the benefits they were enjoying. It was not just the better agricultural returns, but the income from Malfon for the water contributed to the domestic coffers of the mountainous country, allowing Talon to provide governmental services previously not available. Hydroelectric power was Talon's primary achievement in improving the standard of living. Without spending money on military increases, Talon had been able to exceed Malfon's pace in electrifying the country. More improvements were on the way. Talon had never been the basket case their desert-bound neighbor was, but conditions were improving in many ways.

There were advancements in transportation, communication and other areas. These achievements were a source of irritation to the King of Malfon, for his country depended on non-replenishing oil-fired, polluting generators for electricity and Rafan could not persuade, nor force Talon to share their hydro power. Rafan felt that power should be Malfon's to share, since Malfon and Talon were partners in the dam projects. But, Malfon was left to fill its power requirements with the less environmentally sound resources it had.

"Minister Deusein," Rafan began, "don't you think Malfon should have access to the hydro power from the dams in Talon?"

Deusein shuffled his feet as he sat on the chair in the King's office and started to sweat.

"The dams are in Talon," Deusein squeaked. "Our purpose in co-operating on the dams was for the water supply for irrigation and consumer uses, like drinking water and sewer treatment." The minister looked blankly at the purple walls of the room and not at either of the other two people in the room.

Deusein knew he had to answer carefully. Rafan was becoming more difficult for him to deal with lately. He had to handle the opinion he was offering the king in such a way that it didn't seem too obviously in conflict with Rafan's own views. Yet he felt he had to offer his true opinion. It was important for Malfon. But, he knew he wasn't saying what Rafan wanted to hear. Deusein was trying to avoid a Rafan tirade.

King Rafan stared at Deusein, who continued to deny eye contact. "But there is no harm if Talon would choose to share their hydroelectric power," Rafan stated.

"Perhaps there is. Maybe it would strain their transmission capabilities."

"We could help with that," Rafan inserted.

"But, that is up to Talon, sir. They may not want our help. They apparently don't want to share the electricity."

"So Talon is being unreasonable, a bad neighbor," Rafan suggested.

Deusein sputtered, but said nothing.

"Surely you can come up with some way to convince them otherwise," Rafan challenged after a moment. "You're very good at putting things in a convincing way." Rafan smirked.

Deusein wanted to remind Rafan that he was commerce minister as well as king, perhaps it was his job to find a way, but he knew better than to do that. So he said nothing. As an afterthought he realized that perhaps it would be better if Rafan didn't decide to do the persuading himself. Rafan's belligerent side was coming out more and more. Who knew what would happen if he went into a tirade with the Talonites.

"Minister Aturk," Rafan addressed the other person in the room. "Maybe you can determine how to deal with the Talonites."

"I am only the defense minister," Aturk responded.

"Precisely," Rafan countered.

"But, I know nothing of negotiating, or..."

Rafan cut him off. "Who said you needed to do any negotiating?"

Aturk stopped his objection and looked at his king, as did Deusein.

"Surely you're not talking about military action," Aturk said.

The raised eyebrows said that was indeed what he feared Rafan meant.

"We shall see," Rafan answered. "We shall see."

Neither minister could think of anything else worth saying. So, after giving respectful, sincere, or not, farewells to the king, they returned to other work.

***

The president of Talon and his foreign minister were hosting the visiting king from Malfon at one of the dams the two countries had developed together. They were overlooking the spillway as they talked.

President Balthasar envisioned better things for his country, as the Malfony did for his. They didn't quite agree on how these things related to each other however. They had different visions and different paths to them.

The more temperate climate provided by the higher mean altitude of Talon allowed that country to grow more varieties of food for its people and for sale abroad... another bone in Rafan's craw. The increased productivity was only possible because of the water supply Malfon had helped to create. Lack of water had been the only thing holding Talon back before the dams were built. Talon's oil and mineral deposits were superior to Malfon's new found petroleum wealth. But, indeed, the president was not about to overlook any opportunity for further improvements in Talon's economy. He was not content to settle for agricultural and mineral sources for survival of the increased standard of living Talon was experiencing. There was reason to see Talon as the greatest power in their neighborhood, both financially and militarily, now that circumstances stood as they did. Entering into an alliance with Norova and others, as well as shoring up the domestic army, made Talon bold in its projections for the future.

Balthasar's precociousness was not unknown.

"So you see, Mr. President, we would be willing to pay for a portion of your hydro electric infrastructure if we are allowed to share the benefits. I'm talking about only tapping into one segment of your grid. We wouldn't require complete access to your entire production," King Rafan told President Balthasar.

"Yes, I am aware, of course, of your interest in our hydro power. But, I'm not convinced how to control what is considered excess production. I don't think we are interested in the structure of the proposal. Indeed, we really aren't interested in changing our current situation," Balthasar mentioned amiably.

"The technology can be worked out as a mutual agreement by our engineers. We possess the ability to increase your production simply by updating the components of your system. As I understand it, we would draw up to a certain amount of kilowatt hours, then a relay would kick in augmenting the grid with our oil fired generation to meet our needs at any given moment, if they exceed the acceptable limits on what we draw from you. Talon would still maintain the same supply as you now have. There would be no loss of capability on your part."

"I see," Balthasar said. "But, would the benefits to Talon financially offset the ability to expand in the future without consulting and working out new terms with Malfon? I don't see any real gain for my country. After all, we are not Norova. We don't greedily pursue any proposition on the chance of a windfall." Balthasar laughed at the reference to Norova's well-documented greed, and Rafan shared in the laugh. The king's laugh seemed genuine.

"Well, I suggest we let our engineers, ministers, and ambassadors work on that. However, of course, I act as commerce minister for Malfon and I assure you I will be involved in any discussions," Rafan calmly explained and then changed gears. "Now, what about those troops that have been maneuvering along our border?"

"King Rafan, we are only keeping our military in tune. As you can obviously attest, this is a most necessary element of preparing for any eventuality...a part of maintaining a viable military, if you will."

"I am aware that there is some talk of me, perhaps, being arbitrary in some of my actions, Mr. President." Rafan's demeanor was no longer calm. "If such talk is true, I would recommend you progress cautiously in this area of military provocation."

"Is that a threat, Your Majesty?" Balthasar was obviously shaken, as was his foreign minister who accompanied him but had remained silent. "You would be well advised to heed your own advice." The minister finally made himself heard. The meeting was quickly going downhill.

"Is that so?" Rafan asked. "You would be well advised, as well, to seriously consider my proposal on the electricity."

Suddenly a raucous laugh escaped Rafan's mouth. "Not greedy like the Norovans? I'll have to remember that. Do you think your Norovan allies will appreciate that humor?"

Rafan was alone on his visit to Talon's dam site and he just walked away from the two Talonites, back to the car that would carry him into the Talon capital city were his own driver waited.

After King Rafan's departure from this initially fruitless discussion on the hydro power and military build-ups, Balthasar turned to his foreign minister.

"Those oil deposits along the Malfon border," the president began, "is there any reason why we can't tap them from within our borders?"

"As I understand it, Mr. President," the minister answered, "the field runs along the border on both sides for some distance. We could drill on our side and be well within our legal rights by international law."

"I've delayed developing that field in order to keep from antagonizing Rafan. But, now I feel no such reserve."

"That spontaneous laugh of his is disconcerting. He seems to break away from the situation at hand and lose track of propriety. He loses track of reality," the minister observed.

"Yes. I thought it was strange that Rafan didn't mention the oil field while he was ranting about the military," the president said.

"He probably didn't want to draw our attention to it. He's probably hoping we haven't thought of tapping that field and didn't want to give us the idea."

"Does he think we're that stupid?" The minister ignored the question. "Let's do it," the president snapped with a nod of his head. "Let's tap that field."

The foreign minister stared at his president a moment, then said, "Of course King Rafan may be opposed to us doing any such thing. He may see his country's need as greater and try to convince the world community that Malfon should be able to develop that deposit by itself. Malfon did find the deposit first and is already producing from wells there."

The president obviously didn't share his minister's concerns. "I don't care what His Majesty thinks or does in this respect. I don't think the world will get any easier with Rafan because of this. Get the drilling started. He's already verging on starting a war. I won't let fear of provoking him stop me from working to do whatever could possibly help our country any more. More oil for us and less for Malfon would certainly be in our best interests."

Obediently, the minister bowed and set about his assigned task.

CHAPTER 55

Internally, the government of Malfon was in turmoil. Some ministers worried over how to stop Rafan if things truly got out of hand. Others wondered if they should stop him. Surely he had done many good things for their country. Were they incorrect to second guess him? None of the ministers were sure they could stop him if they decided they needed to curtail Rafan's activities.

Segments of the population were sharing the same questions, and they knew little of what worried those inside the palace.

Aturk accosted Commodore M'hut on a chance meeting at the market place in Creche. "M'hut, are you still condoning Rafan's aberrations? How can you, an intelligent and patriotic Malfony, not see what is going on? How can you consider that this man, who is younger than you, can be trusted to always be right in his decisions? He is making all the decisions for Malfon, without any advising. Look what he has done to us in the international field. We are having sanctions leveled against us for unfair demands and practices in the docking facilities we use for our navy. Rafan demands that only our people be used to supply our ships, to tie them up, to pilot them, no matter where they are! We've got sailors scattered all over the area. We are being denied the opportunity to even dock in some countries now. They don't like not being able to give their citizens jobs assisting our ships, and having to give us special treatment.

"You should have been there at the last meeting between Rafan and the Norovans. I, unfortunately, was.

Our king showed no respect for them. None! He actually got down to name calling! He refused to shake hands. He made up a new tradition to follow to explain that. He said it was traditional to bow instead.

"He's drafting our young men away from our industries and farms and putting them in the military. He's proclaimed himself king! M'hut, many of us here have royal blood, but we didn't go out and proclaim ourselves king. I'm talking about Prince Sabu, Malat Sabu, Arat, and anyone else." Obviously Aturk had a personal sore spot on this point.

"There isn't a single country we can call our ally. Not even one! I can't even name one country that isn't against us! If we get into the military struggle that Rafan seems intent to get us into, we stand alone. Yes, Rafan seems set on getting us into a power struggle. That seems to be what he wants," Aturk was ticked off. "This goes beyond our immediate neighbors. The U.N. supports the sanctions against us. Yet, you support him at the cabinet meetings and in private."

"I support the way His Majesty wants it. He is our king," M'hut countered, looking at a chicken hanging from an overhead beam that he was considering buying. "He doesn't want Malfon to have to depend on any other country's help ever again...and don't forget, he has put more of our people to work than ever before. We have a per capita income no one dreamed of only a few years ago, thanks to His Majesty's belief that this country was capable of more than what any of his predecessors had thought it was capable of. Malfon is now the leader in standard of living in the area."

M'hut signaled the shop owner and paid the man as he removed the chicken and handed it to his customer on a thong of sinew. "I don't doubt that the king is still working to do even more for Malfon."

"Then you feel comfortable with Rafan having total control?"

"It's not total control. We have freedom," M'hut objected petulantly. M'hut looked at the skinny chicken swinging from his hand and turned from Aturk and started away from the shop with his purchase. He mused about having seen them wrap this sort of purchase in other countries. It seemed a better idea than carrying raw food around loose. Perhaps he would suggest to the king that the monarch pass a law be requiring more sanitary handling of food in the market place.

"Freedom? Not total control? Rafan takes advice from no one and we have freedoms as long as he lets us have those freedoms. When he sees fit, he decrees new laws to fit his whim." Aturk followed after M'hut. "We must keep an eye on Rafan. You know it. We may have to stop a disaster. You have seen him strike out at ministers, physically. You have heard his tirades, even about unimportant things. You know that there is something wrong with your old friend." M'hut continued to walk away. "We cannot allow him to take away from our country all that we have gained, out of loyalty to an insane leader."

M'hut balked.

"We must have some safety valve. We must find a way to rein in Rafan, for the good of us all," Aturk yelled over the increasing distance between the two men. "Rafan is going to drag us into an unwinnable war with his swaggering and craziness and that won't benefit any of us. I'm not sure what we can do. But, we must have something to fall back on, for security. If we don't admit what we all recognize...he cannot be allowed to run this country on his own. It's inevitable we will have a crisis of one kind or another. There has to be a balance to his power. You know I'm right." Aturk paused. "Have you ever considered what might have happened to your wife?"

M'hut reluctantly turned back and nodded agreement. Of course he had considered Anna's fate. Aturk was trying to put the country's salvation on a personal level for M'hut. If the Commodore could be forced to blame Rafan for his wife's death, perhaps he could admit the king was dangerous. M'hut had adjusted well to the loss of Anna. But, the pain might still be strong enough, Aturk hoped, to get her husband thinking and overlooking his blind spot of allegiance to Rafan.

M'hut sometimes sorted through the events of Anna's disappearance when he was lying alone in bed at night. He tried to get away from those thoughts, those painful questioning thoughts, as quickly as he could. But, there were times when his mind wouldn't let them go.

As he would lie in the now too large bed, he'd remember how frustrating Anna could be. But, he'd remember how supportive she was at times too. During her pregnancy she'd been nearly unbearable. But, the period leading up to that pregnancy had been quite wonderful, he had to admit. Then there was the secrecy. The thing with Rafan, and the meetings with Aturk.

The disappearance and the lack of any increase of public knowledge of an organized opposition had followed his confession to Rafan of his wife's activities. Those two things seemed connected in M'hut's mind. How could he not associate her accepted demise with Rafan's gaining knowledge of a dissident group of which Anna was a member?

Maybe it was a flaw in M'hut's character, but he felt what was done was done and the forward march of Malfon continued. He wanted to be a part of that and to be able to contribute to that march. So, he supported Rafan against any misgivings. He couldn't do anything about the loss of Anna, but he could cement himself on a path of prominence for the future. He convinced himself that losing Anna wasn't such a great loss. She'd been an obstruction in his life's plans. Besides, he still had his son. He still had a family. Anna's mother was still part of that family, a part that he needed to help raise the boy. Thankfully, the mother was more traditional than Anna had been and young enough to be around for some time yet.

As M'hut looked back across an expanse of open market between himself and Aturk, he only allowed himself this moment of reflection, of giving Aturk's words some value.

Aturk, for his part, looked across the newly concrete paved expanse and saw a man that he respected and wished very much would see the light. In their time of working together in the military, as Minister of Defense and Commander of the Navy, Aturk had become more and more convinced that this man was a good man. M'hut had the devotion to his country that Rafan showed, without the ego, eccentricities, and need for personal glory of the king. Aturk might have been a little less respectful if he'd had access to the inner workings of M'hut's motivations.

But, even that wouldn't have colored Aturk's evaluation of M'hut much. Even M'hut's loyalty to Rafan, misplaced though it might be, was a positive quality, Aturk thought. Yes, Aturk was sure Mahumud M'hut was, at heart, a very good human being.

CHAPTER 56

"Este." The king scowled at the use of his first name. "Este, there is concern for your health..." M'hut turned to tell his friend. He had been leaving the king after a discussion in his office and then changed his mind about leaving.

"My health is fine," the king responded. "Who is worried about me? Is it those people who think I'm crazy?"

M'hut hesitated before answering, wondering where Rafan's reaction to a simple question would lead. Was he endangering his associates or even himself? M'hut wondered. "Some of the ministers, and I, myself. We are concerned on your behalf and the country's. There are a few questions from other people as well," he finally answered. "Dignitaries from other countries and our own citizens are concerned."

"Ask my physician. I am fine. Now, let's move on to other subjects, my friend, or are we finished here?"

"Este, as your friend, I have to tell you that I don't think it would hurt you to divert some of your energies to less pressing matters than the ship of state from time to time. There must be something you would do to relax that you aren't doing, something you're denying yourself."

"I've already said that I can't depend on the country to keep on a true path if I am not personally at the helm," Rafan stated flatly. "Malfon won't run itself!"

"Surely there are some that you trust to take the helm for short periods of time, even me, perhaps. Do you not trust me?"

Rafan scowled his displeasure at M'hut. "As I said, let's move on to other subjects."

"Yes, sir," M'hut acknowledged. Leaving was no longer a priority, it seemed.

"How is enlistment in the military coming? Are we meeting our quotas?"

"You mean the draft? We just discussed that Your Majesty."

Even M'hut had a hard time referring to his friend as 'Your Majesty'. He also knew better than make a scene about Rafan's apparent loss of tracking on their just concluded discussion. "Yes, we are filling our rosters," M'hut said sadly. He knew that later it would be his unpleasant duty to inform the cabinet that the futile attempt to persuade Rafan to slow down, using the health issue with him, had failed. There would surely be no surprise among the cabinet membership. Nearly all the ministers had made an effort to do the same sort of thing in their own way. M'hut dissolutely began to slip away. "I have other duties to tend to, Your Majesty. If you will allow me, I need to see to them." With that, he left the room.

CHAPTER 57

"It's just that he's dedicated his life to his country and denied himself. That's bound to take a toll," Commodore M'hut defended his friend and leader when he gave the ministers the news of his effort at convincing Rafan to ease up on his demands on himself.

"Are you trying to tell me that if Rafan had taken a wife he wouldn't be acting like he is?" Aturk wore an incredulous smirk. Then reconsidering, he said, "there has been some credence put on that notion before. Perhaps there is something to it. But, the case is, he didn't take a wife, and he is acting crazy! Whatever he needed to keep from going off the deep end, a woman, a child, an interest in sports, or whatever, he didn't get it. Now it's too late! None of those things or anything else will bring back his sanity. I have always wondered about Rafan, if he ever was sane."

M'hut looked lost for a moment. His gaze was unfocused. "It's possible that those things could have made a difference. They might have kept him from becoming so intensely focused on his goals for the country. He might have had some personal goals... accepted ones, like being a good father, or a good husband. Instead, he only wanted for himself to be king, I guess," the disillusioned M'hut admitted. "Maybe if his parents hadn't died when he was so young they might have guided him to a more normal life. It's a shame, since it was probably the poverty that Rafan hates so much, that killed them." M'hut stopped, then started speaking again. "Maybe he would have taken a wife, but for that."

"His parents died of poorness?" Aturk snorted.

"If they hadn't been undernourished by the poor diet we all had then, they might have lived longer, probably would have. Our life expectancy has improved tremendously since then. Those of us in the military benefited by having the best of everything available. Even so, I have some problems with my bones. Most people suffered much worse."

Aturk mumbled something under his breath and M'hut went on, "His parents' guidance through his adolescence might have had an effect on where Rafan's emphasis went in his life. His parents were very self-sacrificing for him. Rafan told me that they used to leave portions of their figs and dates for him to eat, and find other food for him they did not share."

"Rafan? What happened to calling him Your Majesty, M'hut?" Aturk teased. He seemed to be enjoying the turmoil that Rafan's erratic behavior had fathered, at times. He especially seemed to enjoy the pain it was causing M'hut and other one time supporters of the king. Perhaps Aturk saw an opening to pry apart their loyalty to Rafan and have them fully join the fold of ministers who saw the need to control the king.

"I've known Rafan since we were kids. Anna and I were his only friends. He was always off by himself. None of the other kids liked him. He was too serious, especially after his parents died."

"As I said, if he was ever sane," Aturk cut in on M'hut's comments.

"I think Rafan, I mean His Majesty, was bitter that after their death he was subjected to the same poor standards as most people, no one was looking out for him anymore. No one was giving him their share of food. The elderly aunt and uncle that he lived with until he could join the army gave him no special treatment. I doubt they could have. I asked about them once and he told me he felt no sadness when they died.

"The kids at school who felt he was unfairly given everything they wanted didn't change their attitude or treatment of him after he no longer had those privileges.

"He has never taken any time for himself, as long as I've known him. He was always working on something for the future of Malfon. Anna and I thought he was just dreaming, like the navy idea. But, we all know now that he was planning for today, even then. He's never had any hobbies. I guess his hobby was planning the future, until he had the power to actually control it. He never took a leave from the army. When he was forced to be off the duty roster, he hung around the quarters anyway, looking in corners and cracks for things to be improved. All he has ever done is think of ways to improve Malfon, any part of it he could, and then act on them. Look what he has accomplished!"

"We know all that, M'hut," the squeaky voiced Minister Deusein broke in, "but now he seems to have taken up the hobby of antagonizing the world, not to mention some of his own people. Just this week he mentioned wanting an aircraft carrier, a nuclear reactor, and extending the service term for draftees to three years. His ideas just keep snowballing with no thought to the consequences."

"I know. He mentioned all those things to me too, and even more," M'hut acknowledged. "He told the ambassador from Talon that they should share their melon crop with us because if we hadn't gotten them to move forward on the water projects, they wouldn't be able to grow as many as they do."

"The question is, do we do something about this aberrant behavior, and if so, what," Aturk said bluntly. "I think you know I am sure something needs to be done about these problems...THE problem. But, I don't want to dictate what is done. I'm even willing yet, to hear your proposals in lieu of any I may have. If you, in a majority, think we should do nothing, I will abide by that decision for the time being. But, I am sure the situation will only worsen and we will revisit this question again." Once more Aturk was ducking responsibility for action.

"Perhaps it's not too late to interest the king in something to divert him from his current obsessions," Deusein offered.

"No. I've known him longer than any of you and he's never shown any interest in anything but...I guess you'd call it politics," M'hut reminded them. "I don't think planting tulips would interest him, neither would planting a prostitute in his bed. It wouldn't change anything, except for getting the culprit who pulled the stunt into big trouble. If we could get him to someone...I hesitate to say, 'psychiatrist', perhaps there would be a benefit. But, I know King Rafan would not go along with that!"

"Yes, he does seem to opt for violent reactions when he feels trifled with lately," Aturk noted. "He took a swing at an army major the other day. The officer didn't see him and Rafan felt offended and disrespected, I hear."

"Maybe it's the wrong sex we'd be tempting him with if we opted for a prostitute," someone ventured.

"Not that either," M'hut assured. "There was no evidence of that kind of behavior even as a youth or in the military. Still, I know his monomania, if you will, does make him unusual, in another way, perhaps abnormal. But, does it make him bad?"

M'hut was still pondering his own convictions and loyalty.

"M'hut, how can you still doubt?" Aturk burst out.

"He never has gone deep sea fishing from one of our ships that I've heard," Deusein joked. "Maybe we could interest him in that. It's the kind of kinky idea that might appeal to him." The others didn't share Deusein's laugh. "He keeps trim," Deusein went on, "even without any outside interests he manages that somehow. I'll give him that," Deusein continued on a different track while everyone else was searching their own minds for pertinent thoughts. Deusein finished by looking at his own slightly portly physique.

"He has a complete workout room here in the palace. You know that, Deusein," another minister told 'squeaky'. "That's how he keeps trim."

"Yes, I guess that's sort of a hobby. But, really I think the king considers it a medical treatment. It's quite regimented, his workouts. It's consistent and rigorous," M'hut supplied.

"I tell you, we are not going to divert his attention with hobbies and such," M'hut reiterated.

"His nervous energy keeps him trim," M'hut said. "He is also still very young, remember. Perhaps as he gets older with our capability of overeating now, he will spread out as we in this room, and others of our countrymen have. The lack of diversions is sure to take its toll the older he gets." This time the laughter was spread beyond the speaker.

"If, he gets older," Aturk threw in. It wasn't clear if Aturk was joining in the joviality.

"Minister!" Deusein chirped. "We're not here to discuss radical ideas on his life span. I hope you're not suggesting an unnatural end to his life span."

"My apologies, Minister," Aturk lavishly enunciated.

"He's never been interested in football, as a spectator or a player. He looks like he could be a good center forward. But, sports don't amuse him," M'hut mentioned further, joining Deusein's search for a diversion for the king, even though he didn't believe one existed. "But, why are we concerned about these things? Again, does any of this make him bad?"

"Perhaps the commodore is right. He does seem to have Malfon's interests at heart. The king might be a bit eccentric and have unusual ways of getting things done...perhaps born of past necessity. But, should we be trying to curtail his success?" asked Deusein.

"Yes, perhaps His Majesty's behavior is just temporarily odd, due to the stress he subjects himself to, and can be left to disappear on its own," M'hut suggested.

"I can't believe what I'm hearing. He's not any more stressed now than ever. This eccentric behavior has been going on for a long time! Some of his ideas lately come right down to being harebrained. Digging a canal from the coast, through Norova, so that we can have our naval home port in the middle of the desert. Is that sane?" asked Aturk.

"You mean like a landlocked country having a navy?" M'hut asked sarcastically. "The canal would allow us to have our home port in our own country." M'hut once again defended his friend.

"Okay, so he has gone a bit overboard. I still don't think we want nor need any drastic action. He still has huge, if not total, support among Malfonies, as well he should. We don't want to return to the conditions of the recent past, do we? We need stability. Things will degrade without it. What we need to do is control His Majesty's more unusual plans, just oversee what he wants done. We want to shield the public from his difficult side as much as possible."

"How do you propose to do that?" Aturk asked.

"We'll figure something out. We need to keep his support among the people high. We want to keep national morale high and give the people an image to look up to. We don't need to let people know about all his foibles, and indeed, they could be a temporary phenomenon. As things get better and better in Malfon, changes will come easier. That certainly will take some pressure off the king."

"He'll just make up more pressure for himself. Besides, I'm not sure things will get better and better. His international belligerence is definitely dangerous," Deusein told the group.

"As long as the king is not allowed to cause an uncontrollable problem, we can keep right on doing as we're doing. We can continue to prosper, as we are, and continue to earn a better standard of living and improve our way of life. We can still make use of any ideas of the king's that contain merit," M'hut went on. "He does still have those, you know."

"Maybe the canal is one of them," Aturk scoffed. He watched Deusein shuffle his feet with disbelieving eyes. Deusein seemed to be buying M'hut's plan.

"But, we definitely need to keep an eye on his war mongering," Deusein said to a chorus of nodding heads.

"Well, I guess we would benefit by keeping his public image as unblemished as possible," Aturk reluctantly agreed. "Now that it seems we've agreed we need to control Rafan, how do we do it?"

No one volunteered an answer.

"Is there an idea we can actually use, or is there another choice of direction? Is protecting Rafan's image and controlling him our best option?" Aturk asked.

"Only time will tell us that, Minister," M'hut stated.

Deusein spoke up with a final question. "Has anyone tried to talk to the king about our concern, beyond the health issue? Have we all tried as hard as possible to convince him how serious the situation, like a coming war, is?"

"I've tried," M'hut said. "He won't tolerate any discussion of his policies or himself." M'hut looked up into a choir of nodding heads once again. "It's too bad the general is gone. I think Rafan would have listened to him."

"Yeah, the general would have known how to handle this," finished Aturk. "Even though he was an agitator in his own right, he wouldn't have let Rafan run amuck. He surely wouldn't have let Rafan paint the walls of the palace purple!"

The nodding heads changed to shaking heads as Aturk dismissed the impromptu meeting and those that had been present went on to other business. Aturk knew it would be some time before the citizens of Malfon would realize that changes had occurred in their ruler, and that those changes would make a difference in their lives. This group of officials would work hard to make sure of that, while coming up with ways to control Rafan!

Or find another solution to the problem.

"I can't believe I'm one of those making sure the people support Rafan," Aturk told M'hut as they left the meeting. "If people only knew Rafan has championed aroma therapy candles for rooms in the palace to promote creativity, they would wonder at so many other ideas Rafan puts stock in like playing ocean sounds on the intercom system in a palace in the desert. If they only knew; the public would have no doubt that something is wrong with their leader."

M'hut did not respond.

CHAPTER 58

A few weeks later M'hut sought out the king. "Este," again a scowl from M'hut's old friend on the use of his first name rather than 'Your Majesty'. "There is a growing segment of the public becoming aware of things about your behavior that upsets them. I fear there will be real trouble if your behavior isn't moderated. You need to have good counsel. No one knows what is best all the time..."

"I don't need anything from anyone. I am the king." Rafan looked at M'hut for a moment. "Mahumud, I know about Anna's involvement in the group you exposed to me last year. Even though you shielded it from me, I found out. That group has been silenced."

"Your insistence on pomp and majesty is just the sort of thing that has people worried." M'hut tried to not let Rafan derail him. "I told you Anna was in the group."

"Of course, Aturk eventually admitted that he knew, and his own involvement became apparent. He's never admitted that, but I am quite sure. Who else in the government would go to such extreme measures to undermine me? Surely not the scapegoat he paraded as the group's mastermind. Knowing of Aturk's participation caused me some hesitation. I wasn't sure how much of a following he had, assuming I was right in believing he was setting machinations against me into action.

"But, he carried out his orders and the group is disbanded. I have heard of no other activity, from you, or anywhere else. Aturk continues to do his job. His need for self-preservation outweighed his rebelliousness. He stood down rather than moving forward with whatever he had planned. It's not surprising with his well-established lack of ambition in mind. I feel there is no further danger to me. Both the secret meetings and Aturk's public support have visibly disappeared. So I don't believe what you're saying, unless you have now become the force trying to undermine me."

"No, Your Majesty. It's not me." M'hut gave into the formality Rafan preferred. "The people of Malfon as a whole are losing patience with you."

"Nonsense," the king replied. "That was all false discontent stirred up by Aturk. He has learned his lesson. He won't be causing trouble again. He's not sure what I know about him, but he's not going to do anything to test whether I have any knowledge of his attempts to deter me from destiny. He surely must have figured out that you are the one who told me about Anna's group. That's why he offered up a victim to take the blame as the inside-the-government connection. So if it is not you, there is no opposition."

The king wouldn't listen to facts. The country was destabilizing over worries about coming war, about rising taxes and about rumors of the king's eccentricities. Now, he brought up Anna's death and his part in her death. M'hut added hurt to his building anger.

M'hut was seething. He had no doubt that Aturk was responsible for Anna's disappearance and apparent death. But, he'd just chosen to not let himself think about it. Having Rafan connect it to himself left M'hut unable to not think about what that meant.

"Did you tell Aturk to kill Anna?" M'hut burst out. "I have a child to raise on my own!" He was seeing clearly in his mind, for the first time, what had happened. "Raising him takes a lot of time I might have dedicated to my job, to your programs. Certainly Aturk had been ordered to break up the group of dissidents. But what was he told to do about Anna? If Anna was alive I wouldn't have to leave the palace to take care of my son when grandmother cannot. Was that in your plan?" He was being less than eloquent, but M'hut's emotions were getting ahead of his mind.

"Mahumud, I am sorry about the loss of your wife. But, I had nothing to do with it."

"I cannot believe that, Este. Aturk protected himself, as well as you, by silencing the group, on your orders."

"Believe what you will, Commodore."

"I also know about you and Anna when we were kids."

"What are you talking about? I don't know what she told you, Mahumud, but I assure you nothing happened between me and your wife. We were all just friends, the three of us. Then Anna grew apart from me, to your advantage, I'd say."

"Este, I stood with you against my wife. I convinced myself she wasn't as important to me as the future, your future, my future, the country's future. I made the wrong decision, Este. In spite of the things she told me...things that might have turned me against you, I turned her in...I told you about her opposition group, and you eliminated it...and her." M'hut leaned into the king's face. "But, now I'm warning you, Este, as your friend, step back. I'm not leading any opposition. There is no organized subversion that I know of, but trouble will result if you keep pressing forward as hard as you have been. I'm not talking about a radical group of dissidents. I'm talking about the general public, the people of Malfon...the ones you say you're looking out for. You need to consult with your ministers before you act."

"Is that an ultimatum? How dare you tell me, the king, what I have to do," Rafan roared. Then he sat back, relaxed, and said calmly, "M'hut, I am always right. Isn't that obvious by now? Commodore, I have business to attend to, good day." The king turned back to the papers on his desk, effectively dismissing M'hut.

The naval leader stood fuming momentarily, then left the palace office. His next move an uncertainty to him at the time, his anger cooled. His concern for the welfare of Malfon overcame his personal emotions. It was not long before nearly unquestioning support for Rafan returned, however with more than a small dose of lost respect for the king. M'hut would apply increasing efforts to contain Rafan's actions while dampening the growing despair of futility among the cabinet ministers. He felt that was in the best interests of Malfon. The latter part of the idea, dealing with the other ministers, hadn't yet fully evolved into a plan for implementation.

M'hut felt that standing in Rafan's way was not a good choice. It would be better to redirect any extraordinary actions on the king's part into a harmless pool of stagnation.

CHAPTER 59

The Rafan that the country was aware of was the same old Rafan, but with the public now and then questioning his actions.

The Rafan that had pulled their nation out of poverty into the blissful relative wealth of an oil producing nation in just a few short years, was still their hero. But, the militaristic king, who taxed their prosperity, caused the support to be tenuous.

The internal contention about women's rights and high taxes did ease. With ever-improving lifestyles allowed by household income increases, along with some concessions, people were still not in a revolting mood.

"What will come after Rafan?" Deusein asked his fellow ministers one day.

"We need to worry about now, Minister," Aturk told him. "Rafan's intentions are questioned less and less in the light of better life in the desert. Most people are content to not worry about the future, other than about an unwanted war. This is true even in the light of their fears about their king's overall eccentricities, such as they are aware of them. We will need to address this apathy by our people to obvious problems with the king at some point. In all aspects we must focus on working diligently at defusing any upheaval that threatens to bear fruit, domestically or internationally."

Only those in the upper levels of government constantly questioned Rafan's intentions, only those individuals knew Rafan up close. The remaining cabinet ministers and other top officials knew they had to choose their battles with their unpredictable king. But, indeed, they knew they had to battle at times or all would be lost. He was kept from the dais in the center of the city by every means possible. The less contact with the citizenry, the better.

Sometimes Rafan's instructions were just ignored or undone out of the king's sight. Excuses were made when these constraints were found out. More and more, the eccentric Rafan became less and less aware of these situations. He was no longer thorough in his follow-up to his commands. Perhaps in moments of clearer vision he realized some of his orders were frivolous and chose to let the fact they weren't executed slide from sight. But, it was much more likely he just lost his focus and forgot he'd given the orders. As long as the world community relaxed to only an interested vigil, the ministers declined upsetting the applecart, or fig cart, as it were. All of this subterfuge and disobedience seemed to be doing its job of controlling King Rafan.

Meanwhile in the neighboring nations, discontent with Malfon was rising, even against most of the world's apathy. There were some cases of more than interested vigil.

"This King Rafan is not the Este Rafan we knew when we negotiated for port facilities," the Norovan ambassador told his nation's leadership. "This man is not shrewd, he is crude. He no longer shakes hands, or bows. There is no diplomacy, just demands. There is no respect. I fear that he is up to something dramatic. The Rafan we knew wheedled and bargained for advantage for Malfon. This Rafan is just disrespectful. He even asked me why we allowed our women to go about unveiled. He is a Christian. What does he care? He said he considered it a terrible freedom to condone, and suggested we do something about it."

It was foreigners who expected contact with Malfon's leader who could not be shielded from Rafan's deteriorating mental faculties.

"That may be," Norova's leader answered. "But, as long as Malfon poses no immediate threat, we don't want to cause an escalation by showing our fears, or responding inappropriately to his questions. Be as careful in your comments as we are in our defensive preparations."

"Of course, sir." The ambassador had frequent contact with Rafan and was sure his leader would be more disturbed if he had the first hand knowledge of Rafan he did. "It does seem that the shock waves produced by his title change and all it encompassed have died down in Malfon," he admitted. Why his own countrymen didn't have the same view of their king as he did was a mystery to him. "The people of Malfon revere him as much as ever, I am told. Of course, I get that word from official channels. The people on the streets do seem to be increasingly proud to be Malfonies."

"Yes, of course. There was a need for Malfonies to have something to support as their national identity. Rafan gives them that in himself. They bestowed upon Rafan the pride and respect Europeans heaped on their monarchs for centuries, whether they were worthy of it or not. King Rafan became the face of Malfon for all, domestically and internationally...and I do fear he is up to something that will affect us." The Norovan leader's head was nodding to himself.

CHAPTER 60

Mahumud M'hut was shocked at the latest request for military hardware and personnel. It was one more thing the ministers would have to deal with on a delicate basis. The military was something on which Rafan did keep a close track.

Rafan was not content with the status quo. In his mind there must always be more, and the army and navy were his highest priorities, it seemed. He was making that clear in cabinet meetings month after month.

"You are wondering why I have again called for more military spending. You see no reason to staff our army and navy with a work force that could be making computers, or drilling oil, or raising crops.

"Some of you are worried that I have gone too far. Oh, yes, I hear the grumbling. There are grumblers among you here, and there are grumblers throughout the country. I assure you, I know, though, it is still only a small minority outside of this room that is grumbling. We need a stronger military. I will not waste my time trying to convince you.

"There are those few grumblers who will never be satisfied unless they have everything their way. You know who those among you are." Rafan looked squarely at Aturk. "I am giving the order to M'hut to buy another ship, a small one. I want another airplane. We still don't have a naval air corps. But, that can wait. I want another fighter jet. If we cannot find enough Malfonies for the service, perhaps we can hire loyal mercenaries from somewhere."

Aturk opened his mouth to speak, but Rafan went on, “General Aturk, I see you ready to object. I remind you I am the king. Unless you are ready to oppose me openly at risk of your position, you will assist Commander M’hut. You will do as I instruct you. Both of you.” Rafan’s confusion on the ranks and titles of Aturk and M’hut caused a quiet stir in the room. Things like that were happening more and more frequently.

“Malfon is now able to take its place among the leadership of the world, economically, and militarily. But, we can’t stop yet.”

Murmuring voices could be heard around the room. “What does that mean?” Deusein asked squeakily, speaking into M’hut’s ear. “Surely he doesn’t think we’re a match for the true military powers of the world.”

“Commodore M’hut, I have taken the liberty of ordering our forces to the Norovan border,” Rafan said, getting the rank correct this time. M’hut was jarred back to paying attention to the king’s words. “When we are poised at the border, at my command, we will deploy the army and the navy forces in Norova to take back the coast that was stolen from us. The ports will belong to us again, as they should have all along. We will take no more than what is rightfully ours.”

“What is he doing?” Deusein shrieked quietly.

“Are you declaring war?” Aturk asked boldly.

“Only if the Norovans confront us and start a fight,” Rafan stated flatly.

“After we invade their country?” Again Aturk.

“You can’t do that without my knowledge. It’s my navy!”

M’hut shouted daringly. “You need my approval!”

"Next he'll be telling us we have nuclear weapons," Deusein moaned.

Rafan ignored them. "I know you think I've gone crazy. I've heard that too. But, my actions make perfect sense. We were weak when Norova took the ports. Now, we are strong and we'll take them back."

Deusein and M'hut were looking around as if hoping to find an answer to this dilemma.

"I ask again. Have you declared war?" Aturk insisted. To M'hut he said, "if he hasn't told the Norovans about any of this there's still a chance to stop it before troops attack."

"Where are the navy ships?" M'hut wondered aloud. It was his responsibility to know their whereabouts, but he was afraid he didn't have current information.

"Sir, you can't just take back the piers!" Deusein whimpered.

"Why not? They simply took them from us," Rafan explained. The world scenario was unwinding rapidly. Deusein was sure the room was spinning.

"But, there was a war then," Aturk objected. "The U.N. took them from us, not the Norovans."

"There might be a war now," Rafan fired back. "And we were neutral. Why did we lose anything?" Rafan wanted to know how these people could not see his reasoning. "We weren't really even involved in that war."

"We technically did side with the Axis...Central European heritage and all," M'hut recited the historical truth.

Rafan waved the comment away with his hand. "We befriended a weak Balkan country that didn't even figure in the fighting, that doesn't count," Rafan decided judgmentally. "If Norova doesn't resist, then there won't be any bloodshed. Aturk, do you want to contact them? No, don't let them in on the plan," Rafan asked, then answered himself. "Perhaps we will have war. That's up to Norova. You know, General Umbarik once told me a war might be a good thing for us."

Silence overtook the room. No one believed General Umbarik could have said any such thing. Suddenly no one had any idea of what to say.

"Malfon will no longer be a sheep to go where we're led. Rather, we will be a lion!" Rafan broke the silence, staring upward as he spoke. "The next thing to be done is dispatch a representative to see if Norova will agree to our terms."

"But, you just said not to warn them," Deusein pointed out in distress.

"Their military is no match for ours. They'll have no choice but to agree," M'hut said.

"So, contact them." Rafan changed his mind again. "With our troops massed on their border and our navy at the port, there is nothing they can do but yield to our demands. Send in the army! See to it Minister," Rafan said uncaringly to a nonmilitary minister next to him. With finality that verged on the ludicrous, King Rafan exited the room. The officials left staring at each other knew they had to move quickly. They now formed a united group that needed to step up to save their country from a king who had definitely lost his mind.

CHAPTER 61

M'hut's distress was incapacitating. Rafan was obviously out of control, if not out of his mind. He was endangering his country and his people. He was about to destroy the amenities he had created in Malfon by subjecting the nation to war. It was obvious he had to be stopped, M'hut understood. But, M'hut couldn't forget all the good works Rafan had done in his short lifetime.

He searched for a way to save the monarch, yet stop the damage Rafan was set on causing. M'hut, himself, was only in his thirties and Rafan younger, Mahumud thought. It hadn't been that long since they were kids together. But, Malfon had been completely transformed in their lifetimes. Most of the changes were good, and directly due to Rafan. But, perhaps there was still some maturity missing.

Shortly after Rafan had left them in the purple-walled cabinet office, the ministers were still stumbling to catch each other in the halls as they hurried about trying to stop the invasion of Norova in whatever capacity their authority could allow them. They were quickly consulting about their activities, trying to decide what to do with their king and what to do when they'd done those things.

"The army will still take orders from me, I think," Aturk told M'hut, "especially if I'm countermanding an order the officers can't believe they were given." Aturk marched toward his office and phone to contact his troops, his movement apace with his military attire.

An enlisted man from the navy came up to M'hut and handed him a message. M'hut read it and called after Aturk. "At least I know where my navy is now. They are in port in Norova. The entire fleet. My fleet commander just got an order to start shelling Norova's capital. He's awaiting confirmation from me."

M'hut scribbled a note on the paper and handed it back to the sailor. "Get that to the commander right away," he instructed.

Deusein scurried to his office to call the Norovan ambassador.

Yes, Rafan was probably responsible for the loss of his wife. That was the foremost thought on M'hut's mind. But, even if that had been necessary for the good of the country, M'hut had to admit he could no longer justify that. Rafan had gone too far.

M'hut wanted to talk to someone, to air his tumult. But, there was no one he could talk to about it. Instead he processed his thoughts out loud while moving down the palace halls.

"If Anna hadn't been stopped, she might have succeeded in stopping Rafan's faulty leadership. The other leaders wouldn't have needed to conceal Rafan's eccentricities from the public, and we wouldn't be going through all this," he mumbled. That was all inconsequential, M'hut realized. The only thing to do was clearly in front of his eyes. They had to put the brakes on Rafan's actions. Maybe that would mean putting the brakes on Rafan himself. The avalanche of events that was snowballing had to be stopped, no matter what the cost.

"I knew Rafan must have been responsible for Anna's disappearance," the commodore thought out loud. "But, I thought Rafan had to make a choice and had chosen the right path, as harsh as it was." M'hut had managed to damp down his cause for rage and accept Rafan's choice and shelve his grief.

"Were any of Rafan's choices the right ones on the road to the point the country has reached?" M'hut moaned. His uncertainty crippled him. Regardless, he knew what needed to be done now.

"Anna was right all along," he decided aloud. Maybe intervention would have prevented things from reaching their current extreme extent, he thought. It was possible Anna, her cronies, and Aturk had been the only ones to have seen clearly what was happening.

After almost completely accepting justification for Anna's death, the commodore now excruciatingly accepted this possibility.

"My God," someone said as he ran past M'hut, jarring him back to the present. M'hut was still fairly anchored into inactivity by his ruminations, but regained some of his mobility. "The king hasn't been so violent physically lately, and now he wants to attack Norova? We were better off with him smacking officers and aides!" The running man said.

M'hut had seen Rafan strike out at naval officers and men. He had to blame himself for waiting too long to see the evidence of Rafan's insanity.

M'hut stopped another man running toward him. "What can we do? I mean what are we doing? Where are we?" he asked the stranger. The man looked at M'hut with a question on his face, and then the authority of the commodore's uniform elicited an answer.

"What do you mean, sir?"

M'hut then ignored him and kept walking. It had only been his mind speaking out loud to himself. The man stared for a moment and then turned and began running again.

M'hut had to admit he couldn't forgive Rafan anymore. This wasn't a youthful transgression like the situation with Anna as kids. This was serious business. He knew he had to focus on the call for action. His conscious control was returning from the shock of all the realizations he been making. He would heed the call to take on the king. There would be no more cautions from him. There would be no need to conceal the king's condition. Even with that conviction, the naval man still did not have a clear course of action in mind.

After finally setting aside all his side thoughts and distractive feelings, M'hut found himself at Deusein's office. "Minister Deusein, you don't normally deal with things of this nature. Perhaps my military familiarity might be an asset to you in dealing with the Norovan authorities."

CHAPTER 62

"I knew they were up to something," the Norovan ambassador told his prime minister after receiving a phone call from Deusein.

"I don't know what we can do about it now."

"You knew they were up to something?" The prime minister yelled. "I'd say this was more than just 'something'! If you knew about it, why wasn't something done? How did this happen?" The prime minister demanded.

"Well, I mean, I didn't know what to expect. We knew Malfony troops were assembling on the border. But, all we could do was react by sending our troops there too. We didn't want to antagonize Malfon. We're out-manned and out-armed. Starting something was not in our best interest. But, it was obvious that King Rafan was planning something all along. I just couldn't believe he was planning to threaten an armed attack! But, of course, in hind sight, why else would he have been building up his military all these last few years? I failed to see the depth of the depravity of King Rafan. We should all have seen the basis of his preoccupation with improving Malfon's status."

"And now, his Minister Deusein tells us he intends to ask for us to cede the ports or fight a war," the prime minister said.

"Yes, sir. It seems some of his subordinates are not with the king on this. That's the only reason we've been warned. Deusein asked us to not take on the adverse odds by resisting. He hopes that action by the king can be forestalled permanently, and we will have nothing to fear."

"Is he talking about another coup? Nevertheless, we need to take action. Why weren't we building up our military? How could we have let this happen?" The prime minister wanted to know. "I depended on you to keep me aware. How did we become the weak sister?"

"We were building our army as much as possible. We didn't have the resources to finance the kind of build-up Rafan ramrodded in Malfon. We didn't want to jeopardize the welfare of Norova by putting everything into the military," the ambassador explained.

"But, Malfon had the resources? They had nothing! They only discovered oil recently," the prime minister seethed. "We had the resources! Did sparing them serve Norova well? We did nothing!" The Norovan leader's brain was racing. "Mr. Ambassador, we must follow Rafan's example. We must begin to build our strength at all costs. We don't have a minute to lose. Maybe Mr. Deusein's hope will come about. But, maybe it won't. We have been stagnant too long. The Norovan leader paced around his desk, running his hand through his hair. "We need to stall any further incursions by Rafan. Help him to keep Rafan happy with the least we can give him, if that's what it will take. We can't win an armed conflict. So, let's tap all of our other options. We don't want a war...at least not now...not until we're ready.

"We must find a young energetic man to lead an effort to ignite this country, someone the people can rally behind without flustering Rafan. We need someone like Rafan of our own. We must fight fire with fire. The people won't be happy appeasing Rafan. Who knows what's next?

What more will he want? But, we have to stay under control until the time is right to fight back.

"We need to give our people hope without alerting Rafan to our ultimate goal. We need to promote Norovan pride. Be sure to act quickly, but keep Talon and our other neighbors secretly apprised of our intentions so they don't feel threatened by us, but rather stand by us when we need them."

CHAPTER 63

"Now, see here," Aturk shouted! "You can't do this without our consent...my consent. I am the Minister of Defense. I control the military!" They were again in the cabinet office barely an hour after the king had given the orders to attack Norova. Rafan was aware that his orders hadn't been followed.

"Need I remind you, Aturk, that I am the king?" Rafan fired back. "You serve at my discretion. I can do anything I please. I want our navy to start shelling, and move our troops into Norova. Now, do it! Or, I will do it myself, and tell the ranking officers to ignore you if you try to rescind my orders, because you have been relieved of your position!"

"You can't give orders directly to my people! How dare you? I have not surrendered my position!"

"That can be arranged, Aturk. I just informed you of that. Will it be surrendered or coerced? The choice is yours." Rafan spoke in a calm voice that was both inappropriate for the scene and the total opposite of Aturk's screaming.

"You are provoking an all-out war!" Aturk continued. "You can't believe this is the right thing to do. You have to know you're acting irrationally! You have the Defense Minister and the head of our navy telling you..."

"You and M'hut dare question the decision of the man who brought this country out of the doldrums, into the modern world...the man who taught our people how to feed themselves and make a good living besides?" Rafan was making a speech at a totally out of place moment. "You question the man who built our military to the point we don't have to take a back seat to any of our neighboring countries any more? You question the man who brought electricity and manufacturing to Malfon..."

"We do question him, Your Majesty," Minister Deusein suggested. "We fear you have lost your...objectivity."

"Norova will give us back our seaport. They fear that power I've built. You questioned that. But, it will be the way I said it would...for the good of Malfonies," Rafan illustrated. "There won't even be any bloodshed. The Norovan's aren't dumb enough to fight us. Now, move those troops. Then we'll move them to Talon."

Aturk blanched. "What?"

"We have the same reason there as in confronting Norova. We are protecting our assets. We need the water we get from Talon. We can't gamble on Talon interfering with the flow of water from the mountains any more than we can gamble on Norova not cutting off our port. That port is rightfully ours, and the water is rightfully ours. We must guarantee access to the port and to the water in Talon."

"But, there has been no indication of intentions by Talon to deny us that access any more than there has been of Norova stopping our use of the port. Those countries benefit from those resources as well as we do," Deusein objected.

"And some day they may decide they need those resources more than we do. I can't let them have the option of making a decision to deny us when that day comes," Rafan explained. "That is why, once we get things settled quickly with Norova, we must immediately launch an attack on Talon. Just because we need the water, it doesn't mean they feel they have to share it with us. There have been meetings between Talon and Norova. They are planning something. We must pre-empt whatever they have planned. We developed that water resource, and the port was taken from us. They are ours! Once we subdue both countries there will be no threat from an alliance between them."

"You can't really be planning to attack Talon!" Aturk shouted. "I can't let you do that!" The defense minister stood with one hand on his left hip and the other propped on the bulge of his sidearm holster. The defiant pose didn't deter Rafan.

"Still you question your king?" Rafan was tiring of the discussion. The recently installed air-conditioning was the only sound heard for a moment.

Aturk was more agitated than anyone could remember seeing him. But, Rafan seemed unflustered, only bored and sure of himself.

"This is impossible," Aturk loudly objected once more.

In the brief moment of silence when the argument lagged, Aturk, M'hut, Deusein, and the one or two others who were present, exchanged disbelieving looks. Deusein was noticeably sweating, even in the artificially cooled room. Each of the people in the room knew that nothing was happening at the moment, militarily.

No one was attacking anyone yet. Rafan didn't like that knowledge, but saw that another tactic might achieve his desired results. He decided to try convincing his ministers and military leaders, calmly, that he believed his requests were necessary for the good of Malfon. Perhaps, he thought, he hadn't been thorough enough in selling his vision.

"We need to build our army and navy even larger, stronger. We need to protect ourselves from any confrontation, though I expect none from beyond our region. Can't you see that need? We can handle Norova and Talon, but that is just the start. Having Norova and Talon as strong antagonists on our borders is dangerous. The future will call for us to become mightier. But, this is the first step. With our recent achievements, our neighbors may band together against us, feeling that a necessity.

"They are jealous of what we'd done with our nation. They are envious. That makes them dangerous. They see us as a threat. That has got to be what Norova and Talon have been discussing secretly. We must be prepared, and diffuse any potential action against us on their part. We must make the pre-emptive strikes," Rafan preached. "Our prosperity has caused them to be wary of us. Their wariness is a hazard to Malfon. So we must attack before they become strong enough to challenge us."

"But, no one has threatened us," Aturk shouted. He was not in the least calm. "And it's not the prosperity that's bothering them! It's your belligerence and erraticness!"

"With Norova giving us back our ports, you don't think Talon is going to expect us to act against them?" Rafan went on, "the Talonites know we have as good a reason to attack them as we have to attack Norova, so we have to subdue them before they act in response to our moves in Norova."

"And what reason is that the Talonites know we would have? What would be our reason for attacking Talon?" Deusein squeezed into Rafan's explanation.

Rafan waved the question away. "I've already told you."

Rafan, forgetting that nothing had actually happened yet, said, "you don't think Norova is working on retaliation right now? They may give up the ports, but they don't want to. Now, they'll be focusing on how to get them back. They will seek Talon's help. Norova will convince Talon that we are a threat to Talonites as well as Norovans. It won't take much convincing, as I've explained."

"You want us to be a threat to them," Aturk, yelled, trying to get through to Rafan with volume.

"We must be strong!" Rafan chanted. The veins on his temples were popping out, refuting his calm demeanor. "We must protect the port. We must protect our water supply!"

"I don't like the sound of these things, Your Majesty," Deusein ventured in understatement. He was not yelling, still trying to reason with the king in his own calm, squeaky tone of voice. "Surely, you remember that our European ancestors fled here to escape such thinking, and war. There has been none of that sort of strife here. We've had no wars here, ever. We have Christians and Muslims, and even a few Jews living here peacefully, and even somewhat prosperously...thanks to you. Surely you don't want to jeopardized that and create a regional war. We don't want to be responsible for that," Deusein pitched.

"I can't be responsible for the Norovans if they chose to fight. Besides, the European immigrants were despots. They stole this land."

"But, they were our ancestors..." Aman Deusein insisted.

"No. They were not. Not mine. I am of native nomadic blood," Rafan stated flatly.

Deusein looked puzzled. "But, sir, you've always been proud you were of mixed blood. That royal European bloodline is what gave you the right to be a king. We're all of mixed blood here."

The squeaky voiced Deusein was becoming more confused by the moment and deeply over his head in the situation. He was also more and more convinced of Rafan's insanity.

"Even if the Norovans don't fight..." M'hut started to say, but Aturk broke in before he could finish.

"I am the only pure-blooded Arab here," Aturk spoke up. "I am not of mixed blood."

That statement stopped everyone for a moment as they processed it...even Rafan.

In the temporary silence that followed that statement, the people in that room at the royal palace all came to a mutual unspoken recognition that they could no longer delay. They were faced with a severe crisis, worse than stopping the attack on Talon, worse than taking pressure off Norova to cede the ports.

They had the problem of stopping Rafan finally and permanently. Even M'hut was firmly convinced. They had to do it immediately.

The king had lost his mind. Of course, Rafan did not share this belief.

Aturk went on with his comment. "I am an exception to the mixed European roots of the others in this room and the rest of the country. It doesn't matter." Aturk's tone was suddenly authoritative. Aturk saw the parallels of history more clearly than the others perhaps. His grandparents' homeland had come under a foreign domination which had endured to the present.

"The European heritage that our countrymen share continues to destroy what vestiges were left of the nomadic life Malfonies had known. That heritage is destroying the country itself. The Europeans brought their despotism with them. The life most Malfonies live now is a good one. A return to the nomadic life is impossible, and probably undesirable. But, I cannot consider losing the remnants of that uncomplicated culture, as well as the modern life Malfonies live, to Rafan's lunacy."

Aturk knew he should have done something about Sabu wasting opportunities by lack of leadership when he was in power. Aturk had gone along with Sabu's ennui. He'd taken the easy route in his career. He hadn't taken the noble one. Now, Rafan, the 'king', was destroying his own gains or trying to, by starting a war. It was more than Aturk could take. He wouldn't allow himself to make the same mistake he'd made with Sabu's reign.

M'hut and Deusein looked at Aturk. The defense minister's face was almost frightening.

"I have pulled the country along by its bootstraps, if that is an appropriate reference in a desert nation where many prefer to be barefoot. I am still a young man, but I have already done a lot for this country. In the remainder of my life, how much more can I do?" Rafan went into a rambling brag.

How much of what he could yet do would be harmful, the other men in the room wondered. They had no desire to find out.

Perhaps if his parents hadn't died so young they could have given Rafan's youthful ambition some much needed guidance, M'hut thought. There was a rumor that his parents' had planned for him to be a teacher. Maybe teaching others who might have become the leaders of Malfon would have resulted in many of the same advantages Rafan had brought about as the leader himself, without the personality flaws that had brought the country to its present precarious point in history.

Another leader, conditioned by Rafan, could have chosen a different path to the same achievements the king had produced.

Perhaps that leader wouldn't have achieved as much. But, there was no way to tell if that alternate future would have suffered because of that. Perhaps that eventuality would have been better. Perhaps another leader wouldn't have rivaled Rafan's ambition, and Malfon would still be a backwards desert nation. Would that have been a better outcome? Maybe that leader would have achieved even more than Rafan had. Each of the Malfony leaders gathered together in the time of crisis was having thoughts of this sort.

Indeed, there was no way to tell what would have happened if Rafan hadn't happened. It didn't matter, because Rafan existed.

His Royal Majesty King Este Rafan had happened.

If his mentor, General Umbarik, hadn't left him so soon, Rafan could still have been the best thing that could have happened to Malfon, but without the drawbacks. Perhaps the general would have been the other leader himself. He was experienced, well respected, and already a senior member of the government...perhaps too senior.

With Arat's death, Umbarik could have been agreeable to everyone for assuming leadership. Aturk and even Rafan himself would have gone along with that. Perhaps things would have turned out better, perhaps worse. How could you tell? But, Umbarik had died. These were the thoughts going through Aturk's mind. But, in light of current events, he could only assume nothing as dire as war would have come about under Umbarik, military man though he was. Of course he was too old to have ruled for long, had he been able to take over.

But, perhaps by the time Umbarik's rule had ended, Rafan would have been a leader more capable of making better choices. But then one thing was sure. A living Umbarik would have kept the country on an even course no matter who the leader actually was.

"Este, I wish that you could have found some interest in sports, or women, some kind of social life," Mahumud told his friend. M'hut knew the reign of King Rafan was over even if Este didn't know it yet. "The constant stress of dedication to your causes without another outlet for release, has taken a toll on your well being," M'hut said quietly, still in shock from the snowballing events.

"My private life is none of your concern, Commander...and that is 'Your majesty'." Rafan had not seen the handwriting on the wall. He got M'hut's rank wrong again. He was growing very tired of hearing about concern for his health and sanity. He was carrying on as if he was still in charge. "How can you people be thinking about my health and sanity when there are so much more important things going on, like the attack on Talon? That has to be handled!"

Aturk knew that even he had fallen under the spell of Rafan's enthusiasm at times. The minister had been more active and involved in the government than he had ever been since Rafan had begun his rise to power. Sometimes the activity's purpose was to oppose Rafan, of course. Most of the people of Malfon still loved King Rafan...the one they knew. They had been shielded from his worst episodes of fanatical thinking. Though, it seemed impossible that they were unaware of what the military was doing. Soldiers and sailors talked to their spouses, their relatives and friends. They, in turn, talked to others.

Others in the government had even supported Rafan's causes to the masses, when possible. The increased taxes were explained away and replaced by calls for Malfony pride. All in the interest of what was best for Malfon. Good was emphasized over questionable when it came to decision making by the king.

These officials had played the good game for some time. The officials worked hard at this charade, if it could be called that.

"I know that Malfon will never again be a nomadic homeland. This new world doesn't allow for that," Aturk finally said aloud.

The yelling had stopped, replaced by a somber mien. "Malfonies have to stand together, regardless of their heritage, religion, or any other differences."

"What are you prattling on about, Aturk?" Rafan asked irritatedly. "Get the troop movements going. If you won't, then M'hut, you take over. Let's go to where the activity is." The king commanded without opposition and led the entourage out of the building to a prearranged van waiting at the front entrance of the palace.

"Rafan, I won't let the future of our country be thrown away," Aturk continued as they climbed hesitantly into the van. Rafan seemed to be at another odd undertaking, but no one put a stop to it. "It matters not what happens to me. Malfon will thrive, given a reasonable chance," Aturk went on.

"Well, at least you realize you're putting your own future in jeopardy, Aturk," Rafan insinuated.

Around them the others worried about being away from contacts to their responsibilities in this crisis. What was Rafan doing? they wondered. But, the king was insistent, and he was still king, at least for the moment. Everyone seemed uncertain on how to frame the confrontation.

"Get in so the driver can get going," Rafan urged the last passenger forcefully.

M'hut wondered what Aturk's previous comment had actually meant. Aturk's tone of voice continued to be quiet, out of character for the boisterous minister. M'hut looked from Aturk to Rafan and back to Aturk. Where did his own loyalty lie? M'hut wondered. Where precisely? What kind of handling could he accept in deposing the king?

After a short time the van arrived at an apparently prearranged point in the desert, where the driver stopped and the passengers were told to dismount.

Rafan was talking over the top of Aturk's continuing soft railing as they stepped onto the sand. "M'hut, Aturk seems to be resisting a royal order. Have him arrested and see to it that my orders are carried out with the troops! I'm promoting you to Minister of Defense, effective immediately. Now, see about discussing a military surrender of our Northern enemy..." Rafan was rambling. His voice rasped in an unnatural pitch.

Indeed, they were on the border of that Northern neighbor, Amena. Rafan's order overlooked the fact that they were in a barren wasteland without communications ability to discuss anything with anyone beyond their small group. All they had was a two-way radio in the van.

"But, your Majesty, we've had no conflict with Amena. Amena allows our oil to be piped through their territory. Amena has been most cooperative. Do you realize what you're saying? I appreciate the offer of a promotion, but sire..." M'hut tried to sort his confused thoughts aloud.

There was another moment of silence. No one spoke and only the sound of the wind gusting gently through the sand could be heard. No one coughed or shuffled his feet, not even Deusein.

Each person present was rifling through his own perceptions of what should be done and how they would be involved. Each was interpreting what was going on in his own way.

"I love it here in the desert," Rafan finally said. "It reminds me of the past, this sand." He leaned over and sifted a little through his hand. "This is Malfon, my country."

Then Rafan placed his hands on M'hut's shoulders in the manner General Umbarik had used with his young aide. M'hut shivered at the touch. There was an unfamiliar aspect to the gesture. This was not the Este Rafan he had known nearly all his life.

"We are at war with everyone, Mahumud. Every country in the world..." Rafan's ranting contained tones of insanity, but remained calm. The delivery denied the content.

"We must protect this beloved land." It was apparent to those present that the king's mind was receding further from rationality. This was no temporary set back. There would obviously be no spontaneous recovery. Perhaps this confrontation from his ministers had been the last straw, the last strain his psyche could take. Their resistance, now total, had offered him no retreat, no place to go for respite.

The government officials looked at each other questioning their own resolve and wondering who would act, and what form the act would take. None of them wanted to be seen as a traitor, but neither could they stand by and watch this scene get more and more out of control. Something had to be done. But, what could be done? What should be done?

Was everyone thinking the same thing? M'hut wondered.

How do you remove this man, revered by his country? He no longer possesses his sanity and they all knew Rafan could not be allowed to represent Malfon any longer. But, how could they act against the man that had done so much for Malfon? He could not be allowed to continue his march to the ruination of Malfon. But, how to properly move on, that was the question.

"The devout and excellent leader we knew is undoubtedly gone," M'hut said aloud. "This man cannot be allowed to give another order. But, we must be careful to not turn the country against his successors. Any public announcement denouncing the king would reek of political intrigue. An unexplained disappearance would turn the country into a tumultuous state of confused aimlessness."

"M'hut! What are you saying?" Rafan jolted back to reality.

M'hut went on undeterred. "The country needs someone or something to blame for the loss of the leadership Rafan has provided. There must be a scapegoat, whether chosen by the public or other means. You can be sure of that." M'hut's voice was sad but strong. He was forcing himself to be assertive.

Among Malfon's leaders only one man had the conviction to make the next move, regardless of the consequences to himself. Malfonies had cheered Sabu's demise. They were heartened by Rafan's assention to power. How would they handle the next step in Malfon's history? he wondered.

Rafan was muttering to himself, giving orders to no one who was listening.

As the group stood in the as-yet undeveloped stretch of sand, Aturk's memories of the past flowed through his mind, much like M'hut's had. He'd led an eventful, if not always fulfilling, life. He could bow out of Malfon's leadership without jeopardizing the country's future. No one would really miss him if he were gone from the hierarchy.

The people of Malfon could condemn the new leadership, or they could embrace a change from the sometimes disconcerting steps of Rafan's administration. It all depended on how the passage of power was handled.

"Perhaps M'hut could lead the country," Aturk said. Attired, as usual, in his full dress uniform that he still wore in his ministerial position, which included a pistol in the holster at his hip, Aturk drew the gun.

"I act on behalf of my country!" Aturk shouted, then quickly fired twice into the heart of his majesty, King Este Rafan.

M'hut jumped at the sound of the gunshot, then caught the king, his old friend, as Rafan sank to the sand.

The final look on Rafan's face was not one of surprise. Deep down had he known this was coming? Was that why he chose the desert for this meeting, his last? It didn't seem likely, but perhaps he wanted to feel his beloved Malfon beneath him when he fell. M'hut knew that he was romanticizing the loss of his advocate and idol.

As M'hut released the body, letting it drop at his feet, the wind was already piling sand against it. King Este Rafan was at peace.

Now, it was time to make sure that the country was, as well.

Aturk surrendered his weapon to M'hut, and even though those present were shocked, they admired Aturk's guts in taking the action they couldn't force themselves to undertake. They all realized that Aturk would have to pay the consequence for his actions. He would be arrested and tried. He would probably spend the rest of his life in prison.

"Get us back to Creche," Deusein yelled to the stunned driver of the van. Then M'hut regained his sense of the present and sent out a call for medical help on the radio. Then they all climbed back into the van.

"You stay with the body and wait for the ambulance," M'hut told the driver. "I'll drive."

Aturk's face was sad.

"I can't believe you did that, Aturk," Deusein said.

Aturk was the last of the group to look at Rafan's body. On the trip back to Creche, Aturk said nothing. He just stared at the sand around them as they sped forward.

"We need to reach the navy and army commanders immediately. Get to a phone and call the army, Deusein. I'll call the fleet," M'hut ordered.

They reached the capital quickly. M'hut pushed Aturk ahead of himself and called two nearby palace guards over. Nodding at Aturk, he told them, "arrest this man. He has killed King Rafan."

The men, of course, recognized Aturk, but followed M'hut's orders. Aturk didn't resist.

"For the good of Malfon," Aturk finally said, then closed his eyes. He was grabbed by a guard on each side.

About the Author

Walt Polzin is seventy years old. He's worked as an actor, managed political campaigns, and done freelance writing for daily and weekly newspapers. This work included writing human interest stories. Mr. Polzin has two grown daughters and four grandchildren living in the Northwest. He resides in Medford, Oregon.

CPSIA information can be obtained
at www.ICGtesting.com
Printed in the USA
FSHW01n0707210518
48504FS